W9-AJT-037

WEAVING
WATER

© 2016, Annamarie Beckel

We gratefully acknowledge the financial support of the
Canada Council for the Arts, the Government of Canada through the Canada
Book Fund (CBF), and the Government of Newfoundland and Labrador
through the Department of Business, Tourism, Culture and
Rural Development for our publishing program.

All rights reserved. No part of this work covered by the copyrights hereon
may be reproduced or used in any form or by any means—graphic,
electronic or mechanical—without the prior written permission of the
publisher. Any requests for photocopying, recording, taping or information
storage and retrieval systems of any part of this book shall be directed in
writing to the Canadian Reprography Collective, One Yonge Street,
Suite 1900, Toronto, Ontario M5E 1E5.

Cover Design by Todd Manning • Layout by Joanne Snook-Hann
Printed on acid-free paper

Published by
KILLICK PRESS
an imprint of CREATIVE BOOK PUBLISHING
a Transcontinental Inc. associated company
P.O. Box 8660, Stn. A
St. John's, Newfoundland and Labrador A1B 3T7

Printed in Canada

Library and Archives Canada Cataloguing in Publication

Beckel, Annamarie, 1951-, author
Weaving water / Annamarie Beckel.

ISBN 978-1-77103-092-2 (paperback)

I. Title.

PS8553.A29552W43 2016   C813'.54   C2016-904039-9

WEAVING WATER

A NOVEL

Annamarie Beckel

*To Ineka —
with all best
wishes Annamarie Beckel
January 2019*

killick press
an imprint of Creative Publishers

St. John's, Newfoundland and Labrador, 2016

For Megan and Amy

A human being is a part of the whole, called by us "Universe," a part limited in time and space. He experiences himself, his thoughts and feelings as something separated from the rest – a kind of optical delusion of his consciousness. This delusion is a kind of prison for us.

Albert Einstein, a 1950 letter to Robert Marcus

We must be at our most skeptical when we evaluate arguments that confirm the extremely high opinion we have of ourselves.

Steven Wise, *Rattling the Cage*

CHAPTER 1

Beth sets the kerosene lamp on the kitchen counter above the junk drawer. Tries not to hear the melancholy plink-plink-plink of water dripping into the bowls and pans she's placed on the floor to catch the leaks. The lamp's soft glow illuminates the drawer's contents: match-books, candle stubs, scissors, ball of string, paper clips. She picks up a deck of cards, slides off the red rubber band, and releases the odour of must. The smell of old things in an old wooden drawer: Katherine's things.

When Beth and Alan first arrived at the cabin, there were shirts and dresses still hanging in the closet, white cotton socks and old-lady underwear rolled up and stuffed into a small bureau. The dead woman's clothes made Beth uneasy, and she and Alan packed them away in black plastic garbage bags to donate to the Salvation Army. They kept the furniture though, as well as the dishes and the pots and pans. Beth still isn't sure how she feels about that, but it made no sense to throw out what they can use.

The yellow lamplight casts shadows that shrink, waver, and then grow taller on the grey walls. Beth shuffles the cards and lays them out for a game of solitaire. Cringes when gusts of wind rattle loose shingles. She looks up to see rain streaming down the front window, and the eerie reflection of her own pale face bisected by the masking tape that covers the jagged crack. She tries to laugh at herself. She doesn't believe in ghosts. Of course she doesn't. But it was easier to laugh when Alan was here. He's gone now, back in St. John's. He took the black garbage bags with him.

And she's alone in a dead woman's cabin on a pond in the middle of nowhere.

~

Beth crouches down, pinches metal forceps to lift the crushed carapace of a beetle, teases apart slender, translucent fish bones and fragments of blue mussel shell. The black scat exudes an odour of fresh fish and musk. To her, not unpleasant. She finds an otolith, the tiny round bone from the inner ear that, under a microscope, will tell her the age and species of fish the otter ate. Probably trout, mud trout.

She pulls a labelled zip-lock bag from her backpack. Using the bag like a glove, she collects the scat, zips the bag, and tucks it into the cooler against the ice. Hopes the sample won't degrade too much for DNA analysis before she can get it back to the university. Genetic tests on scats will tell her how many river otters are in the group, how many males, how many females, and how closely related they are to each other.

The crows in a nearby birch caw raucously, like rowdy fans jeering a hockey referee's bad call. Beth hears mocking laughter, as if the crows know her research for what it is: picking through otter shit.

Wiping off the forceps, Beth reminds herself that river otters, like wolves and eagles, are an environmental success story, rebounding from small numbers to become plentiful again. And where reintroductions have been successful, it's research like hers that has made the difference.

Crows 1: Beth 1.

She hears the distant hum of a motor, a hum that grows steadily louder until it's a roar. A small boat rounds the point. The motor stops, creating an abrupt silence until the wake slaps rudely against the shore. Beth raises her binoculars: an Alumacraft, *Black Feather* painted in even letters on the bow. Who names an Alumacraft?

A lone fisherman stands, lights a cigarette, then fiddles with a fishing rod. After a few minutes, he casts. He looks toward Beth and nods. A flush rises into her cheeks. She lets the binoculars drop to her chest, packs up her research gear, and slides into her kayak.

~

The otters glide through the pond, propelling themselves with undulations of muscular bodies and thick, tapering tails. They stay near shore, their steady *uhn-uhn-uhns* like whispers through the grey mist that lies in a downy blanket atop the dark water. The oldest one lifts her head, smelling the air. She chirps to quiet the pups tussling in the water, then comes out on shore and sniffs at the place she marked with scat the night before. There's something new: the scent of human, female, sadness. She hurries back into the water and leads them all away.

~

Beth rises through the gossamer shroud of deep sleep, silky threads of a dream clinging: murky water, a tangle of weeds. She lies still in the dark. Hears snuffling noises just outside the window. *Mfuff-mfuff, mfuff-mfuff.* She stands, as quietly as she can, but the sagging springs groan, the sleeping bag rustles. The snuffling stops. There is only the wind shussing through spruce and fir. She tiptoes to the window. Sees a dark hulking shape near the base of a birch – the same spot where she left stale crackers the night before. She imagines the pink tongue curling around each salty square.

She feels an urgent need to pee, but she can't go to the outhouse with a bear in the middle of the path. She squeezes her thighs together. Why has she been so careless? She could have dumped the crackers down the outhouse hole. But no, she had to put them out for the jays and crows, and the red squirrel. She even spread peanut butter on a few. Stupid, stupid, stupid!

3

She knows a black bear isn't really *that* dangerous. Unless it has cubs nearby or it decides to come inside to search for more food. Did she lock the door last night? Does it matter? She assesses the dimensions of the window. Glances at the chair beside the bed. Calculates. If the bear heads for the door, she should be able to climb out the window – if she can get the screen out quickly enough. If she can't, she'll have to go right through it.

The alarm on her watch beeps, implausibly loud in the dark: 5:00. She scrambles to turn it off. Looks out the window again. The bear's head is raised, angled toward the cabin. Beth holds her breath and tries to ignore the pressure building in her bladder. Releases her breath slowly when the bear lowers its head to the crackers. The bear exhales a muffled *mfuff-mfuff*. Or a low woof?

She reaches for her glasses, slides them on, and sees what might be a long shaggy tail. Watches for another minute, waiting for more light. Groans. It's only a dog. A huge black Newfoundland.

Still in bare feet and T-shirt, she races outside. The broad head comes up and the dog gallops behind her, then waits by the outhouse door until Beth is finished. When she opens the door, the chocolate doggy eyes gazing up at her melt her resolve to be stern.

"Where'd you come from, buddy?" Her voice is raspy. These are the first words she's spoken aloud since Alan left three days ago. She does a quick inspection and determines that *it* is a *she*.

Feet wet and cold, Beth runs on her toes back to the cabin. The dog trots along behind her, pausing momentarily at the saltines, now just a few soggy crumbs. She tries to follow Beth right into the cabin, but Beth blocks her with a knee and closes the screen door.

"Go home now. Back to where you belong."

4

The Newfoundland plops down on the wide top step, chin on front paws. Stares through the screen. Beth can't close the door in her face. She has a soft heart. Mushy, really, when it comes to animals. Her father, a farmer, always told her she lacked iron.

Watching while Beth pulls on jeans, wool socks, and a sweatshirt, the dog lets out a small whine now and again. Very small, Beth thinks, for such a large dog. She considers letting the dog come into the cabin. Knows that would be a mistake.

She builds a fire in the cookstove, black soot smudging her hands and gathering in stark lines under her fingernails. Bursts of light from three different matches flare and die before the kindling catches and she can add more splits. She primes the pump and fills the metal percolator with water. All the while, the whimpers are growing more insistent. She adds coffee grounds to the pot. Spills some across the dark-red counter. Blames the dog. The dog has disrupted her morning routine. Beth places the coffee pot on the stove, adds more wood to the fire, and turns the rocking chair away from the screen door. She sits down and rocks with determination. Hopes the dog will leave.

In just three days alone, Beth has developed a morning ritual. She rises before daylight, builds the fire, then wraps herself in her sleeping bag while she waits for the coffee to perk. The living room window faces east, and she sits, cocoon-like, and waits for the light. When the sun edges over the spruce and fir ringing the pond, she takes up her journal and writes out her research notes: the weight of the pen in her hand, the physicality of holding a notebook balanced on one knee, the scent of real ink and real paper. It's the part of the ritual that makes her feel like her younger self, the self who was full of confidence and purpose, the self who believed she could do research that matters.

The first slow perks. Accompanied by snuffling and whining. Beth avoids looking toward the screen door.

The previous morning she had even dared to imagine herself as Thoreau or John Muir, thinking deep, complicated thoughts about wilderness and human nature. And then was grateful for her solitude: no witness to make her feel foolish.

It has come as a welcome relief to be alone and disconnected: no computer, no email, no Internet, and most important, no news. She's been worrying too much lately, about big problems she can do nothing about – climate change and the loss of more and more wilderness to oil and mineral extraction, the increasingly rapid pace of species' extinctions – and about personal problems she feels equally helpless to remedy. She's goddamn fifty-three. And all she has to show for it are a few minor papers from research she did twenty-five years ago. How the hell did that happen? And when?

She feels like a walking, talking cliché. She also feels cheated.

The coffee pot is perking madly now, close to boiling over, the heady aroma competing with the pungent smell of wood smoke. Beth lifts the pot from the stove and pours scalding coffee into a mug. Glances toward the door. The dog's nose is pushing in, creating a dent in the screen. The sunlight illumines a thin ribbon of drool.

She carries the mug outside. The dog stands, tail wagging, even as Beth nudges her off the top step. When she sits down, the dog settles on the ground beside her. A red squirrel dances in jerky bursts along the woodpile. It stops to release a chattering reproach at them – or maybe just at the dog for eating all the peanut butter crackers.

Beth rubs sleep from her eyes. Sighs. If she wanted a dog here while she was doing her research, she'd have kept Pirate, their three-legged black Lab, when Alan left.

She combs her fingers through the oily fur at the dog's thick neck. Finds a worn leather collar but no tags.

"What am I supposed to do with you?"

The dog lifts her ears and woofs, as if trying to answer Beth's question. She stands, nudges Beth's leg with her muzzle, then backs up and barks again.

When she was a kid, Beth watched *Lassie* re-runs religiously. She knows exactly what she's supposed to do right now: follow the dog wherever it wants to take her; someone might be in trouble. She suspects that's all nonsense. Besides, she doesn't want to follow the dog anywhere. She has work to do.

Newfoundlands are not supposed to bark much, but this one, woofing continuously now, seems inclined to be a breed non-conformist.

"Okay, girl, okay." Beth drains the mug, then goes inside and pulls on sneakers, layers a windbreaker over her sweatshirt. As soon as Beth steps outside, the dog bolts toward a narrow trail Beth hasn't explored yet. She assumes the path leads to the nearest cabin, the only cabin nearby and one of just eight or nine on the entire pond. Judging by her maps, the cabin is about five or six hundred metres to the north.

The trail is rocky and dark. The grey dawn can scarcely penetrate the closely spaced spruce and fir, whose damp fingers reach out to brush her shoulders and arms. The gaps between the branches are decorated with dewy spider webs – the Grinch's Christmas trees. The dog runs ahead but keeps coming back to make sure Beth is following.

In about ten minutes, they arrive at a clearing and a small cabin with dark-red clapboard. The door behind the screen door stands wide open. The dog runs forward and barks. Beth waits, but no one appears. She checks her watch: 6:12. Then climbs the steps and raps several times.

ANNAMARIE BECKEL

Leans close to the screen and cups her hands around her eyes. It's too dark to see anything but the vague outlines of a cookstove and a small kitchen table. An unlit kerosene lamp squats on the table.

Beth looks at the dog and shrugs. The dog scratches at the screen door, deeply marred below the handle, as if she does that often. The top step is hardly big enough for the two of them, and the squirming dog nearly pushes her off. She stares up at Beth.

"I can't just go in, can I?" She knocks again.

Ears forward, the dog continues to gaze up at her.

"Okay," Beth says, "but if we get in trouble, it's your fault." She opens the screen door; the dog squeezes through before Beth can grab her collar. She heads straight for the bedroom.

Stepping inside, Beth releases the door slowly so that it won't slam. Although it feels far too intimate, she peeks through the open door of the bedroom. A person lies supine on the bed, sleeping soundly. Or dead.

CHAPTER 2

Death by natural causes, Beth decides. No evidence of violence. Heart attack, probably. But she's never seen a dead person, except in a funeral parlour. The face is heavily lined, but has an odd waxy smoothness, as if the body has already been embalmed: a polished marble death mask framed by short white hair spiking out in all directions.

The dog nuzzles an exposed hand. The hand moves. Beth jumps back.

"Go away, Muin." A hoarse whisper.

The dog plants her front paws on the bed and licks the death mask, now fully mobile. Eyelids flutter open. Dark eyes stare at Beth for a long moment. "Oh, it's you."

Beth opens her mouth, then closes it. Cannot think of a single word to say.

"Guess I been away a while." A scrawny arm flings off the wool blanket. Thin legs clad in grey sweatpants, elastic at the ankles, swing around. Narrow shoulders stretch back, and long fingers tug at a grey T-shirt several shades lighter than the pants. "Bring the tobacco?"

Tobacco? Beth takes another step backwards. "I … I brought your dog back. She was over at my cabin this morning."

The dog trots out into the kitchen as if to demonstrate her inclination for wandering. The screen door creaks open then smacks shut.

"Morning? What day?"

Beth blinks, hard, as if she could make the scene disappear if she just closes her eyes tightly enough, then opens them again. "Monday," she says finally.

"Hmmm. Time for a cup a tea?" The bare feet slide into worn leather scuffs.

Beth shakes her head. "I just came over to bring your dog back."

"I believe she's chosen you." The dark eyes examine Beth more closely. "Not sure why though."

"What?"

"Sure, you don't understand now. But you will." A quick glance out the window, then back to Beth. "Where you living to?"

"The cabin near here. The one that belonged to Katherine Wells."

"You knew Katherine?" The question is abrupt, almost accusing.

"N-never met her," Beth says. "She was my husband's aunt, but he didn't know her very well. He inherited the cabin when she died."

The white eyebrows arch, as if he, or she, is expecting – no, demanding – more information.

"That was last winter," Beth explains. "A stroke. Apparently she died on the way to the hospital. But we didn't know any of that, or about the funeral, until a month later. We didn't even find out about the will until recently."

The hawk nose lends the face a severity Beth finds disconcerting. She swallows, then rattles on: "My husband thinks there might've been bad blood – or something – between his father and his aunt."

"I spect so."

"Cabin's in pretty rough shape," Beth says. "Could cost us more to repair than to build something new. Might have it torn down."

"Wouldn't do that."

"Why not?"

"Just wouldn't. It's a grand old place." Both hands push against bony thighs, and the person stands. "So

10

we're neighbours then. But you can't stay? Even for a cup
a tea?"

Beth hears longing, maybe even reproach. "Maybe a
quick cup," she says. "But I can't stay long. I have work
to do."

The hand that reaches out to Beth is large and weathered, the palm rough. "Mattie."

"Beth. Beth Meyer."

Mattie stretches, fingertips reaching toward the ceiling.
Just a fraction taller than Beth's own five and a half feet,
she notes, but far more spare.

"So," Beth says, "you were friends with Katherine?"

"Over forty years." Mattie looks at Beth sidelong. "Now
she were always good for a cup a tea and a yarn."

Beth follows Mattie from the cramped bedroom into
the kitchen, which smells of freshly split wood and dried
leaves. Mattie pokes small birch junks and kindling into a
cast-iron cookstove. Beth still can't tell if Mattie is a man
or a woman, sixty or ninety. She looks for whiskers. Can't
see any, but there's a pipe and a pouch of tobacco beside
the kerosene lamp, and on the wall there's a gun rack that
cradles a rifle and a double-barrelled shotgun.

Mattie strikes a match, filling the air with the chemical
stink of sulphur. The dog scratches at the screen door.
"Muin, you are a nuisance. Can you let her in?"

Beth goes to the door and pushes it open. "Moo …
what?" she says to Mattie.

"Moo-een." Mattie exaggerates each syllable, lips pulling forward then back, exposing a left front tooth that is
chipped, almost in half, and a gap behind the eyetooth on
the right. "Mi'kmaq for bear." Long fingers cup the dog's
chin. "Looks like a bear, dontcha think?"

Beth bites down on her lip. "Guess so."

Mattie shuffles to the sink – mottled with black ovals
where the white enamel has chipped away – and primes

the pump. The squeaky complaints are loud in the quiet of the cabin. While Mattie fills the kettle and a bowl for Muin, Beth glances around the room: old black cookstove, kerosene lamp, two straight-back chairs at a small table, and an unfinished weaving in a large loom, the colours similar to those in the weaving that hangs in her own cabin. With the exception of the guns and the loom, the cabin is much like her own: no electricity or indoor plumbing, save for the hand-pump; a combined kitchen and living room; two small bedrooms. And yet, this cabin is somehow older, as if nothing has changed here for fifty years. Not a hint of anything modern, no telephone, not even an old transistor radio or plastic knick-knack. Bunches of dried plants dangle from hooks in the ceiling. Feathers of all sizes – mostly black, brown, and white, some mottled or striped – stand in a mason jar on the windowsill over the sink. In one corner, a rocking chair sits beside a half barrel filled with chunks of wood and antler. A few woodworking tools lie on a low shelf where a dozen carvings huddle together in an unlikely herd: a bear and several moose, a hare, perhaps a lynx, maybe an otter. Beth can't be sure without looking at them more closely. Below the carvings is a long shelf of clothbound books, a few with gold-embossed letters down their spines. They look old and tattered, like something you'd buy at a yard sale for a loonie each.

Mattie places the kettle on the stove. "What kinda work makes you wanna rush off so fast?"

Beth takes off her glasses, carefully wipes one lens on the bottom of her sweatshirt, then tries to clean the other one. Holds them up to the light. The lenses are smeared. As soon as she mentions otters, most people chuckle and tell her a joke: *That otter be otterly delightful. You otter be careful out there.* She slides on her glasses. "It's just preliminary," she says. "A small study on Medicine Rock Pond."

"What kinda study?"

"Ecological. The feeding habits of the river otters here."

"Hmmm. And how do you go about doing that?"

Beth shifts her weight from one foot to the other. "Collect their scats," she says finally, "and examine them for fish bones, broken shells, insect parts."

"I see. Gathering otter shit."

Beth sees the lips twitching, the smile held back. She braces for a stupid pun.

"You must be the lady my nephew seen yesterday," Mattie says. "Dan said you was watching him through spyglasses."

"I wasn't watching *him*. I was watching for otters."

"Said he thought you was uppity."

Uppity?

"No odds," Mattie says, waving a hand dismissively. "But you're some lucky you met me. I knows every otter on the pond. I can tell you exactly what they eat. Trout. Not much else here, except for a few clams and dragonflies. Stickleback or two. And every now and again they dip into the salty water and grab theirselves a lobster or whore's egg."

"Casual observations can be a good start," Beth says, crossing her arms, "but things do need to be verified scientifically. And if I can determine that there are enough otters here on this pond – and on the neighbouring ponds – to justify a full-fledged study, I'll apply for a grant."

"Somebody'd give you money to collect otter shit?"

"The Department of Environment and Conservation has designated river otters a VEC: a valued ecosystem component." Beth tries to speak with the weight and authority she believes her PhD should give her.

Mattie nods. "I see. A valued ecosystem component."

"A sort of 'canary in the coal mine' species," Beth explains. "Otters are top predators. They concentrate heavy metals and other contaminants in their tissues, so they're one of the first species affected by water pollution." She hears herself lecturing and clamps her mouth closed. Slides off her windbreaker and hangs it over the back of a chair. "So what do you do out here?"

"Not much. Bit of weaving, gardening, carving." Mattie turns toward the array of birdfeeders hanging just outside the living room window. A nuthatch clings, upside-down, to an empty suet feeder. "And I watch the birds and animals, specially otters."

The water is blurping away in the kettle. Mattie reaches up to a bundle of dried plants and pulls off some brown leaves. Crumbles them and tosses them into a battered metal pot. Pours in boiling water. "Tea'll be ready shortly, love." Mattie takes two thick ceramic mugs from the cupboard, sets them, and two spoons, on the table, then places a yellow sugar bowl between the mugs. Voluptuous pink roses bloom on one side, a brown crack trailing crookedly between them.

"I sees em all the time," Mattie continues. "Sometimes a loner, sometimes whole families. Usually five or six. Sometimes as many as eight or ten – a big ole family reunion right in front of the cabin." Mattie grasps the wooden handle of the teapot and pours, then sits down and gestures for Beth to sit as well. The dog circles under the table. When she finally settles, Beth has to move her feet aside to accommodate her bulk. A doggy odour, oily and a little fishy, wafts upward.

Mattie spoons sugar into the tea. "See the old grandmother most often."

"The grandmother? How do you know it's the grandmother?"

"Just do."

Beth decides to let that pass.

"She watches over the pond and everything that happens here."

Beth lets that pass too. "The dog doesn't scare them off?"

"Scare them?" Mattie reaches down to stroke Muin's head. "Only thing they want is to play with her."

Beth smiles. "Probably true. I'd sure like to know what all that play is about."

"No big mystery, love. They're just happier than most folks."

Beth runs a fingertip along the rim of the mug. Stops at the rough edge of a chip. *Happy* doesn't constitute much of an explanation for a scientist.

"How long have you lived here?" she asks.

"Hmmm. Must be eighty years or so by now."

"Eighty years?"

"Thereabouts."

"And you're out here all alone?" Beth says.

"Not hardly, girl. Haven't you noticed all the birds and animals?"

"Yes, but–"

"And there's Muin." At the sound of her name, the dog lifts her head, then lays it back down on Beth's feet.

"But there's no one else? No ... spouse?" Beth asks, still unsure of gender.

"Buried a few in my time." Mattie jerks a thumb over a shoulder. "They're out back."

Beth flinches.

Mattie slaps a thigh and guffaws. "Gotcha, didn't I."

The flush starts at Beth's neck and proceeds to her scalp. Her ears burn.

"I knows you been wondering, but I likes to keep people guessing. I enjoys the torment." Mattie sits back in the chair. "Mattie is short for Matthew. Matthew MacKenzie." His eyes crinkle at the corners like an accordion. "And *no* spouse. How about yours?"

"Alan's a vet. He was here for a week, but he went back to St. John's on Friday. We have one daughter. In Vancouver, working in a lab." Beth brings the steaming

15

mug to her lips to stop her flustered chattering. The tea is pale and smells like new-mown hay.

"Vancouver. That's grand." Mattie tastes the tea, grimaces. Stirs in another teaspoon of sugar. "So what do you do when you're not out chasing after otters?"

"Teach."

His face brightens. "Katherine was a teacher! History. Taught in Gander for years."

"I teach biology. At the university."

"University. Big stuff."

"Not really." She's been teaching for more than twenty years. She could do it blindfolded. She'd prefer, in fact, to do it blindfolded, then she wouldn't have to look at the bored faces. She still finds biology awesome, in the old sense of the word: inspiring awe. But she can't seem to convey that to her students. While she lectures, they stare out the window, check their cellphones, and type on their laptops what she's pretty sure are not biology notes.

"You say you see them a lot, the otters," Beth says. "Where do you think I'd be able to watch them?"

"Just a little ways down from Katherine's cabin. Near the old beaver lodge. You haven't seen em yet?"

"I've hardly been here a week. And I only started my project a few days ago."

"Maybe they're staying away for a while. Sure, they can be pretty cautious around anything new."

From the gentle way he says this, Beth suspects he's just being kind to the scientist who can't find her research animals. She pushes the tea away. Her skin feels hot, but also clammy. She pulls off her sweatshirt and lays it across her lap. Begins to fiddle with the metal turnkey on the kerosene lamp.

"So …" She coughs into her hand. "If you've been here for eighty years, you must know the story on Medicine Rock Pond."

Mattie straightens. Eyes that were hazel just moments ago are now bright green with startling flashes of gold. "There's lotsa stories about the pond," he says cautiously.

"About the name, I mean."

His face relaxes. "Oh … that. There's a rock at the outlet. Medicine Rock."

"Odd name."

"Might be Mi'kmaq. Might go all the way back to the Beothuk." Mattie shrugs. "Who knows? Long time ago, people would visit Medicine Rock to pray."

"People prayed to a rock?"

He laughs. "Don't be so foolish. Do people pray to a church? It's just the place where they go to feel close to their god … or creator … cosmic forces … whatever you wanna call it." He clicks a thumbnail on the chipped front tooth. "I've often thought the world would be a better place if all of us had a Medicine Rock. A place to pray, not just for our own selves, but for the earth too."

"I'd say the earth needs our protection more than our prayers."

"Same thing, love. You don't pray for something you don't care about." Mattie picks up the pipe, which looks hand-carved, and opens the pouch of Amphora, stuffs tobacco into the bowl.

Beth lays a finger on the pouch. "When I first got here," she says carefully, "you asked if I'd brought tobacco. And then said something about the dog choosing me."

"Must've been dreaming." He talks around the pipe stem. "I gets a bit confused at times." He strikes a wooden match, holds it to the pipe, and inhales a few shallow draws, expels a cloud of grey smoke. The sweet aroma reminds Beth of her grandfather, of summer afternoons trailing behind him as they walked around the farm, of sitting quietly on the front porch, him rocking and smoking, her sipping lemonade. She fiddles again with the metal turnkey on the kerosene lamp.

"Careful," Mattie says, "gonna break that thing."

She pulls her hand away and tucks it into her lap. Looks down, and then up at Mattie. "So how do you know so much about the rock?"

Mattie takes the pipe from his mouth. "Been here a long time. Oughta know something by now." He sets the pipe in a stand. "And my nan was part Mi'kmaq."

"So you're Mi'kmaq yourself?"

"Not really." Mattie spreads his big hands on the table. "Mostly Irish and Scottish. Bit of French, Welsh, and English thrown in for good measure." He traces a purple vein under the tanned skin on the back of his hand, perhaps considering the mix of currents in that miniature river of blood. "Sure, I'm the mutt," he says. "It's Muin here that's the purebred." The dog's tail thumps against the floor. "How about you? What kinda mutt are you? Sure, you're not from around here."

"Minnesota farm girl. Mostly German, part Norwegian."

"Farm girl! That's grand. Tell you what: I'll help you with your otters if you helps me with my garden. Some kinda worm is eating my cabbages." He points at the tin pot. "More tea?"

"Thanks, but I really should be going." Beth stands. For just a moment, she is dizzy. She grabs the edge of the table. Her vision narrows then clears.

"But I have a story for you."

"I should get to work now."

Mattie touches the back of her hand. "We all live in stories, love. It's important to know which one you're in."

CHAPTER 3

Beth can feel his gaze on her back. Knows that if she were to turn around, she would see Mattie at the window. She hunches her shoulders against his scrutiny and steps onto the narrow trail.

We all live in stories. What story is she in?

Beth stops herself. She might pity his loneliness, but she doesn't have time to sit and listen to the rambling stories of an old man who *gets a bit confused at times,* who believes an old otter keeps watch over the pond. She has to confess to a certain curiosity though. Eighty years on the pond. Watching animals. Mattie probably does know a lot about the local wildlife. Could be useful to talk with him again – if she can just steer him away from his own homespun explanations and get him to speak plainly about what he's seen.

When she gets back to the cabin, Beth changes into shorts and sport sandals, stuffs her research gear into a backpack, tosses in bread and cheese and a water bottle. She looks up. Katherine's rocking chair. Her hands linger on the zipper of the backpack. Friends for more than forty years. Mattie must know a lot about Katherine too.

Anxious to get to work, she grabs an apple but skips breakfast. She has only a couple of weeks before she'll have to return to St. John's to prepare for the start of classes.

She stows everything in the kayak, including a small cooler for samples, and shoves off into a morning that is chilly and overcast. She paddles slowly along the shoreline and enters the small bay just south of the cabin, hoping to find the beaver lodge where Mattie said she could find otters. She lets the kayak drift and scans the water's edge with her binoculars. Finally spots the lodge, sticks bleached, almost hidden by encroaching grasses. She paddles closer. Plenty of droppings on the rocks nearby, some fresh, some old: an otter latrine. They're probably using the abandoned lodge for a den. In a few places, the grass is crushed where they've rubbed themselves dry.

How did she miss that before? She lands the kayak to examine the scats. Pulls out four zip-lock bags and labels each: *02 Aug 10: A5, latrine.* She collects four fresh samples and tucks them into the cooler. Still crouched, Beth counts the scats and records: *02 Aug 10: A5, abandoned beaver lodge (possible den), rubbing site (~3 m northeast of lodge), latrine (~2 m diameter, ~12 m northeast of lodge); 4 fresh scats, 8 old, 4-6 otters.* She photographs the lodge, the rubbing site, and the latrine.

The fir and spruce growing close to shore are dense. She guesses that if she were to come here at dawn and dusk, there's a good chance she could watch them, either from behind the trees or from the kayak. Just like Mattie said.

She lifts her cap to massage her forehead and then her temples. She has a headache and a vague light-headedness she's begun to blame on Mattie's tea.

Beth slides back into the kayak and continues south, slowly, binoculars swinging against her life-jacket. She follows the shoreline until it gradually bends east. The water is the colour of weak tea, but clear: she can see all the way to the rock and sand at the bottom, to the crushed red and blue Pepsi can, the silver Coors Light. She passes through patches of yellow water lilies and gently waving underwater grasses and weeds. Sees black ducks and sandpipers, a chattering kingfisher that swoops from one overhanging branch to the next, but no more signs of otters, no latrines or rubbing places.

After three more hours of slow paddling, she finds a single fresh scat on a flat rock about five kilometres of shoreline from the old beaver lodge. Before she collects the sample, she checks the landmarks against her map: the rock lies well within the one hundred metres of shoreline she's designated section F4. DNA tests will confirm it, but she'd be willing to bet the scat is from one of the animals active at the beaver lodge: otters have multiple dens within large home ranges. In this case, probably all of Medicine Rock Pond, which, despite its name, is more than fifteen hundred hectares. Even after twenty years in Newfoundland, Beth still has trouble using the word "pond" for such large bodies of water. Sixteen kilometres of shoreline: 160 one-hundred metre sections she's labelled A1, her cabin, counter-clockwise through P10.

The ocean is only four or five kilometres to the north, and connected to the pond by a river; it's likely that Mattie is right about that too: the otters are regularly going into the salt water to catch a lobster, mussel, or flounder. Beth puts the sample into the cooler, against the ice.

~

The sky is beginning to darken, but there will be dusky light for at least another hour. Beth slaps insect repellent onto her face and hands – for all the good it will do – tucks her journal and voice recorder into one pocket of her backpack, pencil and binoculars into another, and dons a cap. She paddles to the small bay south of the cabin, wedges the kayak's bow into a rock crevice about twenty metres from the beaver lodge. And waits.

Every now and then, the quiet is broken by the splash of a trout jumping, but Beth doesn't turn toward the sound. She hardly moves except to brush the pesky mosquitoes and black flies from her face and hands.

Half an hour later, she sees the "v" of a muskrat in the still water, its tail waving back and forth in a sensuous "s."

It emerges from the pond with a long cattail, sits on a rock, and manipulates the plant with its front paws until it can chew on the root. Beth congratulates herself on her stillness: the muskrat doesn't even know she's there.

When it's become too dark for observations, she pushes the kayak away from the rocks and starts back to the cabin. She rounds the point of the bay and sees the *Black Feather*, a small green light glowing on its bow. Beth hugs the shore, and when she is opposite from what must be Mattie's nephew, she grins and gives a hardy wave. *Uppity*, eh? He nods. Too dark to see whether he returned her smile or not.

Back at the cabin, Beth lights the kerosene lamp and records: *02 Aug 10: ~16°C, overcast, winds light, observed at otter spot 19:50 – 20:55, none observed.*

She taps the pencil on her journal. Too early to go to bed. She glances at the musty deck of cards and then at the unopened box on the table. One thousand pieces: the pleasure of sorting them by colour and shape, starting with edge pieces first; the simple satisfaction of fitting one piece to another until everything fits. Beth moves a folder of technical papers from the table to the kitchen counter, takes out her pocket knife, and slits the sides of the box.

~

One by one, the otters emerge from the lodge, called forth by the old female's chirps. Hidden in the long grasses, she has been watching and listening, sniffing the air. She smelled the human, then saw her bobbing on top of the water. Strong odour of plastic. She also caught the scent of the man and the boat's stink. She waited until they were gone, and the smells had softened, to call the others from the lodge. They hunt now in the shallows, whiskers detecting fish in the dark. The pups begin to wrestle, prompting adults to join in. *Uhn-uhn-uhn, uhn-uhn-uhn.*

~

Beth wakes early, while it's still dark. Decides to fore-go coffee. Also neglects to brush her teeth, wash her face, or comb her hair. She wants to be at the place she's designated the otter spot before dawn. She shines a flashlight on the plastic thermometer tacked outside the living room window: 14°C. Pulls a windbreaker over her fleece jacket.

This time, she walks. By the time she arrives, the sky is just beginning to pale. She can tell by the absence of fresh scats that they didn't visit during the night.

There is no colourful sunrise: the sky simply light-ens from a charcoal grey to a slightly less sullen shade. Beth sits on shore and waits. And waits. A slender mink appears at the water's edge, dark-brown fur glossy even in the overcast. With a weasel's humpback gait, it leaps from rock to rock, pauses to sniff at the otters' latrine, but doesn't linger. The mink is an interloper on its larger cous-ins' turf. It disappears into the woods.

Small raindrops begin to spot Beth's glasses. Her head aches, and she wishes that she'd taken the time to make coffee. Chilled, and wet, she walks back to the cabin, builds a fire, and fills the percolator. It's raining heavily now, and she rearranges metal pots and ceramic bowls to catch the drips from the leaking roof. She lights the kerosene lamp and looks at the thick folder of articles on the counter – mostly technical papers about DNA extrac-tion from fecal samples, but also articles about the harm-ful effects of the effluent from oil refineries and tankers, about hydrocarbons, heavy metals, and organophosphates showing up in every corner of the globe. She lays a hand on the stack of papers: all those dire warnings, local and global. Decides that she just doesn't have the energy to read them this morning, not with a dull grey sky overhead.

In her worst moments, she can't help believing that people are a blight upon the earth: an aggressive invasive species heedlessly displacing all others. Wouldn't the earth be better off without them?

~

Late afternoon. Still raining hard and the wind is coming from the northeast at a pretty good clip. Cooped up in the cabin, Beth has tried to distract herself with the puzzle and, when that didn't work, with one of the mystery novels she brought with her. That didn't work either. She lays the paperback aside and stands. Every day her knees and hips remind her that she's getting older, that time is running out. And lately, she's been dogged by the suspicion that her so-called accomplishments – her doctoral thesis, her teaching, her scattered publications – are all second-rate. When she went to one of her younger colleagues to seek advice about her project, he'd actually raised his pale eyebrows.

"How long since you've done any field research?" he asked.

"I assisted Martin with his caribou project two years ago. Before that, I did some observations for O'Keefe when she was studying puffins. And for years I've been helping with marine mammal rescues."

"But when was the last time you headed up a research project?"

Beth stared out his office window, at an expansive view that included the university library and the clock tower. "Graduate school," she said.

"And that was?"

She tucked loose hair behind one ear. "Twenty-five years ago."

"Hard to get a grant when you don't have much of a track record." He turned back to his dual computer screens. "My advice is to start with a small request to a local agency."

Beth had settled on a preliminary survey she could complete in a few weeks – without any funding.

She begins to pace. Maybe Mattie and the crows are right: it's laughable. She counts eight long strides from one end of the room to the other, then five in the perpendicular. The count isn't accurate though because she has to step around the bowls and pans.

She grabs her wallet and windbreaker. She needs to get out of the cabin and the relentless drip of water. Beth makes a dash for the Toyota; the door creaks when she opens it. Inside, the stale air smells of spilt coffee.

Town is less than fifteen kilometres away, but driving over the rutted gravel roads and dodging water-filled potholes, she feels like it's at least fifty. The wipers are drumming at full speed. She leaves the radio off, keeping to her no-news rule.

About two kilometres after she finally reaches pavement, Beth spots the service station where she can buy gas and ice on her way out of town. A momentary pinch of guilt. She should call Alan. She hasn't talked to him since he left four days ago. She checks her watch: 16:42. He's probably still at the clinic tending to his four-legged patients. Maybe, on her way out of town, she'll give him a call.

She's tempted to go into the public library, still open on a grey Tuesday afternoon, and check her email, but decides not to break her no-email rule either. Beth passes the Bide-a-Wee, the town's shabby eight-unit motel, and the coffee shop where she and Alan had supper a week ago: seafood chowder that was mostly starchy cream and potatoes. The yellow glow from the front window looks cosy now, more welcoming. Maybe she'll treat herself to a piece of pie before she leaves town.

She pulls into the parking lot of a small grocery, the only grocery, her Toyota one of just two cars in the lot. Hunching against the wind and rain, Beth scuttles inside and grabs a plastic basket from the stack beside the economy bags of Purina and Rob Roy.

She walks slowly up and down the aisles; the only customer. The cashier, a stick-thin teenager wearing a white bib apron over tight jeans – who makes jeans for legs that skinny? – is stacking what looks like week-old iceberg lettuce into a cooler. The outer leaves are already tinged with rust. Overhead, a fluorescent light flickers, repeatedly, and Beth wonders how the girl can work here without going mad.

She scans the shelves for food that's easy to prepare: cans of sardines and Campbell's soups, boxes of crackers and Kraft Dinner, a small chunk of cheddar. Each can and box has a thin layer of gritty dust on top. She adds a loaf of whole-grain bread, some apples, batteries, wooden matches, emergency candles. And a bar of dark chocolate. If all else fails, at least she'll have chocolate.

While she stands at the checkout waiting for the cashier, Beth stares at the covers of the tabloids and magazines: *The National Enquirer, Globe, Us, People.* Doesn't worry about breaking her no-news rule.

The cashier finally comes, her bangs the same shade of red as a stop sign, fingernails enamelled a metallic blue. She glances at the groceries, then at Beth, then out the window, where the sky is cement grey. The Maple Leaf is straight out, snapping a tattoo. The edge of the flag is tattered.

The girl chews her gum thoughtfully. "Not great weather for camping, is it."

"No, it's not."

"Where you staying to?" She hasn't picked up a single box or can.

"The old Wells place."

The premature wrinkles between the girl's eyebrows deepen, then relax. "Oh, I remember her. She was nice. Cabin's out to Medicine Rock, right?" The cashier looks out the window and chews, gum snapping and popping. She turns back to Beth, blue-shadowed eyes wide. "You must be that lady who's here to collect otter poop!"

Beth marvels at the lightning speed of small-town communications. Who needs cellphones?

"Guess there's not much you can do on a day like today though." The cashier picks up a can of sardines and scans the barcode. The periwinkle fingernails click on the metal. "Tomorrow's not supposed to be much better. But you never know." She smiles encouragement. "No TV, no Internet," she says, "not even phone service out there. Nothin." Her eyes widen again at the horror of *nothin*.

"And that cabin's pretty far from everything," she continues. "Good thing Mattie MacKenzie's still out that way." The machine beeps as the girl scans another barcode. "Keeps mostly to herself though. Met her yet?"

"I met *him* yesterday."

The girl chuckles. "Must be up to her old tricks again. Some of the old-timers claim she's a witch. But I don't believe any of that old nonsense."

Beth pinches the bridge of her nose, squeezes hard. "Just a minute," she says. "I forgot something." She walks over to the stacks of dog food and grabs a box of Milk-Bones.

CHAPTER 4

She marches up the trail, light mist dotting her glasses. What in the world prompted her to buy dog treats? She doesn't need to appease anyone. She just wants to ask Mattie why *she* pretended to be *he*. She'd stewed on the possible answers to that question all night long: Poking fun. Pulling the leg of the uppity townie. Another story for Mattie to tell – just like telling everyone about the scientist who's come here to collect otter shit.

As soon as Beth steps into the clearing, Muin greets her with a series of low woofs. The dog runs toward her and prances clumsily around her legs, nudging the box of biscuits. "Okay, girl. Just a minute." Beth is glad now that she bought the Milk-Bones. Muin's not to blame. It wasn't the dog who made a fool of her.

Mattie appears at the screen door, opens it wide. "Come in, love. I'll make us some tea."

"I was in town yesterday. The clerk at Price Chopper asked about you."

"Me?" Mattie steps outside. She is wearing a red plaid shirt two sizes too big. The sleeves hang down to her fingertips.

"The clerk asked if I'd met *her* yet."

Mattie grins.

"Why did you do that?"

Mattie lowers herself to the front step, wraps her arms around her knees. "Simple really. I woke up from a long sleep feeling like a Matthew. Most mornings, I wake up feeling like a Matilda." She looks up at Beth. "Does it matter?"

Beth had asked herself exactly the same question on the long drive from town. What does it change? She couldn't think of a single thing.

"It matters because you pretended to be something you're not," Beth says.

"We all do that, love."

Muin pushes a wet muzzle against Beth's hand. She tears open the package and gives her a treat. It's gone before Beth can close the box.

"When you came by the other morning," Mattie says, "I was just coming back from a dream, a dream in which I was Matthew. I was still Matthew when Muin woke me up."

"But ... dreams are dreams," Beth says slowly, "and life is ..." She holds out her hands, palms up, box clamped under an elbow, "Life."

"Exactly! I knew you'd understand."

Beth's hands drop to her sides. Understand what?

"First time I clapped eyes on you, I knew you were a dreamer." Mattie peers into her face. "You were in the dream too, you know."

"You hadn't even met me yet."

"No odds. Seen any otters?"

Beth turns away and starts to pace. Muin follows the box of Milk-Bones.

On the drive from town, Beth had replayed their first conversation. Then, Mattie spoke with an accent so thick it almost sounded fake. This morning, the accent is gone, and Beth would swear the pitch of Mattie's voice is higher.

She stops pacing and turns to Mattie. "Is anything you told me true?"

"Everything's true ... one way or another."

"But have you really lived here for eighty years?"

"Yep."

"I mean in real life. Not in your dreams."

"Same thing." Mattie pulls at a stray thread on a button-hole. "You talk to them?"

"Who?"

Mattie rolls her eyes. "The otters, girl. You need to talk to them."

"But I haven't even seen any."

"That's why you need to ask them to show themselves. Tell them you mean no harm, that you just want to know a few of their secrets."

"Funny, we never learned that research technique in graduate school."

Mattie examines the foxglove blooming beside the step; the deep throats of the purple flowers are spotted red, like a spray of blood. She touches an oval leaf. "Well, now, there's scientific ways of knowing. Then there's the other ways."

Muin nudges the Milk-Bones. Beth doles out another biscuit but maintains her grip on the box. The dog could eat the whole package, cardboard and all, in a few slob-bery gulps.

Mattie snaps off a spike of the purple flowers and points it at Beth. "You can learn every little scientific fact about otters ... and still not know otters." She nods once, emphatically. "Unless you study them in other ways too."

"Like what? In dreams?"

"That's part of it."

Beth stares out across the pond, the same steel grey as the heavy overcast above. Maybe Mattie does consid-er herself a witch – all those dried plants hanging from the ceiling, the jar of feathers, the Matthew-Matilda busi-ness, foxglove and monkshood growing at her doorstep – decorative, but also poisonous. Maybe there really are spouses buried in the back. Mattie probably has skulls and jars of animal parts stored in the spare bedroom. Beth doesn't believe in witches or in any other such nonsense, but a shiver creeps across the back of her neck and up along her scalp. She pulls her turtleneck up to her chin.

"Come on in outta this drizzle," Mattie says. "I'll make us some tea. I have a story to tell you."

"No, I should get to work."

"No time for a story?" Mattie's lower lip pushes out. "Katherine always had time for a story." She throws up her hands. "But suit yourself."

"By the way," Beth says, "what you told me about the otters. Is any of that true?"

"Parts maybe." Mattie taps an index finger against her nose. "Or maybe not." She stands and steps into the cabin. Muin looks longingly at the Milk-Bones, then turns and follows Mattie. The screen door smacks shut.

~

Beth sits on shore at the otter spot, binoculars in her lap. She spent the day searching six more kilometres of shoreline, found two older scats but nothing new, nothing to collect.

The light is beginning to fade. She's been here for nearly an hour, and so far she's seen nothing but sandpipers, crows, and black ducks. She reaches out and picks ripening crackerberries off the low-growing plants, rolls the red berries in her palm. Tosses them, one by one, onto a flat rock. One red berry smacks against another and sends it bouncing along a crooked path. A silent game of marbles.

You need to talk to them. Mattie is off her rocker, a wingnut. For sure.

~

Her watch alarm beeps: 4:30. Beth hears the long warbling call of a loon, an echoing answer. She rises and builds a fire, pumps water into the percolator. It's early enough that she can make coffee and still be at the otter spot before the sun comes up. It's only a fifteen-minute walk through the woods.

32

When she gets there, Beth can tell from the fresh scats on the latrine that the otters visited during the night, so she's not hopeful she'll see them this morning. She waits anyway; at least she's brought coffee this time and it's not raining.

She sits down among the spruce and fir, arranges her journal and pencil, voice recorder and binoculars. Combs her fingers through her cropped hair. Feels the grease. She's long overdue for a swim and a shampoo. Her hands are dry, the skin rough, and her nails are ragged and out-lined in black soot. She's not even sure she packed an emery board. Not like Alan. He always carries nail clippers and emery boards, a professional necessity. She wonders if he's still in bed.

The night before he left to return to St. John's, Alan cooked the trout he'd caught that day. She set the table and lit the candles. "Your dinner awaits," he said, words spoken with a mock English accent. Alan presented the fish with the flourish of a chef. He'd even garnished the plates with sprigs of pink clover. In the candlelight his face was pale, his peeling nose and blotchy freckles the only evidence that they'd just spent a week in the sun, kayak-ing, fishing, swimming.

He raised a finger and pointed, and Pirate gimped obediently to his bed in the corner, settled in with a groan, and fixed his gaze on their steaming plates.

Alan lifted a fork. "Wish I didn't have to go back." Poked at a boiled potato. "How long do you think it will take for you to get what you need?"

Beth reached for the pepper. "Depends on how long it takes me to find enough samples."

"I could come out next weekend and help."

She sprinkled pepper over her plate, then carefully lifted the backbone away from the fish. "Thanks, but two people bobbing around in kayaks might keep them away and then I won't get any observations."

"I could just go off and fish somewhere. Leave you to your work."

"Being able to focus on my research all day," she said slowly, "every day, means I can get back to St. John's that much sooner." She smashed a boiled potato with her fork. "And I need to know that I can still do this on my own."

"But I'm concerned about you kayaking by yourself."

"It's quiet water, Alan, and I'll wear my life-jacket. Promise." She closed her eyes, took a deep breath, and then said it quickly: "And I think I might need a little time to myself."

He looked out the window and pulled gently at the loose skin under his chin, then turned back to Beth. "For what?"

"Not sure." She tried to smile. "It's been more than twenty years since I've spent any real time alone."

"But I thought you were disappointed that Rachel didn't come home this summer."

"I am, but …" She couldn't finish. Couldn't explain it, even to herself.

They bent over their plates and busied themselves picking bones from the delicate pink flesh. Pirate rose quietly from his bed and walked to the table, clicking nails and three-legged gait audible across the wood floor. With a tentative wag of his tail, he laid his head in Alan's lap and watched him eat. Alan scowled in feigned sternness and then slipped the dog the trout skin. He wiped his greasy fingers on a paper towel. "Call me every evening then?"

"There's no reception here, remember? I'll have to drive into town."

He blinked, his pale lashes barely visible. "Oh, right," he said, nodding. And the nodding annoyed her. She wished she could prod him into an argument, then she could yell at him. But for what? For agreeing with her?

Dinner over, they undressed and climbed into the creaking bed, both sleeping bags unzipped and spread under them and over them like blankets. They'd left the dishes for morning, even though it was only nine o'clock. Alan blew out the candle, then lay down facing her back. He touched her shoulder, and she turned to face him. He kissed her and stroked her breasts, murmured in her ear, "I'll miss you."

She felt her heart shrivel into something hard-shelled and miserly – because she didn't want to return his touch, or his words, but didn't have the courage to say so. She rubbed his chest and reached down to bring him to life, in a ritual that was no longer love-making but just sex.

When it was over, she rolled away from him and stared into the dark. She felt Pirate climb onto the bed and settle between them, a rustling of the sleeping bag then the soft, warm weight. Just before sleep, an image of water and limestone came to mind: the erosion of the bond between them like the steady, underground drip of water on stone, unseen and unremarked. Until this. Not a growing hatred or anger, or even dislike. But an absence, a worn-away hollow.

In the morning, Alan and Pirate left before she'd even gotten out of bed. A peck on her cheek, a slobbery lick to her nose, and they were out the door.

Beth slaps at a mosquito. She picks up the journal and pencil at her side, but then has to pause. Can't recall the date. Thinks it might be Thursday, the fifth, but isn't entirely sure. She scrawls a few notes: *5 Aug 10: ~16°C, clear and sunny, winds light, observed in A5, 5:20 – 7:18, fresh scat from 3-5 animals, none observed.*

None. *This all seems pointless – an animal behaviourist who can't find her animals. And what would it matter if I could?*

She stares at the stark words. Tries to erase them, but the hard eraser makes messy black smears. She crosses them out.

Beth collects three fresh samples, then walks back to the cabin and slips them into the cooler. She eats a quick breakfast of saltines and peanut butter, and re-heated coffee, then loads up the kayak and spends the rest of the morning paddling another few kilometres of shoreline. The sun is warm, almost hot, on her face, and she pictures Alan in his air-conditioned clinic, methodically washing his hands and cleaning his nails before entering an examining room, and then nodding patiently, face serious, while worried pet owners try to explain what they think is wrong with Bitsy or Fluffy or Max. She'll go into town later, she promises herself, pick up more ice and call him.

CHAPTER 5

About mid-day, having searched another four kilometres of shoreline, Beth heads toward the outlet, curious now whether she can identify Medicine Rock. The wind is calm, the paddling easy under a hazy sky.

Approaching the outlet, Beth studies the rocks. They're all different – rust-red, a dark red-black, various shades of grey, some with green or white striations – but none is particularly distinctive. They're millions of years old. Yet, sharply angled, they look new, not ancient, and they're jumbled together as if they were tossed there by a giant hand. Who decided to name one Medicine Rock?

Beth spots a red one that is darker than the others – almost maroon – and a bit bigger too. It stands upright and a little apart. She stares a few moments, squints, finally sees the craggy profile of a man's face. Maybe.

She beaches the kayak and pulls it up onto the rocky shore. A salmon leaps and falls back into the water with a soft splash. About thirty metres away, an eagle watches from a tall spruce. Probably looking for lunch, and Beth has interfered. She raises her binoculars and sees a mottled head and tail: an immature bird. The juvenile, now as large as an adult, spreads its great wings and lifts off.

She sits down beside the upright boulder she has decided is Medicine Rock and pulls a water bottle and bread and cheese from her backpack. She smells fresh water and the faint, sweet fragrance of the wild roses blooming at the edge of the woods behind her. A black and yellow swallowtail lands on the rock, opens and closes its wings, then flits away.

The place where they went to feel close to their god. Well, if she were forced to choose, she'd pick a big red rock beside tumbling water – in a place with eagles and salmon, wild roses and butterflies – over a cathedral any day.

Running a fingertip along a white vein in the rock, she wonders who came here long ago and to whom they prayed. And for what. *Please help us to find enough food for the winter. Please heal the sickness in my chest. Please let this baby be born healthy. Please let my wife – my husband, my mother, my child, my friend – live. Or die peacefully. Please. Please. Please.*

Heartfelt petitions. Not so different then from now. When she was a child she prayed, sometimes fervently, with a child's whole heart. She can't remember when she stopped. Probably when it became clear that no one was listening.

Beth touches the rock again. The surface is cold and rough.

Just what would she pray for if she thought someone were actually listening? A good life and good health for her daughter, her husband, and herself. Of course.

She lifts her face to the sun and closes her eyes. Hears water murmuring and gurgling as it flows around the rocks in its rush to the sea. She would pray for the earth, for the preservation of places like this one.

Her hand drops from the rock. But you can't just *decide* to hold on to childish delusions. No matter how much better they might make you feel.

Two years ago, Beth had actually tried, for Alice's sake. She even tried praying again. And then felt foolish for it. Because no one was listening then either. Her best friend suffered, in the worst kind of way, and Beth couldn't help her.

She swallows the last of her water and realizes she has to pee. There's just one small boat out on the pond, so she won't have to go far into the woods, but as soon as she steps in among the spruce and fir, she has an odd sense of being watched. She looks all around, sees no one, but walks in farther, until she begins to feel absurdly modest. She unzips her shorts and squats down in a thicket of tall ferns. Swats a mosquito from her bare thigh.

As she's zipping up again, she sees a glint. A beer can or discarded sausage tin? She steps closer: it's just a shallow pool of water reflecting the light. But beside the pool, half hidden by sphagnum moss, lie two small shells, cowry shells. Beth stoops to pick them up, but the shells are attached to each other by a corroded metal chain. She pulls, gently, so she won't break the chain, but then has to lift a rock to pull the shells and the chain free.

She doesn't know much about religious objects, but she's pretty sure she's found a rosary, an odd rosary of cowry shells, green glass beads, and bits of carved bone, which she can see now are crudely carved animals and birds. Beth picks shreds of moss off the carvings and, using a thumbnail, scratches soil and corrosion from the chain.

Rosary clasped in one hand, Beth walks back to the outlet. An aluminum boat sits on shore beside her kayak: the *Black Feather*. A man in hipwaders is standing in the fast-moving water. He draws back an arm to cast.

She shoves the rosary into her pocket. "Hi there," she calls out with false cheeriness. "Catching anything?"

"Few rises. Nothing big."

"I saw a salmon jump earlier. Great day," she offers, hoping she's now been friendly enough that she can leave without being called uppity.

He angles his head toward her. "Looking for otters?"

"Just doing a bit of research on the pond."

"Looking for otter shit is what I heard."

"There's a little more to it than that," she says.

"Is there now?" He casts the small fly out over the water, flicks the line, then pulls it in.

"You must be Mattie MacKenzie's nephew."

"Sort of."

"Sort of?"

"Grandnephew. My grandmother was her older sister – by almost twenty years." He shifts the fly rod to his left hand and steps toward Beth. Puts out his right. "I'm Dan. Dan Holloway."

"Beth Meyer."

He is just a few inches taller than Mattie and almost as spare. Under the bill of a red baseball cap, his eyes are the same hazel green. Hair, from what she can see of it, is dark, and generously flecked with silver.

"Mattie tells me you're from the university in St. John's."

In other words: *uppity.*

His gaze travels from her bare toes up to her face again. Beth, in her khaki shorts, black tank top, and sport sandals, suddenly feels both underdressed and over-dressed, as if she's just stepped out of an Eddie Bauer catalogue. She unties the chamois shirt draped over her shoulders and pulls it on.

"Said you were doing some kinda study on otters."

"Just a preliminary assessment, really. To see if I can do a real study here." She turns toward the kayak, says over her shoulder, "Was just taking a lunch break. I should get back to work."

"The shit always calls, doesn't it." Muttered, just loud enough for her to hear.

She spins around, intending a snappy retort, but comes up short: annoyed but empty-headed. Surprises herself then with a question. "Is she okay? Is she ...?"

His smirk fades. "Cracked?"

"She doesn't have Alzheimer's or anything?"

"Nope. Sharp as a tack." He pulls a cigarette from his shirt pocket, sticks it between his lips and talks around it. "Just a bit nuts is all."

"How old is she anyway?"

Dan tilts his head, lips still gripping the cigarette. "Guess she must be in her mid-eighties by now." The cigarette bobbles.

"And she doesn't need some sort of caretaker, someone to help her out?"

"Nope." He flicks a lighter and cups his hand around the end of the cigarette. Exhales a cloud of grey smoke. "I pick up her groceries and cut wood for her. Do a few repairs around the cabin." He loosens a shoulder strap on the hipwaders. "My most important job is taking her weavings and carvings to a gallery in St. John's."

"Really?" Beth chews her bottom lip: Mattie an artist? "When I first met her," she says slowly, "she told me her name was Matthew." She expects Dan to grin just like Mattie did.

Instead, he takes a deep draw on the cigarette, exhales. "She does that sometimes."

"Seems a bit ... odd."

A salmon breaches, and they both turn to watch the disappearing ripples. Beth glances sideways at Dan. His face is angular and weathered, with the same prominent nose as Mattie's. Handsome, she supposes, in a craggy sort of way: the Marlboro Man.

"Matthew was her twin brother," he says. "Died long before I was even born. She claims to be living his life for him." He waves the cigarette dismissively. "Or something like that. I don't ask. Not my business." He looks at Beth, doesn't smile. "None a yours neither." He gently stubs out the cigarette and puts the unsmoked half into his pocket. Walks back out into the water.

~

Beth sips an indifferent merlot and studies the rosary by the yellow glow of the kerosene lamp. She's rubbed the chain with Brasso and scrubbed the dirt off the shells and beads, and the carved animals. The short length of chain for a cross is there, but the cross itself is missing.

After she'd left Dan to his fishing, she paddled back to the cabin and then drove into town, dutifully stopping at the pay phone to call Alan. She fingered the rosary while she waited: one ring, two, three, four, then the answering machine with her own chirpy voice asking her to "please leave a message."

"Hi, Alan," she said. "Everything's going–"

"Good to hear your voice … finally. Glad I didn't miss you." He sounded out of breath. "I was just on my way out the door. Emergency surgery. How're things going?"

"I've collected samples from a few different sites on the pond."

"Great."

"Yeah, but I haven't seen them yet. Not sure I'll be able to get much in the way of observations."

"Observations don't matter that much, do they? Just as long as you can get enough samples."

"I guess. But I'd really like to watch them."

"Well, you said yourself they're elusive little buggers."

She scraped dirt off one of the small carvings. "What's the surgery?"

"Cat. Hit by a car."

She cringed.

"From the technician's assessment, it sounds like we won't be able to save it."

Beth envisioned his fingers running through his sandy hair, mottled now with grey.

"But I'll give it my best try," he said wearily. "Belongs to a little girl."

She could see his lined forehead, his fingers pulling at the loose skin under his chin, and knew that he would try his best. He always did. It's one of the things that made her fall in love. What were the others?

"I should get to the clinic," he said. "Thanks for calling. Good to know that you're okay and that you're getting some samples. Call me again tomorrow? I'll have more time then."

"Not sure I'll be able to get into town again."

"Okay. Well … call me when you can."

"Good luck with the surgery."

Hasty goodbyes. No time to talk about Mattie and the odd he-she business. Or the rosary. Just as well. Too difficult to explain anyway.

She punched in the numbers and called her daughter. No answer, so Beth left a message: "Hi, Rachel, hope everything's good with you. I've started my research, and everything's going great. I'll call again soon. Love you."

Beth made it to the liquor store just before it closed and picked out three bottles of red wine. From there she went to the hardware and bought metal cleaner, an inexpensive scrub-brush, and four dust-covered wineglasses – three more than she needed, but it would be humiliating to purchase only one, like announcing to the whole town that the uppity scientist drinks alone.

She decided then to treat herself to supper at the Morning Glory. She grabbed a novel from the stash in the backseat and sat at the counter, one of only two customers, the other an elderly man tucked away in a corner booth. He nodded and tried to smile when she came in, but the right side of his mouth turned down; the whole right side of his face was slack, as if he'd suffered a stroke.

While Beth ate her salad and vegetable soup, she read the Agatha Christie mystery. And scrupulously avoided eye contact with the man's watery blue eyes, fearing that

43

if she gave him an opening, he'd join her at the counter and regale her with stories of the olden days.

Driving back to the cabin in the golden light of a late-summer evening, Beth surprised herself with her eagerness to clean up the rosary, so eager, in fact, that she didn't bother to go out to the otter spot. Instead, she's spent the last two hours scrubbing and polishing. Beneath the corrosion, the chain is copper. A few of the green glass beads are cracked, and she can tell by the empty spaces on the chain that a few have broken away completely. It's the carvings that intrigue her. It looks as if there may have been ten when the rosary was intact; now there are only seven. The small chunks of bone appear to be a caribou or moose, a bear and a fish, an eagle, a loon, and an owl. If she turns one carving on its side and squints, it could be construed as an otter, or at least she'd like to think so. She lays the rosary aside, swallows the last of her wine, and gets ready for bed.

~

The old female catches a small fish. She chirps at a pup, who follows her out of the water. When she lets go of the fish, it bends and twists – silver flashes over the rocks. The pup paws at the fish and nips its tail, but it flops its way into the shallow water. The old female lunges and captures it again. Bites its head, hard, and leaves it for the pup.

Three of the otters come onshore and sniff at the marking place. Mixed among the scents of plants and rocks, earth and sweet water, are the lingering traces of a female mink, a male muskrat, and two crows, an old one and a fledging that have eaten a rotting fish. Of far greater interest is the strong musk of an unfamiliar otter, young and male but not a pup. Each of the three otters turns, treads both hind feet, and leaves scat over his scat, musk over his musk.

They re-enter the water and all of them swim to the lodge. One by one, they dive, surface inside, and shake water from their fur. They settle in to groom each other: a tangle of warm, wet bodies. The old female touches each one with her muzzle, sniffs each reassuring scent. All of them here. A chorus of *uhn-uhn-uhns* fills the dark, humid lodge.

CHAPTER 6

Rain drumming hard against the roof startles her awake before her alarm goes off. She hopes she's left the pans and bowls in the right places. She's given up putting them away in the cupboards.

Beth closes her eyes to recall her dream, the one that woke her in the middle of the night: A young man sits cross-legged before a fire. Black hair, sun-bronzed skin, blue baseball cap with a bright red C. His hands wield a long bone and a knife that glints in the firelight. She knows, in the way that dreamers know, that he is carving an otter. He doesn't speak or look up, but she also knows that his eyes are bright green and that he is handsome. She hears a branch snap. A bull moose is charging toward her, its broad antlers enormous. She tries to run, but the mud is deep; it sucks at her feet. When she finally pulls free, she crawls, on hands and knees, into the cover of trees and shrubs, and watches the moose through branches interwoven like a spider web. Broad wings sweep over-head, a dark shadow. *Hoo-hoo-hoooo, hoo-hoo.* Then she feels warm breath on her neck. *Mfuff-mfuff.* And turns her head slowly to see a black bear, its golden eyes peering into hers. She edges away, crab-walking backwards, and finds herself in murky water, floating. The sky is geometric patches of green – sage, moss, jade, emerald – that blossom and disappear like patterns in a kaleidoscope. A loon calls in a prolonged, echoing tremolo.

Whiskers tickled her cheek, waking her. *Uhn-uhn-uhn, uhn-uhn-uhn.* The rosary. She dreamed of the animals on the rosary.

Beth keeps her eyes closed to envision the handsome young man. She had wanted him to look at her. She lies still in the warm sleeping bag. It's been such a long, long time since she's felt anything remotely lustful.

~

After she returns from the outhouse, Beth checks the pans and bowls, empties some, moves others. Glances at the table. No rosary. She's sure she left it there, right beside the kerosene lamp and the scattered puzzle pieces. She searches all around the jar of Brasso, the scrub-brush and rags. Lifts the lamp. Nothing.

She builds a fire and prepares coffee, pumping water into the battered percolator. It's then that she sees the rosary on the windowsill above the sink. She doesn't recall putting it there. She rubs her temples. Maybe she had more wine last night than she thought. Beth picks up the rosary and looks again at the carving she thinks is an otter. Lays it back on the windowsill.

While she waits for the coffee to perk, she wraps herself in her sleeping bag and watches the grey morning light illuminate the weaving. She gives it closer attention now that she knows it's artwork worthy of a gallery. Beth studies how the changing light transforms the patterns and colours: azure water, a rose sky bleeding to violet and then to indigo, a row of dark-green spruce, grey rock. Feathers – blue jay and crow, or maybe raven – have been woven into the indigo sky. Embroidery, or maybe crewel-work, Beth isn't sure, overlays parts of the weaving.

Forty years of friendship. Did Katherine buy it? Or was it a gift from Mattie?

Beth pours coffee and turns the rocking chair toward what meagre light the rainy dawn has to offer. She's been alone for a week, but she's not lonely. Not yet anyway. In truth, she often feels most herself when she's alone: no one to worry about pleasing – or disappointing. As an only child on a farm, she'd spent most of her time alone, just her and Jax roaming the woods and fields. She was shy around other kids, often blushed when they spoke to her; sometimes, they called her stuck-up, but it didn't matter. She had the animals for company. She thought of them as friends, even the ones most people didn't like: crows, mice, bats, and barn owls. She'd loved waking up on a spring morning, traipsing downstairs still rubbing sleep from her eyes, and finding a newborn lamb standing in a cardboard box, bleating to break your heart. It became Beth's job to bottle-feed rejected lambs. Until she was nine. That fall, after the lambs had been loaded onto the truck, Beth's father took her along to the slaughterhouse. The next spring, she refused to feed the motherless lambs. Her dad told her she was too soft-hearted to be a farmer's daughter, muttered something about an absence of iron.

Beth hears a scrabbling at the door. A series of woofs. She groans, then throws off the sleeping bag. Cracks the screen door just wide enough to shake a finger. "Muin, go back to where you belong."

The dog uses her muzzle and then her massive head as a wedge to push her way in. Trots into the bedroom and sniffs at the bed. Comes back out, sits down by the counter, and stares at the box of Milk-Bones and then at Beth.

Beth shakes her finger again. "Don't even think about it. I will not reward this."

Muin circles and settles near the cookstove. The odour of wet dog fills the room.

"Okay, you can dry off, then it's back you go."

Muin looks at Beth as if gauging her seriousness. Beth wonders what she's thinking – what the dog knows. She doesn't look especially intuitive, or intelligent, but then Newfoundlands rarely do. And yet, they're one of the most dedicated and courageous of all rescue dogs, willing to swim untold distances through the coldest and roughest water to drag someone to safety. Blind instinct? Or something else? Just what's going on between those floppy black ears?

Muin lays her head on her front paws and closes her eyes, as if she knows Beth's mushy heart for what it is.

~

Three hours later, when the rain has slowed to a drizzle, Beth follows Muin up the trail to Mattie's cabin. The rosary is tucked in her pocket.

Mattie opens the door before Beth can even knock. "Give up being mad at me?"

"I wasn't mad," Beth says, "I was … disappointed."

"Disappointed?"

"Okay, sure. I was pretty annoyed with your little trick."

Mattie chuckles.

"What? Are you someone different today?"

"Nope, still feeling like Matilda." She winks. "For now." She opens the door wider. "Tea?"

Beth steps into the cabin, Muin pushing in ahead of her. "Just water for me," she says.

"No tea?"

"Last time I came away with a headache."

"Nonsense. Just plain old Labrador tea. Harmless." Mattie pulls two mugs out of the cupboard. "But suit yourself. How about some Red Rose then?"

While Mattie prepares the tea – making a show of pulling the teabags from the box – Beth studies the unfinished weaving in the loom: a combination of cobalt, ochre, and ivory threads form an abstract pattern; woven within are real feathers – duck and gull? – and small pieces of driftwood. Dark green yarn has been wound around a spool. To be woven into the warp and weft, she guesses, although she can never remember which is which.

"Met Dan yesterday," Beth says. "He told me he takes your weavings to a gallery in St. John's."

"I'm just glad people like em. Helps pay the bills."

Beth points at what looks like a stylized spider web in one corner of the weaving.

"A nod to the master weaver," Mattie says before Beth can ask.

Mattie pours black tea into two mugs and brings them to the table, where a spike of foxglove stands in a mason jar. She sets the yellow sugar bowl between the mugs. "Haven't seen any otters, have you." It's a statement, not a question.

Beth straightens her glasses. "I've only been searching for a few days."

"They're keeping themselves away," Mattie says, sitting. "You try talking to them?"

"I haven't tried talking to animals since I was eight years old." Beth pulls out a chair and sits down. Muin leans against Beth's shins as she settles under the table.

"That's the trouble, see. Children know stuff we grown-ups forget." Mattie moves the jar and the spike of purple flowers from between her and Beth. "You scientists think seeing is believing. It's the other way around." She winks again. "Believing is seeing."

Beth snorts a laugh. "And that's exactly why people are always seeing spaceships and aliens, Sasquatch and other weird things. They already believe in them."

"So you don't believe in anything you can't see?"

"Of course there are things we can't see, but there's always some kind of evidence. You can't see gravity, but you can certainly see it at work."

Mattie stirs sugar into her mug. "You study animals. You believe they have souls?"

"I'm not even sure people have souls."

"What if it turns out that we all have souls?" Mattie puts her elbows on the table and interlaces her fingers. "And that we're accountable for how we've lived on this earth? For how we've treated its occupants? All of its occupants?"

"Accountable to whom?"

Mattie shrugs. She picks up a box of matches, slides it open, then shut again, the cardboard rasping. She taps the drawing of the glowering seal on the top. "It's us who need them, you know. Not them who need us. Maybe they don't want you watching em."

Beth takes a swallow of black tea, then reaches into her pocket and pulls out the rosary. She holds it out on her palm, green beads and chain dangling. "I found this yesterday. Near the outlet. About fifty paces back in the woods, just lying there beneath some moss."

Mattie touches one of the green beads. The muscles in her jaw tighten, but when she looks up at Beth, her expression is neutral.

"Any idea who it might have belonged to?" Beth says.

"Yours now."

"Mine?"

"You found it."

"But who do you think lost it?"

"How would I know?"

Beth rubs the small bone owl between a thumb and middle finger. "Maybe I should put it back where I found it." She lays the rosary on the table.

"Maybe you should." Mattie stands and goes to the loom, picks up a wicker basket and brings it back to the table. "I have a story for you."

"Mattie?"

"No worries. It's not long. And it's about studying animals." Mattie sits down and pulls a spool and a skein of dark-brown yarn from the basket.

Beth wraps her hands around the hot mug, watches steam rise in wispy curls.

Mattie begins to wind yarn onto the spool. "There was this youngster, see, who spent all his time outdoors, always out in the woods or by a pond or a river. His grandmother fretted about him getting lost or hurt. She prayed for him. The boy loved his nan, but like youngsters everywhere, he didn't have time for her worries. Or her prayers. He just wanted to be out in the bush, watching animals. He began carving them too, not from pictures or memory, but from the way he saw them. He could see their souls. Even carved his grandmother a rosary of animal souls."

Beth touches the carved otter, then glances toward the menagerie on the shelf.

Speaking softly, Mattie watches her fingers wind the yarn onto the spool. "After a while he begins trying to mimic Bear's huff-huff and her cub's bawl, Raven's deep cronk and Owl's hoo-hoo-hoo. He practices and practices, but only when he's alone, see, so the animals won't be confused." She looks up at Beth. "Or maybe he was afraid they'd laugh at him. Some folks worry about looking foolish, you know."

She pauses to untangle a knot. "When he finally thinks he's ready, he speaks. Raven hops closer, turns her head sideways, and peers at him with her black, black eyes. Bear and Owl stop what they're doing, and listen. The boy knows then that he can talk to them!" Mattie nods once, emphatically.

"One day he's out in the bush looking for a yellow moccasin flower to bring to his grandmother." She lays down the spool to pick up her mug. "Ever see one? Lovely. But not much smell to them."

"I've seen them," Beth says. "Usually in bogs."

"That's right. Too late in the year now though. All dried up." Mattie sips tea and turns to stare out the window at the birdfeeders, at the juncos and chickadees coming and going. She turns back and picks up the yarn and spool again, silently winding the yarn.

"What about the boy?" Beth asks, looking over the rim of her mug. "I believe you were trying to teach me how to talk to the otters."

"Hmmm. Where was I now?" Mattie rubs her nose. "Oh, yes. The boy goes farther and farther into the woods, into the bog, searching. Gets himself all turned around. Doesn't know which way to go. Gets scared then and runs one way, turns back, runs off the other way. Does this again and again, until there's no way he can retrace his path; he's trampled everything around him."

Beth pictures the sameness of bog all around, the black spruce and tamarack, the trampled moss. But if the boy was experienced in the woods? "What about the sun?" she says.

Mattie frowns as if she's annoyed. "Oh, it's cloudy, see. No sun. And it's beginning to get dark. The boy sits down on a log. He's worried now that he'll have to spend the night in the woods, and that makes him hungry, and scared. He's staring down at the moss now, feeling sorry for himself."

Her fingers stop moving between the yarn and the spool. She looks at Beth. "Then he hears a deep, gruff voice: 'Follow me, b'y.' He looks all around to see who spoke. Can't see anyone. He stands on the log. Still can't see anyone. Then he hears a rustling sound. A branch snaps. He turns and catches a glimpse of a big brown arse ambling off through the juniper: a moose. And he knows then that animals can talk to him too. And he can see that following the moose is the way he should go. Even finds three yellow moccasin flowers on his way home."

Beth arches an eyebrow. "And of course, Bullwinkle spoke with a Newfoundland accent."

"Was a Newfoundland moose, wasn't it." Mattie slaps the table, chuckling. "Don't be so foolish. The moose didn't say one word out loud. The boy heard it all in his head."

"Then why can't you just say that the boy imagined the words? That the moose just happened to be there? That's a simpler explanation."

"Simple isn't always right. Besides, that wouldn't make for a very good story now, would it." Mattie raises an index finger. "And I know you're wondering. It's a pirn, not a spool. That's the proper name."

"Dan told me you had a twin," Beth says quietly. "Was he the boy who carved the rosary?"

"It's just a story, love."

"Dan said he died young."

Mattie takes a deep breath, lets it out slowly. "Matthew drowned when he was just seventeen. In this pond."

Beth wants to ask how, but the sadness in Mattie's face stops her.

"We're very close," Mattie says. "Two halves of a whole." She drops the yarn and pirn into the basket. "What else Dan have to say?"

"That you ... live Matthew's life for him." Beth's voice rises on the word him, as if she is asking a question.

"Mostly in dreams." Mattie is staring at Beth, who nods as if she understands. But doesn't.

Beth coughs into her fist. "I had a strange dream last night." She tries to laugh, but her throat is too tight. "The animals on the rosary and a young man carving."

Mattie touches the back of Beth's hand. A touch like the flutter of moth wings – or the skitter of spider legs. "You should take it back to where it belongs."

Beth pulls her hand away.

"The rosary brought you that dream."

"I suppose you could put it that way," Beth says carefully. Muin rises from beneath the table, stretches, and lays her heavy head in Beth's lap. She strokes the oily black fur. "Most of the animals on the rosary were in the dream."

"That's not what I mean."

"What else is there?" Beth's fingers find a small knot behind Muin's ear. "Dreams are just a jumbled mix of the things we think about during the day."

Mattie picks up the rosary and examines each carved animal. "Don't you ever wonder if it's your dreams that are real? That it's your dreaming self that conjures your waking self into being?"

"All children think about that at one time or another."

"Maybe youngsters are more open to understanding possibilities."

Beth takes a long swallow of the cooled tea. Sets down the mug. "The weather's cleared. I should get going." She begins to stand, but stops halfway. Hanging from a hook by the door is a dirty blue baseball cap. With a faded red C. "Where did you get that?"

"What?" Mattie twists around in the chair.

"That blue cap."

"Matthew's had that forever. The Cubbies. Everybody's favourite losers. That's what he always says." She turns back to Beth. "Minnesota farm girl like you oughta recognize a cap from a Chicago team."

Beth knows she probably saw that cap on her first visit; it just didn't register until it showed up in her dream. But still.

Mattie holds out the rosary. "You best take this back to where it belongs."

CHAPTER 7

It's been raining on and off all day, and by late afternoon, Beth has spent nearly four hours cruising the shoreline and found only one fresh scat. She goes back to the cabin to change into dry clothes and then – unable to stomach the thought of another can of soup heated on the woodstove – decides to drive into town.

When she walks through the door of Price Chopper, she sees the same flickering fluorescent light and the same cashier with the bright red bangs, but today there are several other customers roaming the aisles. Beth picks up a package of coffee and a jar of peanut butter, then, while she waits for the cashier, studies the postcard rack. She spins it around: fishing boats, the triad of Newfoundland berries, icebergs, the classic photo of the little boy in kneepants standing between two enormous cod, a moose and her calf, and a sea otter floating on its back with an urchin on its chest, *You otter be here!* printed on the front. Beth sighs. There has never been a sea otter in Newfoundland. It's a Pacific species. What Newfoundland has are river otters that exploit marine food sources, a scientific inconvenience happily ignored by the makers of postcards and promoters of tourism. Beth lays the postcard beside her coffee and jar of Skippy. She'll send it to Rachel. She'll get the joke.

The cashier comes to the register. "How things going?" She leans forward, puts her hand to her mouth and whispers, "With the collecting, I mean."

"Fine," Beth says.

The girl picks up the postcard and scans the barcode. "Cute. I like otters."

Beth doesn't try to explain.

The girl's forehead furrows beneath the fringe of red bangs. "How do you get into your line of work? I mean, do you have to go to school to learn how to collect animal poop?"

Beth can feel the person waiting in line behind her come to attention. "Yes," Beth mumbles, "you do."

The girl's eyes widen. "Really? Like university?"

"Something like that."

"Wow! Who would think?" Still nodding in thoughtful wonderment, she places the coffee and peanut butter into a white plastic bag.

Beth grabs the bag and the postcard and walks to the post office. Inside, she goes to the counter against one wall and jots a quick note to Rachel, then steps to the main counter. The postmistress, her thinning hair dyed a severe black, turns around.

Beth lays the postcard on the counter. "Stamp, please?" She digs in her pocket for a loonie.

The postmistress picks up the postcard. "Cute," she says. She looks from the card to Beth, squinting over her glasses. "You must be that lady who's collecting otter ... droppings."

Beth lays her coin on the counter and tries to smile.

~

As soon as she walks through the door of the Morning Glory, she sees Dan, and before she can turn around, he nods. It would be rude not to acknowledge him. *Uppity.* But Beth positions herself so that her back will be toward him when she slides into the booth.

She slips off her rain jacket. "Hi, Dan."

"Saw your kayak out on the pond earlier. How's the research going?"

"All right," she says. Then, having already heard enough comments about her collecting, she quickly adds, "Catch anything yesterday?"

"Nope. Midday's not the greatest time for fishing. But hey, I'll use any excuse to get out on the water." He gestures toward the other side of the booth. "Join me?"

Beth hesitates. She could claim she has something important to read, but all she's brought with her is an Agatha Christie novel. She hangs up her jacket and slides into the booth.

The teenage waitress drops a coffee-stained menu onto the Formica tabletop. With her swizzle-stick build and bright red bangs, she could be a sister to the cashier at the grocery.

Beth skims the menu. "What did you order?"

"Special."

"Which is?"

"The roast beef plate."

"Hmmm."

They both laugh. "Yeah," he says, "I wouldn't recommend it."

She finally settles on a grilled cheese sandwich and pea soup. Something she could have made on the woodstove, she thinks ruefully.

Dan sits back and lays an arm along the top of the cushion, taps his fingers on the red leatherette. "Stopped in this afternoon to see if Mattie needed anything. She said you'd been by."

"She happen to mention that I brought her dog back ... again?"

"No, but then she wouldn't." Giving her a half-smile, he shakes his head. "She loves that dog. Lets her wander all over creation." He sits forward and folds his hands on the table. "She always went back and forth between their cabins ... Mattie's and Katherine's. That's why she's over at your place all the time. It's her second home."

"Great. Does that mean I'll have to take her back to Mattie's every day?"

"Just let her be. She'll go back on her own. Eventually. She always goes where she likes." He picks up a water glass and takes a swallow. "Four or five years ago, she just showed up on Mattie's doorstep."

"No one claimed her?"

"I asked around, but nobody'd lost a Newfoundland. Vet thought she was a purebred, about one or two years old, but nobody knows for sure." He rotates the water glass in a puddle of condensation. "She can be a real pain in the ass at times, but she's company for Mattie. Specially now that Katherine is gone."

Beth decides he looks better without his hat, even if his forehead is divided in half – tan half stopping just above his eyebrows, pale half to the hairline, which hasn't retreated. He takes a pack of Macdonalds from his shirt pocket, lays it on the table, turns it up on one side, then onto the other. She folds down the corner of a napkin, once, then twice.

"So," she says into the silence, "Mattie says she's been on the pond for eighty years."

"Her whole life."

She folds the napkin a third time. "So, have you lived here your whole life too?"

"Only about five years or so." He taps the red and white pack of cigarettes on the table. "Recently anyway. Grew up here – in my grandma's house – across the pond from Mattie's. But soon as I could, I joined the army."

Beth smoothes the napkin. "And that would have been …?"

"1970." He laughs, just once. "I was joining up just about the same time the Yanks were coming here to stay out."

Beth does a quick calculation. If Dan was eighteen in 1970, he's somewhere around fifty-eight, four years older than Alan, although he doesn't look it. He has more hair, even if it is turning silver, and, despite the cigarettes, he looks very fit.

"What brought you back?" she says.

"Pretty simple, really. Nan left the cabin to Dad, and he left it to me. When I retired, I decided to come back. I like it here now. Mostly."

"Mostly?"

"Miss the city stuff sometimes, and the travelling. It's great in the summer, but I'm not sure I'll stay here year-round after …" He rotates the glass again.

"Mattie dies?"

"She's pretty healthy, so that could be a long time yet."

"Nothing else to tie you here?"

Dan cocks his head. "You're full of questions."

"Scientist in me, I guess."

He gives her another half-smile. "No wife or kids, if that's what you mean."

"No, no, of course not," Beth says quickly, too quickly. "I didn't mean to pry."

He looks at her, a spark of devilment in his green eyes. "How about you?"

"Husband's a vet in St. John's," she says. "Our daughter Rachel is in Vancouver, working in a lab."

The waitress approaches, balancing a tray. As she's placing their plates and bowls in front of them, the old man with the drooping face steps slowly through the door.

Dan nods. "Hey, Clive. Why don't you join us?"

The old man shuffles toward them, props his cane on Dan's seat, leans both hands on the table, then slides into the booth beside Beth. Glances at Dan's plate; the left side of his face grimaces. When the waitress comes with the menu, he waves it away. "Just tea," he says gruffly.

Dan gestures toward Beth. "Beth, this is Clive Hiscock. Clive, this is Beth …" He holds up his palms. "Sorry."

"Meyer." She can't remember Dan's last name either.

"From St. John's," he adds. "Here to do some research. On otters."

Clive turns a red-rimmed eye on Beth. It looks huge and watery behind the thick lens. His right eye stares off into space. "Otters, eh?"

"Just a preliminary study on Medicine Rock," she says.

"Clive's lived here near as long as Mattie," Dan says. "Maybe he knows something useful. And what he doesn't know, he'll be happy to make up."

The left side of Clive's mouth grins. "Never a word of a lie."

"Beth's staying at the old Wells place," Dan continues. He lifts his knife and fork and cuts through the mound of beef and mashed potatoes.

"Katherine Wells," Clive says slowly. "Passed now."

Beth's not sure if that's a statement or a question. "Last winter," she says. "She was my husband's aunt. She left him the cabin."

"Always liked Katherine." Clive's speech is very slow but only slightly slurred.

"Go on, b'y," Dan says. "Everybody knows you were in love with her."

Clive waves his good hand at Dan. "Don't be so foolish. She were a lovely, educated lady, teaching history to numbskull kids like you. Waste of her fine intelligence, I say."

Waiting for each of his words is agonizing.

"And Mattie sure enjoyed her visits." He tips his head toward Dan. "If you knows what I mean."

Dan points an empty fork at Clive. "Gossip. Small-town gossip."

"What would you know?" Clive turns his whole upper body toward Beth, nods sideways at Dan. "He were just a youngster when Katherine first come here. Then went off into the army when he was still a pup." He dabs at the right side of his mouth with a napkin, then winks at Beth with his good eye. "Live here long enough, you get to know things."

Dan shakes his head. "Clive, you're full of it."

Clive chuckles and points to his nose. "I knows what I knows."

The waitress brings a pot of hot water and a cup and saucer. Clive struggles to open the teabag, then drops it into the metal pot. Beth clasps her hands in her lap to keep herself from reaching out to help him.

"So, you're out there close to Mattie," Clive says, closing the lid on the pot. "Met the old witch yet?"

Beth recoils. Dan smirks. "First time Beth met Mattie," he says, "she thought Mattie was a man."

Clive guffaws, his whole body shaking.

"Mattie told me *she* was a *he*," Beth says. "I didn't necessarily believe it." She picks up a spoon and plunges it into the soup. "Actually," she says to Clive, "it was Dan who told me that Mattie had a brother who died young, that Mattie sometimes pretends to be him." She gives Dan a pinched smile. To hell with his *none a your business*.

"Drownded," Clive says.

"How?"

"Overturned a canoe. Didn't know how to swim, see."

Beth looks at Dan.

"Long before my time." Dan bends over his plate, forks mashed potatoes and gravy into his mouth.

"Let's see now," Clive continues, "guess I must've been about nine or ten." He pulls the teabag out of the pot. "I don't look it, my dear, but I'm eight years younger than Mattie. Damn smokes is what done it. You should quit," he says to Dan, "while you still got time."

He drops the sodden teabag onto the saucer. "Story

was that his pretty little girlfriend had something to do with it. She almost drownded too, but Mattie saved her."

"Really?" Beth stirs the now-cold soup. It has the texture of newly mixed cement.

"Yep. Mattie didn't become a witch till later." Clive chuckles again, then grows serious. "Might've been better if the girl had died. She lived like a zombie for years."

Dan looks up. "Her, I do remember. She was damn scary when I was a kid. She must've died what ...? Forty years ago?"

Clive looks toward the ceiling and taps his fingers on the table. "Forty-eight," he says. "Katherine come here just two years after Emma died."

"And I guess *you* wouldn't forget that," Dan says.

Clive points to his temple. "I got a good memory." He pours the tea and adds sugar. Stirs, the spoon trembling in his hand.

Beth picks up half of the grilled cheese sandwich. "So the girlfriend lived for years after Matthew drowned?"

"If you can call that living," Clive says. "Her own people – fancy types from St. John's – wouldn't have nothing to do with her after. Damaged goods, see." He seems to be enjoying having an audience. He holds Beth in suspense while the cup makes a shaky journey to his lips.

"Way I heard it," he continues, after the cup has come to rest safely on the saucer again, "Emma's family never wanted her mixed up with Matthew at all. They was all high Anglican, see, and he were a Cat'lic." He leans toward Beth and whispers, "And there was a few said he might be part Micmac. Who knows? Don't matter much now, but it did then."

Dan shakes his head. "Clive, you'd make an epic out of a road-kill moose."

"I was there, b'y. You weren't even a thought yet." Clive passes a hand over his own damaged face. "Emma were in far worse shape than me. Staring straight ahead with those pale blue eyes. That's what I remember: the eyes. Like looking into the face of a ghost." He studies the painting behind Dan – a moose and her calf – as if it were a portrait of the dead woman herself.

"Emma's people probably gave her money," Clive says, "but Mattie was on her own. Can't begrudge her the bit of happiness she had with Katherine, I spose." He points at his ear with an index finger, makes little circles, slowly. "Even if she is cracked."

Clive dabs his mouth with a napkin, then fixes his good eye on Beth. "Be careful. Don't trust her." He places both hands on the table and pushes himself to his feet. Dan hands him his cane.

"You kids enjoy your supper, now," Clive says.

Beth waits until he is out the door. "Any truth to what he says?"

"Mattie likes to tease people, but she's not dangerous."

"What about the rest of it?"

Dan pushes his plate away. "Clive's an old busybody. Loves telling stories to anyone foolish enough to listen."

"That doesn't answer the question."

He shrugs. "Don't know. Don't care. Not my business." He picks up the cigarettes and drops the pack into his shirt pocket. "None a yours neither."

CHAPTER 8

Fingertips gritty and stinking of musty wood, Beth searches the contents of Katherine's junk drawer for something small and pointed. Katherine and Mattie. Dan didn't deny it. Maybe that's why Alan's family so rarely came out to the cabin when he was a boy, why Alan hardly knew his aunt. From what Beth can remember of Alan's father, he seemed like someone who'd have disapproved of something like that. A lot.

She grabs a paper clip and pushes the drawer, but the wood is warped and she has to jiggle the drawer from side to side to close it. She moves the kerosene lamp from the counter to the table, picks up the rosary, and sits down in the rocking chair. As soon as she gets it cleaned up, she'll take it back, although it seems a shame just to leave it to rot in the woods. She bends the paper clip open and pokes an end into the smaller links of the chain to clean out the last bits of dirt.

Her thoughts are scattering in a dozen different directions: Katherine and Mattie; Matthew's drowning and his damaged girlfriend; Mattie's heroism, both in saving the girl and then taking care of her for years; Clive. Dan. And not one of those directions has anything to do with her. Are, as Dan would say, *none a her business*. She drops her hands into her lap. She should forget all of them and get back to her research. She doesn't have time to waste. Beth lays the rosary beside the puzzle she's barely started and considers the stack of unread technical papers on the counter. She pushes herself up from the chair, packs her gear, and walks to the otter spot.

~

Beth sits on shore and watches the pink and lavender sky deepen through shades of violet. When she first arrived, several blue jays delivered a raucous scolding, and she wonders if the otters heard the birds, if they knew by their calls they'd seen something alarming, and so are now staying away.

She slaps at a stout buzzing around her ear. Can feel an itchy lump already rising. But at least she's warm and relatively comfortable. Not like when she did her doctoral research in Minnesota: she'd spent two frigid winters watching otters. There were mornings when clouds of steam rolled off their wet fur as they tumbled in and out of the river and onto the ice, feeding and wrestling, seemingly carefree, even when the mercury dipped to -30°C, and Beth, bundled in layers of down, had to keep her tape recorder tucked inside her parka, close to her body, just to keep the batteries working.

She would never admit it to any of her university colleagues, but she's always been a little enchanted by otters. To her, they have a *joie de vivre* that's rare among animals. They're like perpetual adolescents – complete with attitude. She knows that's anthropomorphic, but she's not sure how else to think about it. When she was in graduate school, scientific holy writ explained all animal behaviour as instinct and stimulus-response learning, à la B. F. Skinner. Talk of animal feelings was taboo. Now, most behaviourists acknowledge that animals think, that they feel pain, pleasure, anger, and fear, maybe even love and grief. Who's to say? It's impossible to know the mind of another person, let alone the mind of an animal.

She pulls at the grass, twists it into tufts, digs a finger into the dirt. She'd give almost anything to get inside an otter's head and that metre-long body, just for an hour, to learn how it senses and perceives its world, to know what

68

it thinks and feels. They hear, see, taste, and smell – and possibly imagine – what people cannot. Some animals' sensory worlds are so rich they seem to have ESP. Beth thinks of it as ESSP, extra-sensitive sensory perception: dogs that can diagnose cancer in people more accurately than a pathologist, and detect blood sugar levels that are dangerously high or low, and sense chemical and electrical changes that signal an imminent seizure. Elephants have specialized organs in their feet that can sense seismic vibrations made by elephants miles away. Dolphins can recognize and remember the unique sound signatures of hundreds, maybe thousands, of other dolphins, and have sonic conversations that may be more complex than humans can ever fathom.

So just what are the otters saying to each other with their chirps and *uhn-uhn-uhns?* What can they perceive and understand that humans cannot?

Beth hears footsteps behind her, branches snapping. A moose? A bear? She turns her head very, very slowly. A sloppy wet tongue bathes her face. She releases her breath and pushes Muin away.

"Lovely evening," Mattie says, lowering herself to sit beside Beth. The tip of a black feather pokes out from her shirt pocket. She points at the binoculars. "Mind if I have a look?"

Beth lifts the binoculars from around her neck and hands them to Mattie, who puts them to her eyes and adjusts the focus. "Haven't seen em yet, have you," she says.

Muin noses at the backpack. Beth digs out a piece of cheese left from lunch.

Mattie scans the shoreline. "These are pretty damn good," she says. "You can see a lot." She lowers the binoculars. "But a lot you can't." She hands them back to Beth. "Talk to em yet?"

Beth offers the cheese to Muin.

"You should call their name."

"Their name?" Beth says.

"You know … address them. So they know it's them you're talking to." Mattie wraps her arms around her knees. "Course calling them by the name 'otter' might not bring em out. Sometimes you've got to call an animal by the name it's known for hundreds, maybe even thousands, of years." She strokes Muin's head, scratches behind her ears. "The old grandmother is the one you need to talk to. And maybe she doesn't know the name 'otter,' or thinks it's silly. Maybe she knows herself as *giwnig* or *edru*."

Beth hears *kee-o-nig* and *e-droo*. Mi'kmaq words? Or something else?

"Or maybe she wants to be called 'Grandmother.'" Mattie cups Muin's chin and speaks to the dog. "Or maybe she wants to be addressed as 'Valued Ecosystem Component.'"

"Very funny."

"You think I'm joking? Well … maybe just a little."

Muin picks up the backpack and lays it at Beth's feet. "Sorry, girl," she says. "No more cheese." A wet circle is spreading across the brown canvas. The dog sits down beside her. Beth drapes an arm around her and stares out across the water, watches an osprey. The hawk hovers, then glides closer to shore and hovers again. Dives. Flies off with a small fish in its talons.

"You're going about it all wrong, you know," Mattie says.

Beth tightens her arm around Muin.

"It's not more little facts we need. But a grand change in the way we think about animals. Nothing wrong with facts. They're just not enough." Mattie straightens her legs and leans back on her hands. She's wearing thick-soled hiking boots.

"What you scientists have got to understand," she continues, "is that the otter – and everything else – is a whole lot more than just facts." She leans toward Beth, her voice a whisper, as if she is confiding secrets. "The otter is special, see. Maybe even magical." Mattie holds up three fingers, points to each one in turn. "A creature of three worlds: water, earth, and air. The otter knows what's under the earth and what's under the water. All that lies beneath."

Muin snaps at a stout buzzing around her head. Misses. Beth lifts the binoculars and scans the darkening water.

Leaning back on her hands again, Mattie says, "She's a creature of that special time when day becomes night and night becomes day: a creature of transformation." She nods at Beth. "But she's a trickster too. Likes her games. So you gotta be careful."

"All great fun to speculate about," Beth says, "but everything you've said comes from mythology – ideas people have imposed on otters."

"Maybe." Mattie pushes herself up and rubs her hands together to brush off the dirt. "Maybe not." She puts her hands to her waist and stretches her shoulders back. "We should get going. These old eyes aren't what they used to be in the dark." She bends her neck from side to side, working out the kinks. "Why don't you come over for supper tomorrow?" she says. "Bound to be better than anything you can get at the Morning Glory."

"I should be out doing observations tomorrow evening."

"But you won't see anything."

"How do you know?"

"Just do," Mattie says. "So you might as well come over. Bout seven or so?" She turns to Muin. "Come on, girl."

Beth listens to their noisy retreat, then sits while the sky deepens from indigo to black. She watches the stars blink on, one by one.

It's all nonsense. She's not even tempted to call out their name.

~

Dark water ripples in front of her. A pup paddles at her side. The pup nudges her cheek with its muzzle, paws at her face, then grabs her around the neck. Quietly, they roll and tumble. The old female dives. Powerful stroke of tail, flick of back paws. Bubbles stream out behind her as she shoots through water the colour of night. The pup follows. When they rise up, she lifts her head and sniffs the air: fish and musk, earth and grass, the lodge, where the others are just beginning to stir.

The wind carries the lingering scents of dog and human. The dog and the old one are familiar. Safe. The scent of the new one is strong. Uncertain. Angry.

~

Beth takes out her journal and jots a few notes by the dim glow of a flashlight: *6 Aug 10: ~23°C, clear, winds light, observed at A5, 20:05 – 22:32; interrupted by Mattie ~20:30 – 20:45; none observed.*

She has been sitting still for nearly two hours since Mattie left. It's dark and there's no one around, so she strips down, lays her glasses and watch atop her clothes, and steps into the water before the mosquitoes can muster an attack. The rocks are slippery and the sudden cold makes her inhale sharply. Then she releases herself to the water, to its sensuous caress on her naked skin. She swims out from shore and slips beneath the surface. Shoots smoothly through dark water. Beth blows air out her nose and bends into a somersault, feels the giddy flip of her stomach. For a few otherworldly seconds, she is suspended, weightless and silent. She floats to the surface and gazes up at the stars. Locates the crooked W of Cassiopeia, Queen of Heaven.

A low *uhn-uhn-uhn* close to shore. Beth lies perfectly still. *Uhn-uhn-uhn, uhn-uhn-uhn.* Relaxed conversation.

At least two. She wants to raise her head and look, but she can't risk scaring them away. She's waited so long.

A high-pitched chirp. Another. If she didn't know better, she'd think the sounds came from a nocturnal bird.

A snort then. Her heart jumps. They've scented her.

Slowly, she brings her feet down and keeps her head low. She's rewarded with a glimpse of amber eyeshine, a grey muzzle, the arch of a tail. And then they are gone. The water forms silver wavelets around the shadow of their absence. Beth feels exhilarated – and bereft.

She swims to shore and uses her sweatshirt to dry off. Shivering violently now, she pulls and tugs at jeans and T-shirt, the dampness of her thighs like Velcro against the slide of denim. Wrestling her sweatshirt over her head, she steps into her sneakers, grabs her backpack, and runs to the cabin. She strips off her damp clothes and wraps herself in her sleeping bag.

As soon as she can grasp a pencil and hold it steady, she records: *6 Aug 10: Observed/heard at least two otters in A5, ~30 m northeast of beaver lodge, ~22:40 – 22:43. Judging by the grizzled muzzle, one is old. Heard grunts, two chirps, and a snort.*

Finally, she has seen them, if only for a few minutes. She lays the journal aside, then stands and picks up the kerosene lamp and her novel. Sees the rosary and decides to move it to the straight-back chair she's using as a nightstand so that she can look at the carving of the otter.

She strips down to a T-shirt and crawls into the sleeping bag, trying not to remember that this is where Katherine slept. She opens *Endless Night* and reads ... until she gets to the part about the old woman the villagers call a witch. She lays the novel aside, grabs the flashlight, and makes a final trip to the outhouse. Inside, the halo of light reflects off a large web spanning an entire corner. An orb-weaver, a filigree pattern of brown and white on her back, sits in the centre, waiting, as still as death. Beth stares at the en-shrouded flies, caught and bound in silk. *Master weaver?* More like master predator.

~

The dreamer glides through pools lit by a silver moon. Amber eyeshine all around. Musk in her nose, smell of dank earth. She nestles into a cradle of thick roots, comfort of warm, wet fur all around. *Uhn-uhn-uhn, uhn-uhn-uhn.*

Then she is hiding behind trees. From behind the web of branches, she watches her brother. He is pushing a rotary lawnmower across a vast expanse of green. The blades whir. A girl in a yellow sundress splashed with huge pink roses steps from the veranda. She is carrying a glass of lemonade. Cubes of ice clink as she steps across the new-mown grass. Her bare feet stain green.

She sees the girl through her brother's eyes: milk-white face shade-dappled by a straw hat, small swell of breast. Up close, the girl's eyes are a crystalline blue, a blue light-er than he's ever seen in anyone's eyes. He thinks that if he were to bring her wrist to his nose, her skin would smell as sweet as the roses on her dress. He tugs at the bill of his baseball cap, says his name, and when he takes the sweating glass from her hand, he wraps his tan fingers over her pale ones. The Kewpie-doll lips form an O of surprise, ivory skin flushes. The girl pulls her hand away, but when she turns to leave, she glances back and smiles.

The dreamer lets go of the branches. They snap back into place. She and her brother are close: two halves of a whole. The girl is an intruder.

CHAPTER 9

The alarm beeps. Beth turns it off and gives herself a few extra minutes. Dozes. Then slowly shakes herself awake and gropes for the matches, strikes one to light the lamp. Sees the green glint of the rosary on the chair beside the bed, the small bone carving of the otter.

She pulls on jeans and a sweatshirt and goes into the kitchen to make coffee. While she waits, she flips back to the notes she made the night before – just to confirm that she really did see them, that the otters weren't a dream or a phantom of her imagination.

Beth walks to the otter spot just as the sky is beginning to pale. It's unlikely they'll be back so soon, but she wants to take another look, then she'll be satisfied to search more kilometres of shoreline for scats.

She sits on shore and waits. Watches grey clouds creep in to smother the fragile sunrise, the pond's still surface reflecting both the innocent light and the sinister clouds. She listens to the morning chorus: a raven's deep quork, a chickadee singing its own name again and again, the jungle cackle of a northern flicker.

Her yawn brings tears to her eyes. She slept only a few hours the night before. Half awake, half asleep, a hazy dream of amber eyeshine and the smell of musk, all tangled around Clive's stories.

A high-pitched chirp, an answer. Beth raises her binoculars and spots four – no, five – in the water. She reaches into her backpack for her voice recorder and begins to dictate, quietly: "6:02. A5. Observing from fifteen metres. Five otters, swimming and wrestling about

75

twenty metres northeast of beaver lodge. Chirping while wrestling."

When the otters emerge from the pond and chase each other, Beth can see that at least two are pups. The otters wrestle in twos and threes, in the water and out, tussling, grabbing, pretend biting, chirping. She soon loses track of who is who, but keeps dictating. Now and again, an otter abandons the wrestling to dive, sometimes surfacing with a fish in its mouth. The crunch of bones is audible in the morning stillness, and Beth wonders if she'll be able to hear it when she transcribes the recording.

"One adult is swimming to shore with a large fish. It comes out about six metres northeast of the latrine. A pup follows. The adult releases the fish – twenty to twenty-five centimetres long. The pup bites near the fish's tail. The fish wriggles free. The adult catches it again, bites its head, then goes back into the water, leaving the fish for the pup. This same adult, which is relatively small and slender, comes out on shore at the latrine, arches its tail, treads both hind feet several times, urinates – probably a female – and deposits black scat. It returns to the water."

Even when Beth is not whispering into the recorder, she leaves it running so she can time the behaviours. After another minute, two adults emerge from the water, shake, and then rub in the grass to dry themselves. They settle side by side to groom – themselves and each other – dark-brown fur glossy in the sun that's just beginning to emerge from behind the clouds. Beth can hear their steady *uhn-uhn-uhns*, which seem to be quiet assurances to each other that everything's okay – almost like cats purring. A wet pup approaches them and shakes water over them, but neither adult snarls or growls, or even harrumphs. They merely rearrange themselves to accommodate the pup, who has plopped down on top of them. One adult begins to groom the pup, nibbling at its head and neck.

Beth smiles. No curmudgeons in the otter world.

"One pup and one adult are still in the water about ten metres from shore, three metres apart. Adult periscopes. Snorts. All five look in the same direction, northeast."

Beth watches and listens, and after a long minute, hears the distant whine of a motorboat. By the time it rounds the point and enters the small bay, the otters are long gone.

The *Black Feather.* Beth steps back behind the trees before Dan can see her. No luck. He dips the bill of his cap toward her. She turns away, no nod, no wave. Doesn't give a damn about being called uppity.

~

She refills her mug with the last of the coffee in the percolator and sits down to expand on the notes she's just transcribed from the voice recorder: *7 Aug 10: ~16°C, overcast > pt. sunny, winds light, observed at A5, 5:30 – 6:18, 5 otters appeared near latrine at 6:02.*

Sixteen minutes. That's all she got. Damn. Why did Dan have to show up? Of all the places he could go to fish, why there?

She sits back in the armchair. Okay, okay. She shouldn't be angry with Dan. She and the otters don't own the pond. No curmudgeons allowed, she reminds herself. Then writes: *The 5 otters included at least 1 adult female (probably) and 2 pups. At 65-75 cm, the pups are about 2/3 as long as the adults and more slender. Probably 4-5 months old. The pups are now proficient swimmers.*

She suspects the old beaver lodge is the second natal den. The birth den would have been more secluded and higher in the watershed since pups can't swim when they're born. When they're about three months old, the mother moves them closer to the water to teach them to swim and to catch their own food.

Beth reconsiders a note she made from the voice recording: *The adult caught and released a large fish, 20-25 cm. The pup tried to grasp the fish by the tail, but lost it. The adult – the mother? – killed the fish and left it for the pup.* She taps the pencil against the page. It's likely that it was the mother who caught the fish for the pup, but she can't be sure. A few studies have shown that other adult females sometimes share food with pups, but no one knows whether these "helpers" are the pups' aunts or older sisters, or are completely unrelated.

Using a paring knife to sharpen the pencil, Beth lets the shavings fall to the floor. So many unknowns. No one even knows the role of the father in the wild. In captivity, the mother is so fiercely protective of her pups that when she gives birth, the adult male usually has to be removed from the enclosure – for his own safety. He can be put back in when the pups are three to four months old, and for the most part, adult males are gentle with pups. Yet radio-tracking of wild otters shows that adult males don't have much to do with pups. They remain solitary or live in all-male groups whose members share dens and may even hunt together – in a highly unusual social arrangement for a member of the weasel family.

Beth is hoping the DNA analyses will tell her the composition of her group, but she'd love to be able to identify who is who while she's watching them. But their ears are too small for coloured tags, they'd chew off any kind of wristband, and their necks are thicker than their heads, so collars would just slip off. And with no funding, Beth can't live-trap them to mark them or surgically implant radio-tracking devices. She doesn't want to do that kind of invasive research anyway.

She re-reads another note: *The 5 otters wrestled in 2s and 3s, in the water and out, frequently changing partners, chirping almost continuously.* Beth closes her eyes to imagine the exuberant physicality of wrestling – not so different from children chasing and tussling, playing so hard they have to stop just to catch their breath. But it's not just otter pups that wrestle and chase; adults do too, and not just with pups but also with each other. Otters are one of the superstars of animal play. They're like domestic dogs and cats who've been bred to behave like perpetual pups and kittens.

Closing the research journal, she lays it on the arm of the chair and drums her fingers on the cover. Just what is all that play about? She knows play makes endorphins flow, so it probably does feel good. Endorphins – opiates within the brain – are a gift of evolution: an opiate reward for performing a behaviour that increases the chances of surviving to reproduce. It's easy to see why endorphins would flow when animals are seeking food and sex, but not so easy to see when they appear to be wasting time and energy in play. And a behaviour with no purpose, no function, poses a serious problem for evolutionary theory. There's no reason for it to exist.

Beth pictures Mattie's slap of the thigh and guffaw, her easy dismissal of scientists who worry about such things. *No big mystery, love. They're just happier than most folks.* But the people who study play do worry; they spend considerable time at it. And so far, there's been lots of theorizing, but researchers aren't much closer to understanding play's purpose, especially among adult animals, than they were twenty-five years ago when Beth was writing her doctoral thesis and documenting lots of otter play but could only speculate about the reasons why.

She picks at the burgundy threads unravelling on the arm of the chair. Feel-good endorphins. She wouldn't mind a few of those right now.

Maybe that's what otters feel when they settle into one big otter-y pile to groom each other – simple physical contact that makes endorphins flow. Maybe they're like close friends, or a mother and daughter, lying on the beach together, talking, and then touching each other's hands and shoulders and hair in an intimate conversation that needs no words.

She thinks of Rachel – all grown up now and on her own – and feels the ache of her absence. This is the first summer she hasn't come home to work in Alan's clinic. Beth decides that she'll go into town this evening and call Rachel. She needs to hear her voice. She's like mama otter: *uhn-uhn-uhn.* She needs to hear that everything's okay.

Beth swallows the last of her coffee, gritty grounds on her tongue, the last dregs from the pot. Dan has probably left by now, she thinks. She can go back to the otter spot and collect some fresh samples. Since the otters were at the beaver lodge last night and then again this morning, they'll be on the move tonight. How did Mattie know that?

CHAPTER 10

Beth is standing on Mattie's doorstep before she even notices the black pickup in the driveway, rust eating away at the wheel wells. As soon as she opens the screen door, she sees Dan sitting at the table. He nods, but not warmly. Since she didn't acknowledge his greeting this morning, he's probably added stuck-up and humourless to the pool of adjectives he uses to describe her. Muin trots over to inspect her hands, and Beth wishes she'd remembered to bring treats. She retrieves a chair from the corner.

"Heard you were out watching this morning," Mattie says, dishing up salt fish and potatoes from the pots bubbling on the cookstove. From a cast-iron skillet, she spoons pork scrunchions and fat into a bowl. The windows are wide open, but the kitchen is hot and steamy. "What did you see?"

"There were five there before—"

"I showed up?" Dan lifts an empty fork in a salute. "Guess the otters and I both know where the best fishing is." His voice softens. "I'll try to stay away from there for a while. Don't want to get in the way of *research*."

"Thanks," Beth says, a little surprised at his easy concession.

Mattie sets three plates and the bowl on the table, hands both of them paper towels, then sits down opposite Dan. She wipes sweat from her brow with the back of her hand. "Glad to hear you've finally seen em. Call their name, did you?"

"No, I didn't." Beth picks up the bowl and spreads a spoonful of scrunchions and fat over her fish. She passes the bowl to Dan, then picks up a fork and stabs a boiled potato. "Did Dan tell you we saw Clive yesterday at the Morning Glory?"

Mattie snorts. "Saw? Or heard? Nobody can yammer on like Clive Hiscock." She spreads the scrunchions over her fish and potatoes, then turns to Beth. "Don't believe half of what he says."

Dan laughs. "He said the same about you. Even called you a witch."

"See what I mean?" Mattie says to Beth. "Born trouble-maker." She shovels potato into her mouth.

Muin settles under the table, resting her head on Beth's feet. Beth takes a small bite of fish, chews, and swallows. Mattie and Dan busy themselves pulling bones from the white flesh. Beth takes another bite, then another. All of them are concentrating on their plates.

Beth brings a paper towel to her lips and clears her throat. "He said that Matthew had a girlfriend?" Voice rising in a question.

Mattie stiffens. "The drowning wasn't her fault."

"He never said it was. He said that you saved her."

Mattie wipes her greasy fingers on a paper towel, doesn't look up.

"And that you took care of her for years afterwards," Beth adds.

Mattie lays down her fork, turns, and stares out the window. In that moment, she looks twenty years older. Beth sees, more than hears, the deep sigh. "Fed her and kept her clean," Mattie says. "Was the least I could do for Matthew."

Dan keeps his eyes fixed on his plate.

"Must have been hard," Beth says. "Clive said—"

With a loud scrape, Dan pushes his chair back from the table. "Tomorrow's supposed to be a grand day," he says. He leans back, propping the chair on two legs, and puts his hands behind his head, elbows out. "Wanna go fishing?"

Beth stops mid-chew. "With you?"

The right side of his upper lip curls, like an aging Elvis Presley. "Well now, I don't guess Clive'll be going out any time soon."

The blush starts at her kneecaps and proceeds to her hairline. She hopes her red face will be blamed on the heat in the kitchen. Flustered, she deliberates quickly. She's explored most of the pond in her kayak, but it could be useful to get a different view of things from a motorboat. Might also put to rest adjectives like stuck-up, humourless, and uppity.

"Okay," she says. "What time?"

"Five-thirty? Unless that's too early for a St. John's girl."

"Five-thirty's just fine. Maybe five would be better."

"Nope. Five-thirty's good. I'll stop by in the boat." Dan stands. "Thanks for supper," he says to Mattie. "If you need anything, just put out the flag." Then he is out the door, plate still half full.

The creak of the truck door opening is followed by a rattling slam. The motor turns over but doesn't catch until the third try. The gears grind as Dan backs out the driveway.

Mattie stands and puts her plate, and Dan's, on the counter. "Gone off for a smoke. Wish he and Matthew would stop that business." She takes two mugs from the cupboard. "Tea?"

"I really should be going. I need to get some ice. And I want to call my daughter. I haven't talked to her in days."

"Sure, you can spare a few minutes for a cup a tea." Without waiting for an answer, Mattie crumbles papery brown leaves and flowers and tosses them into the teapot. "So you saw five this morning?"

"An adult female, I think, and two pups, plus two others, but just for a few minutes."

Mattie pours boiling water into the pot. "What did you see?"

"Wrestling and grooming. Fishing. One of the adults caught a fish for a pup."

"That would be the old grandmother. Or the pup's mom or auntie."

"Mattie, I don't even know for sure that the one who caught the fish was a female. Or even that it was an adult. It wasn't much bigger than the pup."

"The old grandmother then. What did you hear?"

"Chirps and grunts. Snorts when they heard Dan's boat."

Mattie pours tea into the mugs. "Nothing else?"

"No," Beth says warily.

Mattie reaches into the cupboard for the yellow sugar bowl. Sets it on the table. Beth blinks. Pink roses. Just like the ones on the yellow dress in her dream. All afternoon, while she was out in the kayak, she'd recalled more fragments, but never enough to make any sense. She pushes her plate, and the uneaten food, aside. Mattie sets a mug in front of her. She leans away from it.

"Go on, girl. Nothing in there to hurt you." Mattie sits down, looks at Beth, then tips her head to the side. "You got something besides otters on your mind?"

"Not really." Beth picks up the mug and sips the dark tea. It tastes like sweet clover. Over the rim of the mug, she sees the blue cap hanging by the door. Feels spider legs creep across the back of her neck.

Mattie follows her gaze. "That cap is Matthew's favourite. I gave it to him when we were sixteen. Sent away for it. Mail order."

Beth takes another swallow of tea.

"Matthew's still here, you know," Mattie says. "Or maybe you believe that's just old foolishness."

Beth toys with the spoon beside the mug.

84

"And by taking that rosary, you brought him to you." Her lower lip pushes out. "Take it back yet?"

"I need to go now." Beth stands, but the room tilts. She sits back down and puts her elbows on the table, leans her face into her hands. The cabin feels hot and claustrophobic.

"It's like we all walk around with bags over our heads." Mattie's words are muffled by the cotton in Beth's head. "Can't see what's right in front of us."

Beth wishes she had a bag right now, because when she uncovers her eyes, the light is too bright. She peeks out through interlaced fingers.

Mattie gestures toward the bookshelf. "Sure, I've read about the Big Bang and evolution. They're probably true. But lots of other things are true too. Things you scientists call superstitions." She picks up the matchbox. Opens it and takes out a single match. "Every culture that's come before us has had some notion about ghosts." She strikes the match and watches it flare: yellow, ethereal blue at the base.

Beth catches a whiff of the acrid stink.

Mattie blows out the flame before it can burn her fingers. "Takes a lot of arrogance to dismiss all that as superstition just cause we don't understand it."

Beth lowers her hands. She's beginning to feel less dizzy. Was it the heat? Or the tea?

Mattie stands and goes to the basket beside the loom. She picks up a skein of ivory yarn and a pirn. Turns back to Beth. "Katherine was a lot like you. A hard-nosed history teacher. We had some good arguments." She chuckles. "Whenever I'd be getting on about ghosts, she'd say, 'You go on home now, Matilda, and send Matthew over. He's got better sense.'"

Beth stands. "I *really* need to go."

"But I've got a story for you."

"I need to get to town."

"Sure. Go on then. But it's a story about otters." Mattie brings the yarn and the pirn to the table.

Beth takes a deep breath and sits back down.

Mattie sits down across from Beth and begins to wind the yarn onto the pirn. "Matthew used to watch them for hours. Got so they knew him, and talked to him." She peers at Beth. "They gave him the greatest gift animals have to give: a whole new way of being alive to this world." Her eyes narrow. "And he got all that just from spending time with them. And listening."

Mattie sits back and clicks a thumbnail against her broken front tooth. "Seems to me you're watching, but you're not listening."

Without a word, Beth pushes herself up from the table and leaves.

~

As soon as the cool air hits her face and she breathes it in, her head clears, her thoughts unmuddle. She rubs her temples. She's been spending far too much time with someone who believes she knows everything there is to know about otters, who thinks Beth is going about her research all wrong.

Stepping onto the narrow path, she looks back over one shoulder, glad it's not dark yet – and then wants to slap herself. Getting spooked by a lonely old woman who believes in ghosts!

And yet she can't help marvelling at how Mattie manages to connect her nutty ideas into an illogical chain that ends with a conclusion Beth can agree with: Western society has become too arrogant about what it thinks it knows. Ghosts aside, Beth has always been annoyed by the smug – and erroneous – idea that humans occupy some sort of pinnacle, that evolution has been working toward some goal and humans are it. People forget that it's humans who decide what constitutes evolutionary success.

She pushes a branch out of her way. Well, if there's an apocalypse in the offing, she'd place her bet on cockroaches and rats.

Beth steps over raised tree roots and exposed rocks. She's just as impatient with the assumption that humans have arrived, at this point in the twenty-first century, at the *correct* world view, that radical changes in the way we think about ourselves and the world ended with the Copernican revolution in the sixteenth century, the Darwinian theory of evolution in the nineteenth, and theories of quantum physics in the twentieth. People talk with condescension about what humans believed just a few hundred years ago; yet these same people never seem to wonder what their descendants will shake their heads at. She suspects that future generations will be appalled at how the current one has treated the earth.

Her thoughts gain momentum as her feet stride along the path. Maybe people would be less arrogant if they understood that their own world view is shaped by the limits of their senses, literally, their view. We experience the world not as it is, she thinks, but the way our brains construct it. Mattie's not far off the mark to talk about everyone walking around as if we all have bags over our heads. Even when we're paying attention, we perceive only a small fraction of what's around us. How differently might we conceptualize the world if, like otters, our dominant sense were smell rather than vision? Beth smiles. *I smell what you mean. I can smell it in my mind's nose. I didn't even recognize him, he just didn't smell like the man I used to know.* We'd navigate by smell not sight, and instead of written language, we might have some sort of complex olfactory code for preserving information: libraries for odours. And if we had four digits on each hand and foot, then eight, not ten, would be the base for our numerical system. If, like migrating birds, we had a visual map of the earth's magnetic fields, or, like insects, we could see ultraviolet light and infrared, it would change the way we see each other, our artwork, our architecture, the way we travel – the way we live on this earth.

It's dusk by the time Beth arrives at the cabin. She has used her internal rant to distract herself from admitting just how unnerved she is by Mattie's talk of ghosts and the rosary. When she goes inside to grab her car keys and wallet, she can't help peering into every shadowed corner and hoping desperately, stupidly, that Matthew – or Katherine – doesn't put in an appearance. Beth is doubly eager now to hear Rachel's voice, to talk with someone who is sensible and rational, someone who would scoff at the very idea of ghosts.

CHAPTER 11

Driving as fast as she dares, Beth bumps along the pot-holed roads. When she finally arrives at the Irving – and the pay phone – she fishes a calling card from her wallet and punches in the numbers. The sanity of the woman's voice politely asking her to press 1 for English and then to enter her key code calms her. Step by step. Logical. The voice tells her, to the penny, how much money is left on the card, and then requests that Beth enter the phone number she wants to call: Rachel's. She listens to the tinny ring – five times – and then to Rachel's voice telling her that she's "busy right now. Leave a message if you want to."

Beth leans her head against the phone cubicle. Almost weeps. *Rachel, where are you? I need to know that you're okay. To know that I'm okay.*

Struggling to control her voice, she leaves a message: "Just calling to say hi, sweetheart. Hope everything's okay and that your lab work is going well. I'll try again soon. Love you." When she hangs up, she feels a familiar tightening in her chest, cords pulled taut. It's been more than a week since she last talked with Rachel. *What if something's happened?*

She smacks her forehead. "Stop," she says out loud. "Just stop." If anything serious were to happen, Alan would come out. It's only a four-hour drive. She doesn't need to worry.

But she can't stop herself. The umbilical cord still pulses with warm red blood.

Should she call Alan? Yes, no. Yes, no. She wishes she could call Alice. Alice would make her laugh at herself. But she can't. Her best friend is dead.

Beth punches in the calling card numbers again, follows the commands, then enters the number of her home phone. Alan picks up on the second ring: "Hello?"

"Hi," she says.

"Oh, hey. How's everything going?"

"Fine. Have you talked to Rachel recently?"

"Just yesterday."

Beth breathes out. "How is she?"

"Fine, as far as I know."

"Did you ask about her research?"

"Of course."

"How about that new guy she's seeing?"

"What new guy?"

Why does he always make her do all the worrying? "Alan, how do you know everything's okay?"

"Because she said so, Beth. How's *your* research going?"

Beth slides the calling card back into her wallet. "All right. I have quite a few samples now. In fact, I should make a trip into St. John's Monday or Tuesday to get them into a freezer."

"It'll be good to see you. Planning to stay overnight?" A brittleness in his words.

"Probably. I'll try to do some observations in the morning and then drive in while it's still light."

"So you've been able to watch them?"

"Some." Just sixteen minutes, but there's no need to explain about Dan and his stupid boat.

"Anything useful?"

"Pretty much the same stuff as when I did my thesis research."

"Well, you can't expect too much at this stage, right?" He hesitates. "I mean ... it's early yet."

"If I could just mark them," she says, "so I could know who was who, the observations would be a lot more useful."

"But that's hard to do, right?"

"Impossible without live-trapping them." Beth runs her finger down a row of numbered buttons, 1-4-7, then across, 7-8-9. "And I don't really want to do that."

"But maybe that's something you'll have to consider."

As if she hasn't already. She hears Pirate barking in the background. "How are things there?"

"Fine."

Fine. Everything's always *fine*. "Did the cat live?"

Silence. "No, she didn't," he says finally. "And I had to tell the little girl myself."

Beth visualizes him leaning against the stainless-steel refrigerator and staring down at the black and white tiles.

"I promised her that when the next litter of kittens comes in, I'll let her have first pick."

"That was nice, Alan."

"What else you gonna do?" He sighs. "In a weak moment, I even told her mom I'd do the neutering for free."

Beth smiles. "Always the astute businessman." Just like when he did the surgery, free of charge, for the stray dog who'd been caught in a leg-hold trap. And then adopted him. Her shoulders begin to loosen. "I met the neighbour."

"Neighbour? Just one?"

"An old woman and her dog. Claims she's lived on the pond for eighty years."

"Really! And she's there by herself?"

"Yeah. Maybe for too long. Seems a bit strange." Where to begin? There's no way to explain Mattie and the story about her twin. And the ghosts. Alan would think she's gone bonkers. Maybe she has. "She claims to know everything there is to know about otters."

"There you go," he says. "No need to mark them. Just talk to her."

"That's exactly what she said."

Alan laughs, then says, "That cabin's pretty isolated. I'm glad there's at least one other person out that way." He pauses. "Strange can be okay." He laughs again. "As long as she's not homicidal."

Beth laughs with him, then says, "It's good to talk with you, Alan, but I should get going. It's a long drive back to the cabin, especially in the dark."

"Promise me you'll be careful, Beth. I know you can handle a kayak. And it's quiet water, but …"

Beth waits, then speaks into the silence, "See you soon. Love you. Bye."

She drives around to the gas pumps. The buzz of the bright lights overhead is loud, drowning out all other night noises. The air around the lights is thick with insects. She lifts the nozzle, the gas fumes pungent, but familiar and almost pleasant.

Gas pumped, she goes inside and uses a credit card to pay the young man behind the counter for the gas and a bag of ice. His surliness, and his quickness to return to his small-screen TV, make it clear that he's not about to engage in conversation. Beth lingers anyway, looks longingly at a TV show she doesn't even recognize, listens to laughter that's not even real. She hates TV sitcoms, but she's reluctant to leave, to be alone again, in the dark.

"Something else?" he asks sharply.

She spins away and walks up and down the aisles, passing shelves of chips and snacks, refrigerators filled with soda pop and energy drinks, milk and beer. She studies the lip balms and the stale glazed doughnuts and blueberry muffins left from that morning – or maybe the morning before. Finally, she selects a pack of Dentyne and brings it to the counter. The young man flicks greasy hair out of his eyes and sighs hugely when he takes her coins.

It's dark now and Beth has to drive slowly, always on the alert for moose. She breaks her no-news rule and turns on the radio, but the announcer's cheerful voice only makes her feel more alone. She flicks it off.

Mattie's ghosts, she thinks. Nothing mysterious or scary about them. Not really. Mattie lost her twin when she was a teenager. She's lonely, especially now that she's lost Katherine too, and just trying to bring back the people she can't bear to live without.

Who would Beth bring back? Not her father, that's for sure. He was a harsh, unforgiving man when he was alive. She grew up believing that he didn't even like her all that much, that she was a disappointment to him. Her mother loved her though. She was kind-hearted and well-meaning, but ultimately, ineffectual. Beth doubts she'd have much wisdom to offer from the other side.

She peers into the darkness, headlights reflecting off pale birches. Knows there is a ghost she'd bring back if only she could: Alice, her best friend for more than twenty years. Gone now for two. God, how she misses her, not just their long conversations but also the times when they needed no words, when a single sidelong glance or raised eyebrow stood in for thousands. And the laughter, Beth misses the laughter. When Alice got going, she sounded like a donkey braying, incongruous for such an elegant, graceful woman. She'd try to stifle the guffaws, but her efforts only made them both laugh even harder, until their sides ached and tears ran down their cheeks. Alice was the sister Beth never had, and Beth still hasn't filled that void. Doubts that she ever can. And she's terrified that, in the end, she may have disappointed Alice too. Beth had taken her to the appointments, wept with her when her copper curls came out in handfuls, and sat with her. And sat with her, and sat with her some more. But it wasn't enough. Beth couldn't give her what she needed. When Alice asked, Beth couldn't let her go. And she wasn't there at the very end, when Alice needed her most.

Beth sees a sudden movement at the side of the road. A great-horned owl rises up before her. The broad wings span the width of the Toyota. A limp hare hangs in its talons, and, for a split second, the owl's yellow eyes stare into hers. Beth slams on the brakes, skids on the gravel, and comes to a grinding stop. Her mouth opens then closes, no sound, like in nightmares when her screams are stopped at the back of her throat. What is wrong with her? It's only an owl. But it isn't. It's the one thing Alice asked for that Beth could give her: A feather from her collection. A feather from the bird that can fly safely through the darkest night.

By the time she finally pulls into the driveway she has stopped shaking, but the headlights shining on the trees cast eerie shadows that dance over the red clapboard with every gust of wind. She reaches into the glove compartment. No flashlight. Of course not. Beth leaves the car idling, headlights on, and runs to the cabin. Unlocks the door. Inside, she fumbles around for matches and then lights a candle. She wrestles with the kerosene lamp until that's lit as well. She grabs the flashlight from the counter and runs back outside to turn off the car, and the headlights. Forcing herself to walk calmly, she returns to the cabin, hugging the bag of ice to her chest. Once inside, she locks the door and leans against it.

Beth drops the ice into the cooler with her samples and uncorks a bottle of wine. Tries to ignore how the lamp creates shadows that darken the corners and change the colours in the weaving: rose to blood-red, indigo to black. Her hand trembles as she lifts the glass to her lips. What a comfort Pirate would be right now. She thinks of Jax then, the collie-shepherd mix who was her childhood companion. That's another ghost she'd bring back. The old farmhouse and barn could be scary at night, especially the barn. Small animals crept or flew through the shadows, sheep shuffled in the straw, chewing their cud, breath steamy in the cold night air. But Jax was always right there with her, protecting her, loving her.

She takes a sip of wine. Maybe she should have kept Pirate here when Alan left, just for the company. But what would the old Lab do while she was out in the kayak? She'd hate keeping him closed up in the cabin all day. Besides, he's Alan's dog, not hers.

Scratching at the door. Beth freezes. Stares at the door for long minutes. Can hear nothing but her own heart: thump-thump, thump-thump, thump-thump. Too fast. Hears a bark, then a whine. She steps quickly to the door and cracks it open, sees the now-familiar chocolate eyes. Muin noses her way in and Beth stoops to hug her.

When the dog licks her face, Beth laughs and wipes away what could be a tear. "I don't know why you're here, girl, but I'm some glad you are."

Beth sits on the floor. Muin stretches out beside her. She keeps a hand in the warm fur, and when she finishes the glass of wine, she takes the dog with her to the out-house. Then, settling in for the night, she pats the bed, encouraging Muin to jump onto it. Doesn't care that the dog's length and bulk push her to the edge of the mattress.

She checks, one more time, to make sure the flashlight is on the chair beside the bed, then leans in to blow out the lamp. Stops. No rosary. She moves the flashlight, her novel, and the lamp, then she stands. Muin jumps off the bed. Beth searches the floor all around the chair. Shakes out the sleeping bag and then the clothes on the floor. She sweeps the flashlight's beam and then her hand under the bed. Nothing. She sits back on her heels. Muin sits down beside her. Nothing is out of order, but the rosary is gone.

Holding the kerosene lamp like a torch, she goes out into the kitchen and living room. Muin follows. Beth checks the windowsills, moves both the rocking chair and the armchair, then the stack of articles on the counter and the bottles of insect repellent and sunscreen. Nothing. She even searches around the pans and bowls on the floor.

She pushes the jumble of puzzle pieces aside and sets the lamp on the table. She sits down in the rocking chair, elbows on her knees. Okay. What's logical? She's certain she didn't move the rosary from the chair beside the bed. And it couldn't have disappeared into thin air. Could someone have taken it? Matthew's ghost? Ridiculous! Mattie? She probably still has a key to the cabin.

Beth looks suspiciously at Muin. "Were you and Mattie here earlier tonight?" The dog's ears lift forward, her head tilts.

But that makes no sense … unless Mattie somehow knows that Beth hasn't taken it back, and she's angry. *Take it back yet?* Beth never answered, so how could Mattie know? Rocking backwards, Beth picks at a splinter on the arm of the chair. Surely Mattie's not trying to make her believe her weird ideas about ghosts. Why? The splinter pricks her index finger, and Beth watches blood rise into a single bead on her fingertip. Maybe there is no rational explanation for what Mattie does. Beth looks to see if the blue baseball cap is hanging by the door. That would be just like her. Then she'd claim that Matthew's ghost left it there when he took the rosary. Beth sees only the empty hooks.

She blots the drop of blood with a tissue, then checks once again to make sure the door is locked. She takes the kerosene lamp into the bedroom and sets it on the chair. Placing the flashlight close at hand, she crawls into the sleeping bag and calls Muin onto the bed. Fully awake now, she picks up the novel and reads a few pages. When she realizes she has no idea what she's just read, Beth lays the book aside, blows out the lamp, and snuggles into Muin.

~

A slim crescent moon sits just above the horizon: silver light and shadows on dark water. Waves curl, then roll and crash against massive rocks, drowning out the sound of the otters' chirps and *uhn-uhn-uhns*. Two of them wrestle. Chirp. A pup joins in. Chirp. Poke to belly. Chirp. Nudge to cheek. Chirp. Paws grab. Turning. Twisting. Tumbling through foamy water.

Rocked back and forth by waves, they hunt then. Underwater, long whiskers detect movements of fish and lobsters. Sensitive paws probe rocks for mussels. When their bellies are full, they swim to the river and rinse their fur in water that does not taste or smell of salt.

CHAPTER 12

She is wearing the yellow sundress and sitting on a blanket spread over newly mown grass. The young man's lanky arm is draped around her shoulders, and they gaze out over silver water that glistens with reflected sunlight. From under the brim of her hat, she steals a shy glance at his face, and knows that he is only pretending not to see her looking. Without his blue cap, his hair has the ebony sheen of a raven's feather, a violet iridescence.

He turns to her and lifts the straw hat from her head. Lays it aside and pulls the pins from her hair, slowly. Kisses her face and her lips as he removes each tortoiseshell pin. One by one, he lays them carefully into the bowl of the hat. Platinum curls cascade down her back. He lifts the curls and kisses her neck, then gently pushes her down and lies beside her. He puts a hand to her narrow waist, slides it up to her breast. He unbuttons the top two buttons of her yellow dress. She lays her hand against his jeans.

The waves suddenly rise and sweep over them. Her mouth opens, but her scream is muffled by the water. She holds her breath and hears the echo of a scream. Flails in the murky water, knows that he can't swim. She tries to find him. Her lungs are bursting. She opens her mouth.

Beth wakes, gasping, the metallic tang of muddy water on her tongue. She swallows. Stares into the dark and waits for her heart to slow. Listens for Muin's soft breathing. She puts a hand to the dog's fur and then reaches to make sure the flashlight is still there. Her fingers find her watch: 1:12. She considers getting up and lighting the lamp, reading or working on the puzzle. She lies still in the dark and breathes, the warm weight of Muin's long body next to hers.

~

Staring straight ahead with those pale blue eyes. The face of a ghost. Dan's voice is soft. His green eyes are shadowed by a blue baseball cap. Beth is looking at his face through a spider web. She can hear the whir as the spider spins silk thread. Then, she and Dan are sitting on a blanket by a pond. She sees murky, roiling water. Remembers. But he puts an arm around her shoulders, gives them a reassuring squeeze. He kisses her neck. His fingers fumble at the snap on her jeans. He yells her name.

A loud banging startles her awake, someone shouting her name. Beth lies still. Dan! She leaps out of bed. Muin is already at the door.

"Just a minute," Beth calls out. She slides on her glasses and sorts through the mound of clothes on the floor for something reasonably clean. Hops to the door on one foot, still tugging at her jeans. Opens it to soft grey light and Dan's smirk.

"Guess five-thirty *is* too early for a St. John's girl."

"Forgot to set my alarm." Beth can't bring herself to look at his face, fears she'll blush scarlet and he'll know, somehow. "Just need to go to the outhouse, brush my teeth …" She bites her lip. "And make coffee?"

"No worries. Got a thermos in the boat."

Muin pushes her head out the door.

"What's she doing here?" Dan says.

"Showed up late last night. Think we should take her back before we go out?"

"No, she'll find her way home." He lifts his cap and pushes it farther back on his head, puts his hands on his hips. "But as soon as she sees the boat, she'll wanna come with us."

~

It's a perfect summer morning, cool and clear with just enough wind to keep the bugs away. The sky is deep rose where the sun is rising, apricot tinged with gold beyond.

For the first hour, while Dan fishes, Beth is content to sit, arm draped around Muin, and nurse the coffee Dan poured for her. It's heavy with cream and sugar, and Beth prefers black, but at least it's coffee.

He's already caught four good-sized trout and laid them in a cooler half-filled with ice. He's returned three smaller ones to the water. They've hardly spoken, but Dan seems comfortable with the silence. Beth is still avoiding looking into his face, but when his back is turned, she watches him, the clean, graceful movements of his shoulders and arms when he casts. She can't help comparing him to Alan. Dan is about the same height, but in better shape; he doesn't have that little paunch, and his face is tanned, not pasty. His prominent nose gives him a rugged, serious sort of look. But Alan is more intelligent, more interesting. Maybe. She doesn't really know that; she's just assuming. And Dan is certainly sexier, or at least in the dream he was.

When did Alan become unsexy? When did she and Alan become so … boring? They didn't start out that way. She was working on her doctoral thesis in Minnesota when they met, Alan his veterinary training. They shared common interests in animals and the outdoors, a deep concern for the environment. There was lots of laughter, and teasing. Few fireworks though, no drama, no fighting. Theirs was a calm, solid kind of love. Or at least she thought so. After they married and finished school, they moved back to Alan's home province, to St. John's. To Beth, already pregnant, it seemed like a romantic adventure in an exotic locale – a fantasy that didn't outlast the pregnancy. Alan joined a veterinary practice; Beth started teaching at the university; Rachel was born. They were busy, doing all the things that young professionals with children do, but now they just seem … boring. And somewhere along the way, they'd stopped laughing.

Beth studies Dan's back and wonders if she's missed something huge in her life. A grand passion. Or is that just in schmaltzy movies and novels?

After another half-dozen casts without a rise, Dan lays down the fly rod and pours coffee into the thermos lid, refills Beth's mug. He lights a cigarette. The three of them sit, staring out over the calm water. Dan has only to lean toward her and whisper: *Staring straight ahead with those pale blue eyes. The face of a ghost.* He has only to touch the waistband of her jeans …

"Lovely morning," she says.

He nods. Takes a swallow of coffee, then a draw on the cigarette.

She wishes she'd remembered to bring her binoculars, then she could pretend to be scanning the shoreline. She thinks of the rosary then. In the bright light of day, its disappearance seems less ominous. "Does Mattie ever play tricks on you?" she asks.

"She does some odd things, but I wouldn't call them tricks." He takes another draw on the cigarette. "Why?"

"Just wondering. She seems like the kind of person who might." Beth snaps the lid of the plastic mug off, then back on. Off. On. "Does Mattie still have a key to Katherine's cabin?"

"Doubt it. Neither of them ever locked their doors." He cocks his head. "What? You worried that Mattie will come in uninvited?"

"No, no." She hesitates. Dan is looking at her, his head still canted to the side. She tries to speak casually, but her voice catches. "It's just that Mattie has said some strange things about Matthew and ghosts. It's giving me the creeps."

"Don't worry about it. Mattie's always getting on with stuff like that."

"But it seems important to her that I believe her."

"Trust me." Dan raises a hand, as if he were in a courtroom swearing an oath. "Mattie doesn't give a damn what you believe. She just enjoys tormenting people. Look at that whole Matthew-Matilda business."

"Yes, just look at that whole business. Doesn't that tell you something?"

"Go on, girl. After she says something weird, she just laughs and says it's probably all nonsense." He tosses the cigarette butt into the bottom of the boat. "She misses Katherine, so what's important to her now is having someone to talk to. She never cared whether Katherine believed her." He laughs. "And she knows I don't."

"I think," Beth says carefully, "that Mattie may have done something to try and *make* me believe her about Matthew's ghost."

"Like what?"

Beth looks at Muin, who returns her gaze, brown eyes innocent. "Taken something from my cabin," she says.

"Like what?" he repeats. He takes a mouthful of coffee.

"An old rosary that Matthew made."

He spews out the coffee. Wipes his mouth on his sleeve. "A rosary? That Matthew made?"

"Mattie said he made it for their grandmother when he was a boy."

"So why's it in your cabin?"

"I found it near Medicine Rock. When I showed it to Mattie, she said I should take it back."

"And you didn't?"

Beth runs a hand through her hair. Tugs at a brown and grey lock behind her ear. "Haven't had time."

"So why would Mattie steal it?"

"To take it back herself?" Beth says. "Or, more likely, to make me believe that Matthew's ghost took it. She said the rosary would bring him to me."

Dan shakes his head. "She says some pretty weird shit, but Mattie would never steal anything. And she sure as hell wouldn't go to the trouble of hiking all the way to your cabin just to take an old rosary. No matter who made it."

"Maybe you just don't know that side of her. You didn't even know about her and Katherine."

He lets out a long, exasperated sigh. "I knew. I just never thought it was any of my business." He swallows the last of his coffee and screws the lid back onto the thermos. "Listen, whatever happened, Mattie did *not* steal anything."

"Do you drink her teas?"

"Her teas? Sure." He squints at Beth. "What? You think there's something strange about them too?"

"Don't be ridiculous."

"Beth, I'm not the one being ridiculous."

"Never mind."

"No, tell me."

"Well …"

"Come on," he urges.

"I always feel dizzy and headachy when I drink them."

He puts a hand to his mouth and coughs, as if stifling a laugh. "No offense, but I think that's just you. And your imagination. It's just Labrador tea she gathers herself. And raspberry, maybe some rose hips." He touches the bill of his cap, pulls it lower. "You're letting her weirdness get to you. She'd love that."

Beth wishes she'd never mentioned it, any of it. Spoken out loud, everything does sound crazy, and now Dan probably thinks she's paranoid *and* a hypochondriac. She studies the soggy cigarette butts floating in the bottom of the boat. Small waves make little slapping sounds against the hull. She wishes she could think of something funny or interesting to say, something that doesn't make her sound like an idiot.

Dan lifts the lid of the cooler to check the trout. Muin puts her head in, sniffs. "Stop that now," he says, pushing her away. He closes the lid, his hand a dark tan against the stark white.

"So …" Beth says. "Are you really part Mi'kmaq?"

He snorts a laugh. "A very, very small part. Might as well call myself Beothuk. That seems to be all the rage now." He takes off his cap, wipes his forehead with the back of his hand, and puts it back on. "Okay," he says, "so some great-great-grandmother, way back when, was half Mi'kmaq and half French. Myself? I'm a whole lot more Irish. Doubt that anyone in Dublin would consider me Irish, so I don't spect the folks in Conne River think I'm Mi'kmaq."

He shakes the thermos. "Coffee's near gone, so I guess it's time to head back. Wanna couple trout for your supper?"

"You caught them."

He looks into her face, hazel eyes assessing. "Could be you're spending too much time alone in that old cabin. Can make you think some strange stuff when you're not used to it. Why don't you come over for supper? I'm not a terrible cook."

Taking her stunned silence for a yes, Dan slides toward the small outboard. "I'll come over in the boat about five and get you." He raises an eyebrow. "Set your alarm this time."

"No, no, that's okay. It's just a short paddle across the pond."

"Suit yourself. Just look for the green bungalow directly east of your cabin. Tall junipers on either side of the deck." Dan starts the engine with one clean pull.

CHAPTER 13

Beth spots a red flag fluttering from a metal pole on the pier. She points, but Dan is already turning the boat toward Mattie's cabin. He cuts the motor and uses an oar to guide the boat into the pier. Muin jumps into the water and swims to shore, comes out and shakes herself off. Dan ties a rope to the flagpole, then turns and offers a hand to Beth, but she is already climbing the short ladder onto the pier.

Mattie appears on the front step. She is wearing the blue baseball cap. She dips the bill toward Beth and Dan. Muin gallops toward her.

"Seen the boat go out with Muin," Mattie says. "Thought you'd be stopping by."

"Here's your dog," Dan says. "Again."

"Any luck?"

"Nothing big," he says, "but enough for supper."

Mattie raises a finger. "Before I forgets, you should pick me up some dog food next time you're in town." She jabs the finger into his chest. "And none a that cheap stuff neither."

Dan glances at Muin. "No, we can't have that horse eating the cheap stuff."

"A bag of bird seed too. Black sunflower."

"Certainly. Can't have the hordes going hungry."

"Don't be saucy," Mattie says. "Time for tea?"

Before Beth can blurt out a no, Dan says, "Sure." When Mattie turns around, he leans toward Beth and whispers, "I'll watch her hands to see if she slips anything into your mug."

"Very funny," Beth says, turning toward the path to the outhouse. She thinks about making up an excuse and just walking back to her cabin, but then decides that she wants to ask Mattie about the rosary, in front of Dan. Then he'll see.

A few minutes later, she steps into the kitchen. Mattie has set out three mugs.

"Just water please," Beth says, sitting down.

"Oh, yes," Mattie says, "I keeps forgetting that I'm trying to poison you." She pours tea into two of the mugs.

Dan takes the third one to the sink and works the squeaky handle of the old pump. "Wonder when they'll get around to putting electricity out this way." He fills the mug with cold water.

"Don't need it, do we, Beth?"

"I'm not so sure about that. It would be nice to have an indoor bathroom and a refrigerator, a real stove."

"No need of it," Mattie says firmly. "Katherine and I don't want it."

Beth gives Dan an *I-told-you-so* look, but he is turned toward the rocking chair. The floor around it is littered with wood chips and shavings. A long, hollowed-out cylinder of wood and a knife lie on the bookshelf. "Carving this morning?" he says, sitting down at the table.

"Woke up as Matthew and felt like working on a flute." Mattie sets out the yellow sugar bowl. Muin is already ensconced under the table. To avoid her sprawled legs, all of them have to push back their chairs.

"What's this I hear about Matthew making some sort of rosary?" Dan winks at Beth. "Never thought he was all that religious."

"I'm not," Mattie says. "Made that for Nan when I was just a youngster." She jerks her chin toward Beth. "She found it. Or it found her." She tastes the tea, then adds more sugar. "But it's missing now, isn't it."

"Yes, it is," Beth says, looking straight at Mattie.

"Don't know why you thinks I took it," Mattie says.

"I never said that." Beth turns to Dan.

"I didn't say a word." He raises his hands, palms out. "I swear I didn't."

Mattie chuckles. "He didn't have to say nothing, love. What you thinks is as plain as the nose on your face." She grins. "Matthew's probably just having a bit of fun with you. He's got a sly sense of humour."

Beth folds her hands and lays them on the table. "Or maybe it's you who's having *a bit of fun* with me."

"That's just what I said."

"So you didn't come over to the cabin and take it?" Beth says. "You ... or Matilda or whoever?"

"Nope."

Beth stands. "I should get back to work."

Mattie raises her mug in a salute. "Yep, you got lotsa work to do yet."

Dan starts to rise. Beth puts out a hand, gesturing for him to stay seated. "Thanks," she says, "but I can find my own way home."

~

Beth rocks slowly, creaking forward, then back. Looks at the kerosene lamp, seeing it, not seeing it. Why would Dan lie? So that he and Mattie could share a good laugh at spooking the scientist? On the other hand, maybe it was just a lucky guess on Mattie's part. It's hardly a stretch that she would assume that Beth would know it was she who took the rosary. Beth rubs her palms on the rough fabric of her jeans, picks at a loose thread on the knee. Wishes she'd never found that stupid rosary. She'd be out in her kayak right now, doing what she should be doing: her research.

She decides to search the cabin one more time. Just to be absolutely sure. She looks first in the kitchen and living room, even though she's certain she left the rosary on the chair beside the bed. She looks at the table with the unfinished puzzle – a stereotypical mountain scene from the Canadian Rockies – then moves all the dishes, boxes, and cans off the counter and puts them away in the cupboard. She lifts the folder of scientific articles she hasn't read yet, then rifles through all the clutter: matchboxes, research journal, voice recorder, pens and pencils, insect repellent, sunscreen. Nothing. She checks both windowsills and all around the hand-pump and sink. Moves all the chairs and the table, as well as the bowls and pans she set out to catch the drips. She gets out the broom and sweeps the floor. Ends up with a pile of bread and cracker crumbs, wood debris, pencil shavings, and a fistful of black dog hair.

Beth carries the broom and the dustpan into the bedroom, pushes back the tan curtain hanging in front of the empty closet. Nothing but metal hangers on the wooden rod and a scattering of sand on the floor. She lets the curtain drop. Clears everything off the chair she's using as a nightstand: flashlight, matches, wineglass with a dried red circle in the bottom, paperback novel. She lifts the sleeping bag and shakes it, picks up all the discarded clothes from the floor, shakes out each piece, checks every pocket, and lays the clothes on the bed. She searches all around the chair, then kneels down and sweeps her arm under the bed as far as she can reach. Nothing but gigantic dust bunnies. She decides to move the bed. Pulls on one corner, then another, inching the heavy metal frame away from the wall.

Glint of green beads! Tucked into a dusty corner behind a metal leg. Beth picks up the rosary and, with a sick feeling in her stomach, knows that Mattie never took it at all. She has been a complete and total idiot.

She sits down on the edge of the bed and lets the beads and chain slide through her fingers. In her flustered hurry to grab her car keys and get into town last night, she must have knocked the rosary to the floor and kicked it under the bed. Beth puts a hand to her forehead, not sure whether she's more embarrassed or angry. Mattie wasn't assuming anything. Dan must have told her about Beth's suspicions, and in doing so, he has multiplied her humiliation tenfold.

Beth rubs a thumb over the small carving of the otter. She'd left Mattie's in a huff. Does Dan still expect her for supper?

She sits up straighter, rolls her shoulders back. She'll go. There will be those first awkward moments when she has to tell him that she found the rosary, but then she'll ask him again, and keep asking, until he finally confesses that he did tell Mattie.

Tomorrow, she'll have to go to Mattie and apologize.

~

The sun is high above, warming their fur as they rub themselves dry in the grass. Bellies full of fish, all six lie close to the lodge and to each other. Two begin to nibble through the fur on each other's head, shoulders, and back. A pup joins in. And then another adult, until finally, all six are grooming themselves and each other. Comfort in the touch. They listen to their own *uhn-uhn-uhns*, as well as to the long grasses rustling, the robins warbling, the juncos chirping, and to the jays and crows calling to each other. Nothing alarming in their calls.

The old female breathes in their familiar scents, the distinctive musk of each one and the fishiness of their muzzles. She breathes in the fragrances of earth, sky, and water, the smell of the lodge and the rocks and grasses around it. She detects the scent of the watcher. Knows by its faintness that she is far away. And yet her presence lingers.

CHAPTER 14

Precisely at 16:30, Beth slides into the kayak and heads east across the pond. She will not be late this time. The sky is overcast but there's no heavy wind to buffet her boat, and it will be light for another four hours. Plenty of time to have supper and then paddle back.

She's prepared her speech. Has pictured the scene a dozen different ways and practiced exactly what she will say: She's sorry. Yes, she jumped to silly conclusions. But then Mattie's very strange and says odd things. Even Dan admits to that.

Trying not to envision his self-satisfied smirk, she's given a lot of thought to how, without sounding whiny, she can confront him about telling Mattie – and then lying to her about it. He needs to apologize too.

Damn. Even her thoughts sound whiny.

Immersed in her own debate, she paddles steadily, hardly noticing the sky or the pond, but then she spots a pair of loons in the distance, a grey chick swimming between them, small for this time of year. She lays the paddle across the kayak and lifts her binoculars. Rising up from the water, one loon flaps checkerboard wings, throws back a sleek black head, and releases piercing warbles that reverberate across the pond. No matter how clichéd it may be, to her, the call embodies wilderness. Yet, even here, the human world intrudes: the snarl of a chainsaw and the monotonous low hum of a motorboat, beer and pop cans on the bottom of the pond, a yellow plastic bag waving gaily from a tall spruce.

Within thirty minutes, she sees the bungalow with the dark-green clapboard, a deck with sentinel larches on either side. No lawn, just trees and shrubs that almost hide the house. The *Black Feather* is tied up to the pier. Beth beaches the kayak, unzips her life-jacket, and tosses it into the cockpit.

Dan steps out onto the deck. He is drying his hands on a dish towel. "Wasn't sure you'd show up."

She walks up the path toward him. "I found the rosary," she says.

"Kinda thought you might."

"Listen, I'm really sorry that I said anything about it, that I even suggested that Mattie might have taken it. I'm–"

"No worries," he cuts in.

"I'm sorry," she insists, "but why did you have to tell her? Now I'll have to go to Mattie and apologize."

"I didn't."

"I bet you two had a good laugh about it."

"I swear, Beth, I didn't tell her a thing." He throws the dish towel over one shoulder and leans on the railing. "There's no easy way to explain this, but sometimes, Mattie just seems to know what you're thinking."

"What? She reads minds?"

"Don't have a better explanation."

He sweeps an arm toward the open patio door. "Let me show you around and then I'll start cooking."

Beth decides she'll let him change the subject. For now. Because she's not sure what her next question would be: Why are you lying to me? Or, What's your evidence that Mattie can read minds?

She slides off her wet sandals and leaves them by the door. When she steps inside, Beth has to hide her surprise. Given the state of Dan's battered pickup and his standard uniform of worn blue jeans, flannel shirt, and rubber boots, she'd expected a décor of shabby but functional.

Instead, she is greeted by neatness and quality. A real estate agent might describe the house as well-appointed: hardwood floors, tiled kitchen, large windows onto the pond, overstuffed sofa and chair in a colourful print that verges on tacky, but actually looks good with the latte-coloured walls. Tall bookshelves stand on either side of a stone fireplace, and a weaving incorporating Mattie's signature spider web and a stylized raven hangs over the mantel. There's also a black and white etching of a raven that looks to be Haida or Tlingit. A foot-tall carved raven perches on one of the bookshelves. Beth picks up the carving and runs a finger over the feathers. Turns it over: *Matthew MacKenzie*. She looks up at Dan.

"She signs all her carvings that way. I don't ask. Not my business." He slides the screen door shut.

Not my business. Dan's mantra. Maybe that's the only way to stay sane when you're dealing with Mattie.

Beth places the carving back on the shelf. In the quiet, she hears the refrigerator's hum start up. A refrigerator. With a freezer. She tucks her hair behind one ear. Smoothes the damp cloth of her shorts. Takes off her glasses and cleans each lens on the bottom of her shirt. Slides them back on. If she could just store her samples here she wouldn't have to drive them back to St. John's. Can she dare ask?

Dan lays a hand on the countertop that separates the living room from the kitchen. "Get you something? Beer? Wine? Rum and Coke?" He grins mischievously. "Or tea maybe?" She lets herself laugh with him. Decides that he looks more attractive when he's smiling. "Wine, please," she says.

"White or red?"

"White."

He opens the refrigerator and pulls out a bottle of wine and a Black Horse. "I just drink beer, but I picked this up in town today. George – the guy at the liquor store

– recommended it." He glances at the label. "A Chilean Chardonnay okay?"

"Perfect."

While he uncorks the wine, she scans the shelves of books: basic how-to's, detective novels and thrillers, some old classics, but also a few contemporary novels she recognizes as literary, which surprises her. And then she wonders why. Why has she assumed that Dan isn't a serious reader?

Grasping a beer in one hand, he gives her the glass of wine. His fingers, brushing hers, seem to linger. She glances up, but he's already turned away and is pointing the bottle toward the hallway.

"When I came back here I had the old place torn down," he says. "Then built this one. Did most of the work myself." He speaks with pride edged with uneasiness, as if embarrassed by his own enthusiasm. "Small, but it's all I need."

Beth follows him into a study. A heavy wooden desk with an old computer sits in front of the large window onto the pond. The desk is uncluttered, as if he doesn't use it much: no sticky notes, no office knick-knacks, not even a container for pencils and pens.

He opens the door across the hall. He has made what was probably designed to be a small bedroom into a cosy TV room. Two matching La-Z-Boys sit opposite a flat-screen TV. One chair looks well-used. A pile of *Maclean's* and *Canadian Geographic*, as well as a clean ashtray, sit on a small table beside it. The other La-Z-Boy still looks new.

"Mostly for news and hockey," Dan says. "A movie now and again." He steps away and opens the door to the bathroom. Spartan, but clean. Beth notes that there is only one toothbrush in the holder. The walls are blue-grey; cream tiles cover the floor and shower stall, which she contemplates with longing. She looks in the mirror and tries to straighten the collar of her wrinkled shirt. Wonders if she smells bad. She's gone swimming nearly every day, but hasn't showered for more than two weeks. Would it be too intimate to ask if she can shower here now and again?

She follows him back to the kitchen. She hasn't seen a photograph of him – or of anyone else – anywhere. "No dog or cat?" she says.

"Nope. Don't want the bother." He places a cast-iron skillet on the stove. "Just look at Mattie. She's always having to do something for that dog."

Yes, but? Beth thinks of Pirate and of how much she'd miss him if he weren't around. "Don't you ever get lonely out here?"

"Not really. Had my fill of people – and obligations – in the army. I came back here to relax and fish – not to have to do things I don't really wanna do." He turns on the burner and pours oil into the pan. "It's all I can do to keep up with what Mattie wants."

Dan spreads flour on a plate and sprinkles a few herbs from unmarked bottles onto the flour. He takes the gutted trout from the refrigerator and dips each one into the flour. Places the fish gently into the hot oil. "So how's the research going?"

"Okay. I've observed them a couple times near the old beaver lodge." She pauses. "Well … once, actually."

"When I showed up yesterday morning?"

"Yep." She sips the wine. "I probably should've gone out there again this morning instead of going fishing. Should be out there right now, I suppose."

"Hey, a scientist has to take it easy sometimes. You know what they say about all work."

"Guess so," she says. "But at least I have almost enough samples for an analysis of food habits. And for the genetic tests. Those will tell me who's in the group using the beaver lodge."

Dan flips one of the trout, bright pink flesh turning pale. "Just ask Mattie. She knows all that."

Beth smiles. "Or thinks she does." She clicks her fingernails against the chilled wineglass. Studies her bare toes and the lines of dirt that outline where her sandal straps go. "I've been keeping the samples on ice," she says carefully, "but I should get them into a freezer soon. Actually, I was planning to drive into the university tomorrow." She takes another sip of wine. "But if I could find a freezer here where I could store them ..."

Dan's eyebrows lift. He turns another fish. "You wanna store otter shit in my freezer?"

"I'd double-bag it."

He exhales through pursed lips. "For how long?"

"No more than a week," she says quickly. "Well, maybe just a little longer."

"Otter shit in my freezer," he says, shaking his head. "Don't you dare tell anyone. Clive'll never let me – or anyone else – forget it."

"I really appreciate this, Dan." She wants to hug him, but she's not sure he'd welcome it.

"And I want it triple-bagged." He turns the last trout, the hot oil sizzling. "Just another week? Then it's back to St. John's?"

"Guess so." But the thought of going back fills her with a familiar melancholy. She'll be returning to city dirt and city noise, and even worse, to the daily barrage of news – from CBC, *The Telegram*, her colleagues – about climate change, fracking near Gros Morne, chemical and oil spills, plastics showing up in every corner of the globe. And so few people who give a damn. She's begun to think that people just can't allow themselves to care – because they feel so helpless to do anything. She feels helpless. And hopeless.

Stop, she thinks. Just stop. She takes another sip of the chilled wine. "But I still need to get out to some other ponds yet," she says, "just to make sure there are enough otters in the area to justify a full-fledged study."

Nodding, but only half-listening, Dan lays out place settings on a table set near a window halfway between the kitchen and the living room. Beth watches as he puts out butter and fresh rolls from the grocery in town. She rubs the stem of the wineglass with her thumb. When she gets back to St. John's, she'll be taking up her life exactly where she left it: teaching Biology 1001, interminable staff meetings, as well as meetings of the Newfoundland and Labrador Environmental Network, which she'd joined in hopes of making a difference, but where she inevitably learns even more about all the environmental destruction going on around her.

And she'll be going back to Alan: same as always. *Fine.*

And Alice will still be dead.

Why can't she stop herself? Just for one evening? She upends her wineglass.

"I think they're ready," Dan announces. Deftly wielding a spatula, he lays the fish onto two plates. "A little skimpy, but if you'll get the potato salad and coleslaw from the fridge, there should be enough for the two of us."

Beth retrieves the salads, still in clear plastic containers bearing Price Chopper stickers. She holds them out in front of her, unsure whether to set the containers on the table or to put the salads into serving dishes. Opts for the former.

Dan refills her wineglass, grabs himself another beer, and they sit down. He jumps up again to get the salt and pepper and some paper towels to use as napkins.

Beth spoons potato salad onto her plate, then points the serving spoon toward the bookshelf. "So you like ravens?"

"Yep." Dan grinds pepper onto the steaming fish.

"There's some really interesting research coming out on how intelligent they are."

"Is there now?" He reaches for the tub of coleslaw, pauses, tub in mid-air. "Mattie's ideas might be pretty weird sometimes, but I think she's right about one thing: there's a lot more going on with animals and birds than scientists ever give them credit for." He buries a serving spoon in the coleslaw. "Or maybe, as a scientist, you don't believe that?"

"I agree there's a lot we don't know," she says carefully, "yet." She takes a forkful of trout. The flavour is delicate but savoury. Dan's a better cook than Alan.

"But you have faith that we will eventually," he says.

"I wouldn't call it faith."

He takes a swallow of beer. "What would you call it?"

She thinks a moment. "Confidence," she says. "I have confidence in the scientific method. And I'm agreeing with you: there's more going on than we've been able to figure out—"

"Tough to figure out if it turns out they're smarter than us."

She barks a surprised and abbreviated laugh. "This is starting to sound like a conversation with Mattie."

He teases out the backbone and accompanying small bones from the pale flesh. Doesn't look up.

"All right," Beth concedes, "I agree with you that there's probably more going on with animals and birds than most scientists think. But Mattie takes it way too far."

"How's that?"

"When she says the otters are waiting until I call them by their proper name to tell me their secrets. That the old grandmother watches over the pond."

The right side of his mouth turns up in a half-smile. "That's just Mattie." He scoops more potato salad from the plastic container. "Most of the time I don't even listen."

Not my business.

"And all that stuff about Matthew's ghost." He splits a roll with his fingers, butters one half. "That's just her way of coping. She never got over Matthew's death, and her way of dealing with it is to pretend he's still here. Keeps him alive for her, I guess." He bites into the roll.

"I get that. But it gives me the creeps when she says the rosary will bring him to me."

"Why are you even listening to that stuff? You're the one who's supposed to be the scientist."

"You truly didn't tell her that I thought she took it?"

"Christ, Beth. Why would I? She's tangly enough as it is."

"Then how could she know I couldn't find it?" She shakes her head. "Sorry, but I just can't buy that she's a mind reader."

"Can't explain it any better than that." Dan reaches for his beer.

"But then why–"

He clinks the brown bottle against her wineglass. "Here's to your otter shit," he says. "Hope you find what you're looking for."

CHAPTER 15

They are sitting at the table drinking coffee. They've talked mostly about the news, in a conversation that has been polite, but not much else. Dan has been guarded, and Beth has followed suit. Neither has mentioned Mattie again.

It came as no surprise that she'd missed nothing important in the national or international news. But what did startle her, when the reality sank in, is that it's been less than ten days since Alan left for St. John's. It feels like a month. She's known Mattie for less than a week, Dan for just a few days. What surprises her too, when she finally notices the cool breeze raising goosebumps on her forearms, are the dark clouds boiling in the west. Why has Dan said nothing? He must have seen the ominous sky.

She jumps up. "Oh my god! I've got to get going."

"You can't go out on the water in this," he says. "I'll drive you back." The words are hardly out of his mouth before the rain starts, fat drops hammering against the windows.

"You haven't had too much beer to drive?" Because she's certainly had too much wine.

"Nope." He closes the windows and the patio door, efficiently but not hurriedly.

"Can we load my kayak into the back of the truck? I'll need it first thing in the morning."

Dan peers out at the rain, which has become a deluge. "We'll get soaked." He glances at the clock over the sink: 7:12. "You could just wait until the storm passes. I can drive you and your kayak home then."

A move? Or is she just flattering herself?

~

Beth sits in the armchair and listens to water drip into the pans and bowls. She stares at a candle, at the small halo of light against the dark.

While she and Dan waited out the storm, they cleaned up the kitchen, and then, while he had a cigarette, she went into his office to check her email. She'd already broken her no-news rule. She drummed her fingers on the desk while she waited through all the beeps and buzzes of the dial-up connection, then she opened her inbox and scanned the scores of unopened messages – mostly spam and notices from the university she didn't even bother to open. Also three from Alan. But none from Rachel. True, she'd told her daughter she'd be out of touch for at least two weeks, but still.

She signed into Facebook. Saw that Rachel had posted a funny status about her lab work only hours earlier. Her daughter was fine. Fine without her.

Beth posted a cheery comment, then opened the first email from Alan, sent the day after he got back to St. John's: *Not sure when, or if, you'll get this. Hope the research is going well – and that you're getting the 'alone' time you need. Miss you. Love, Alan.*

She opened the second one, sent three days ago: *Sorry we couldn't talk long, but I'm glad to know you're okay and that you're getting some samples – and I hope by the time you read this that you've also been able to observe them – if only so you can come home sooner. I miss you. Pirate misses you. Love, Alan. P.S. The cat died. Too badly injured to save.*

Beth sat back in the leather chair. Pictured laundry piling up, the refrigerator empty, balls of dust and dog hair rolling like tumbleweed. Of course Alan misses her. Stop. She knows there's more to his missing her than just the chores going undone. And yet, sometimes, when he scowls just like her father used to, she suspects that she's disappointed him too, but she doesn't know how or in what way. Maybe he finds *her* boring.

She leaned forward and clicked on his third email, sent just last night, right after they talked: *I know you're probably not getting these, but it feels good to write them. I'm looking forward to seeing you. If you do get this, and if you can get away early enough, let's go out to India Gate for supper. And talk – about whatever it is you've been thinking about during all those hours alone. Love, Alan.*

She closed the messages without answering. Couldn't tell him by email that she's not coming home tomorrow. She'll have to do that over the phone. Beth ran her hands down the arms of the chair, felt guilty just for being at Dan's, like she'd been unfaithful, when, in truth, everything had been perfectly innocent. Disconcertingly innocent.

When he finally drove her home, Dan concentrated on the road, on the huge puddles and potholes. The truck rattled with every jarring bump, and the kayak, though tied securely, bounced around in the back. The trip around the bottom of the pond took nearly thirty minutes. They didn't talk much, just listened to the steady beat of the wipers, the right one leaving so much water on the windshield that Beth could hardly see the road.

By the time they arrived at Beth's cabin, the rain had slowed to a drizzle. Dan left the headlights on while she unlocked the door and went in to retrieve the samples, which she slid into another plastic bag. She handed them through the truck window, and Dan accepted the bag gingerly, grasping the top with just a thumb and forefinger.

They unloaded the kayak. He slid back into the truck and, with a simple "See ya," was gone.

Beth stares hard at the candle. She should be relieved that he spared her the embarrassment of having to ward off an unwanted advance, or even the suggestion of an advance. Instead, she has to confess to disappointment.

Here's to your otter shit. Hope you find what you're looking for.

What is she looking for? Her project is beginning to feel like a last-ditch effort to rekindle the idea that she can still have a career, that she can still do research that matters. But she can't. No matter what research she does, she'll still be just as old, and the earth and all its wild places will still be imperilled.

Another depressing thought: she'll have to go to Mattie tomorrow and apologize.

~

She wakes, flat to the bed, palms pressed into the thin mattress, fingers gripping the edge. She'd been scaling a cliff above the ocean, the sunlight brilliant on the water. Someone she couldn't quite see was peering over the top, watching, only a bit of forehead and the bill of a blue baseball cap visible. Suddenly, the rope released from her harness. Her grip failed. Beth woke just before she hit the rocks below.

She sucks in air and listens to the wind shussing through the birches, the tap-tap-tap of rain hitting the leaves. Hopes the pans and bowls don't overflow.

~

She propels herself through dark water by languid undulations of body and tail. Paws grab her from behind, a whiskery snout presses into her cheek. A game. Rolling in black water. She turns and twists, releasing herself from the paws' grip. Swims. Swims hard, following a silver path laid down by the moon. Fish scatter, tinfoil bits of light. Heart thumping, muscles taut, she surfaces to breathe. Hears a flute: silver threads of moon woven through indigo sky.

126

Beth wakes, an image of dark-blue sky and moonlight fading, the silky slide of water soft on her arms. She can still hear the flute, the strains profoundly odd, more like the calls of birds and animals, or an infant's thin wails.

The music stops. She gropes for her watch, stares at the green glowing numbers: 4:32. Who would be out with a flute at this hour? She sits up on the edge of the bed, slides on her glasses, and strikes a match to light the kerosene lamp. Carrying the lamp before her, she goes into the kitchen to light a fire and make coffee, quietly. Listens hard for the sound of a flute. In the bright light of Dan's kitchen, Mattie's ghosts had fled, but now? Now she wishes Muin would show up at the door.

~

Two cups of coffee, a clear head, and a golden sunrise have helped Beth to realize that she was still enmeshed in her dream, and not quite awake, when she heard the nighttime serenade. She sits up in her kayak and squares her shoulders. This morning, after she goes to the otter spot, she'll take the rosary back out into the woods and leave it where she found it. She will visit Mattie and offer an apology, and then be done with all these distractions. She won't even see Dan again. He showed her last night where he keeps the spare key. She'll put any new samples she collects in his freezer when he's not there. From now on, she's sticking to her research. She will make it something that matters.

Paddling steadily, she listens to the satisfying swish of water against the hull. Within minutes she is at the otter spot. She balances the paddle in front of her and lets the kayak drift. Waits, binoculars and voice recorder ready, and doesn't move. There is only the piping of shorebirds and the *peent-peent-peent* of a nuthatch. She hopes the jays and crows won't call out a warning.

The wild roses blooming on shore remind her of Rachel, beautiful but tough, nothing fragile about her. Of course Rachel doesn't need Beth's mothering the way she once did, and Beth has resolved to be glad that her daughter has become so competent and independent. There's a certain freedom in that. For both of them.

Maybe that's how an otter mother feels when she watches her pups become proficient at catching their own fish, when they're finally ready to leave her: a sense of accomplishment. But maybe there's an ache too. Maybe she recalls every pup she's ever birthed. Remembers the peculiarities of each cold black nose and silken head, each clumsy first swim.

Beth groans: she's being anthropomorphic. And sentimental.

The kayak bobs gently. She hears a raven's *cark-cark-cark*, but no chirps or soft grunts. There's hardly a ripple on the water.

Anthropomorphic and sentimental maybe, but Beth's pretty sure there's more to animal emotions than people want to believe. Most people – if they think about it at all – want to believe that pups are out of their mother's mind as soon as they're out of her sight, and that the pups forget their mother as well. But that belief is no less speculative than believing that the mother and pups remember each other. Neurologically, otters are very similar to dogs, and people want to believe their dogs still love them and remember them when they're out of sight. Otter pups stay with their mother for at least a year, maybe longer. Why, then, wouldn't an otter mother remember her pups? Or a pup its mother?

Horrible images spring to mind, and Beth is helpless to stop them: a young otter caught in a drowning set or a leg-hold trap. Do the other members of the group crowd around in panic and grief? Watch as their companion or child dies? A slow, painful death if it's a leg-hold trap. And if it's a nursing mother who's caught, the pups are left to starve. Beth can't even think about it without tearing up.

She lifts the paddle and quietly turns the kayak to keep herself facing shore. She scans the water's edge. Nothing. She should steel herself, go to Mattie, and get her apology over with. But then she sees a lone otter, swimming quietly along the shoreline.

Funny how you never see them coming, Beth thinks. They just appear.

She notes the time: 6:42. Lifts the binoculars even though the otter is less than five metres away. Too close to use the voice recorder. It looks old, the muzzle silvery grey. The otter is swimming lazily. It turns toward the kayak and, paddling languorously with one back paw and guiding itself with a front paw, swims closer, so close that Beth can hear the water ripple against the kayak.

Slowly, she lowers the binoculars and stares into eyes that are round and dark behind a bulbous black nose that bears a small white scar. Long grey whiskers curve down into the water. The otter floats, staying in place with an occasional flip of a back paw, a gentle wave of a thick, tapering tail. And then quiet conversation: *uhn-uhn-uhn, uhn-uhn-uhn.*

Beth keeps her mouth closed and tries to mimic the sound deep in her throat: *uhn-uhn-uhn, uhn-uhn-uhn.* It doesn't come out right.

The otter periscopes, its head and neck coming high out of the water. Snorts an alarm.

Beth sits perfectly still. Doesn't look at her watch, but it feels as if they stare at each other for a full two minutes. What *is* that otter thinking?

Uhn-uhn-uhn, uhn-uhn-uhn.

Who is it talking to? This time Beth stays silent, just watching and listening. And then she hears it. *Hope.* The word is as clear in her head as if someone had spoken it aloud. The otter periscopes again, and this time, gives a high-pitched chirp and disappears beneath the water.

Beth waits a few minutes, then takes out her journal: *9 Aug 10: clear and sunny, winds light, ~17°C, observed at A5, 6:20 – 6:50. One otter appeared close to shore at 6:42 (about 5 m away), an old one with a grey muzzle and a small white scar between its nostrils; swam slowly along shore. Quiet series of grunts. Came to within 2 m of the kayak and …*

And what? Whatever she writes would be embarrassing if any of her colleagues were to read it: *The otter and I locked eyes. I felt like I was looking into the eyes of a sentient, intelligent being. I was on the verge of understanding something important about the way animals think and feel. I heard the word "hope."*

Did she really hear that? Now she's not quite sure.

She writes: *It looked at me and grunted. I tried to imitate the sound. The otter periscoped and snorted, then watched me (~ 2 min), grunting quietly. Finally, it periscoped again, chirped, and dived.*

Beth slides the research journal into her backpack and lands the kayak near the latrine. She marks a thick plastic bag with the date and location. Collects one fresh sample, slides it into a second marked bag, and places it in the cooler.

CHAPTER 16

Mattie is sitting near the pond in the soft light of mid-morning. Muin is out in the water, but as soon as she sees Beth, she swims to shore and gallops toward her. When she is two feet away, the dog stops and shakes.

Beth brushes water off her shorts. "Sit, Muin." She pulls a Milk-Bone from her pocket.

Mattie pushes herself up from the deep chair. She is holding a long, hollow cylinder of wood and a knife. Shavings lie scattered on the grass. "Was just having tea," she says. "Want some? Plain ole black, right outta the box."

Beth can tell by the pitch of her voice, and the blue baseball cap, that she is Matthew this morning. "No thanks," Beth says. "I'm good." She gives Muin another treat and scratches her behind the ears. While she's still bent over, she says, "Listen, I'm sorry–"

"Found it, didn't you."

Beth straightens. "So Dan was by already this morning?"

"Nope." Mattie sits down and points the knife at the Muskoka chair beside her own.

"You sure?"

"I might be old, love, but I'm not senile. Not yet any-ways." She rests the knife and the wooden cylinder in her lap.

Beth doles out the third, and last, Milk-Bone.

"Come on now," Mattie says, "sit down and stay a while."

"I took it back."

"Good."

Beth slides into the chair.

"Might be too late though." Mattie picks up the knife and taps the butt of the wooden handle on the arm of the chair. "You might've started something you can't stop."

Beth looks at her sidelong. "Like what?" she says quietly. Muin noses at Beth's pocket. Beth holds out her empty hands and lets the dog sniff them.

"Hard to know." Mattie points the knife toward the grass, and Muin circles and plops down. She takes off the blue cap and lays it on the arm of the chair, fingers lingering on the soiled bill. Her hands seem larger this morning, rougher. Beth blinks and looks away, toward the tall monkshood and evening primrose growing near the cabin, and then at the expanse of fireweed in the clearing, bordered by goldenrod and interwoven with vetch: a riot of purple, yellow, and pink.

Muin stands and puts her head in Beth's lap. "It's no small thing," Mattie says, "when an animal chooses you."

"Mattie, I don't know what that means."

"Simple. She wants to go with you when I cross over."

Muin's tail wags as if to confirm her choice.

"Are you telling me you're dying?" Beth says.

"Course I am. I'm old."

Beth leans forward. "What's the doctor say?"

"Don't need a doctor to tell me what I already know." She turns to Beth. "Looking forward to the rest, really. Though I'm sorry to leave Muin behind. Glad she's finally picked someone."

"I can't take your dog."

"You have to."

"But why me? Why not Dan?"

Mattie guffaws. "Don't be so foolish. Dan's a nice boy, but …" She rubs her beaked nose with a thumb and middle finger. "When he was young, he looked just like Matthew, so I've forgiven him a lot." She lays a hand over Beth's. "No need to worry about it now, love. When the time comes, Dan'll give you a call."

"Don't I get a choice in this?"

"You don't want her?"

Muin looks up at Beth. "I'll leave you my number," she says.

Mattie shades her eyes with an open hand and watches a chattering kingfisher swoop from a nearby birch to a spruce overhanging the pond. "So what's new in the world of otters today?"

"Not much," Beth says. "Early this morning, I saw a lone otter near the beaver lodge."

The kingfisher plunges into the water and comes up with a small fish.

"The old grandmother," Mattie says.

"You can't know that."

"Had a scar on her nose, didn't she."

"That doesn't prove anything," Beth says. "In a few months – when the genetic tests are done – I'll know who's in the group."

"No need of all that. It's the grandmother, two of her daughters, and one daughter's pups. And sometimes a male, or another female, just passing through."

Beth presses her lips together. No point in arguing, especially with an old woman who's dying. Muin turns and presents her haunches for scratching.

"What else you see?" Mattie asks.

"The otter swam very close to the kayak and looked at me. That's about it."

"She's trying, love." Mattie tips the mug and studies what's left of the tea. "Course, your dreams'll help too."

"Dreams?"

Mattie puts on the blue cap, tugs on the bill. "Don't tell me you haven't been dreaming of em."

"The only thing I remember from my dreams," Beth says, "is climbing a steep cliff above the ocean. You released the rope from my harness and I fell."

Mattie laughs. "Weren't me, girl."

"And there was some odd flute music," Beth says, pointing at the cylinder in Mattie's lap.

"I plays the flute."

"You weren't out in the middle of the night, were you?"

"In my dream I was."

"That's not funny."

"Weren't meant to be." Mattie sits back in the chair and picks up the wood and the knife. "You're here to help her, you know."

"Who? Muin?"

A shaving falls to the ground. Beth hears a whisper. "Matilda, girl. Matilda."

~

The Toyota rattles over the washboard road. She stops at the Irving, then decides that before she calls Alan, she will try one more time to get Rachel. It's lunchtime here, early morning in Vancouver: Rachel should be getting ready for work. Beth enters her calling card number and, while she follows the verbal commands, studies the patterns in the dirt below the pay phone. People waiting – happy, angry, worried, hopeful – have used the toes of their shoes to build small mounds of dirt and pebbles. Beth places herself in the hopeful group and uses her whole foot, rotating from the heel, to leave a windshield-wiper pattern of scraped dirt bordered by ridges of grey pebbles.

She punches in Rachel's number. After five rings, Beth gets her voice mail. Why isn't she answering? Rachel always has her cellphone with her: it's like an added appendage. Beth places herself in the angry group now. Imagines Rachel hearing the phone, knowing it's her mother calling, and then ignoring the insistent rings.

Beth does her best to leave a cheery message: "Hi, sweetheart, hope everything's good there. My research is going really well. Hope to talk with you soon. Love you."

She steels herself to call Alan. Punches in the numbers of his cellphone and listens to the buzzing ring. Hopes he's busy with a patient and she'll get his voice mail.

"Hello?" Garbled, mouth full, probably eating lunch.

"Hi, Alan."

"Hi." A quick swallow. "How's it going?"

"Fine."

"You sound tired."

"No, not really." She pushes at the dirt and pebbles with her toe. "I found a freezer where I can store my samples." Shoves them into a narrow grey pile. "So I guess I won't have to make a trip back to St. John's after all."

"I was looking forward to seeing you. I was hoping we could go out to dinner."

She can see his face: brow furrowed, disappointed, but irritated as well.

He laughs once, harshly. "Where in the world did you find someone willing to store otter shit in their freezer?"

"Met an old guy at the Morning Glory. He's interested in my research."

"Well ... glad you found a freezer. I guess. Can't you still make the trip back?"

"I could ..." Beth leans her forehead against the phone, looks down at the ridge of gravel and dirt. "But driving back and forth would use up two whole days. If I just stay here, I can get the research done that much quicker."

Silence.

"Although to be honest," she adds quickly, "I'm not sure that any of it really matters."

"Of course it does, Beth. Scientists know almost nothing about the behaviour of otters. Except, of course, their extreme cuteness." Trying to lift her spirits. Maybe his own too.

"But does any of it matter?"

"Guess you *are* feeling worn out. Listen, you never know what's going to matter in the end. And studying otters isn't the most useless thing you could do. Some academics spend their whole professional lives studying ancient Byzantine dialects."

Thanks for that vote of confidence, Alan. "Easy for you to say," she argues, "you know your work is useful."

"People pay for it, yes. But does vaccinating people's dogs and cats, selling them flea collars and anti-dandruff shampoo, matter in the long run?"

She closes her eyes. "I don't know, Alan. Sometimes I feel like I don't know anything anymore."

"How much longer do you think you'll have to be out there?"

"I need to get out to at least a few other ponds to take samples, and I'm not sure how long that will take."

"I miss you, Beth."

"Me too." She flattens the mound of pebbles with her foot. "Well, I should be going now." A long moment of silence, some crackling on the line.

"Love you," he says.

"Love you too. Bye."

Love you. So easy to say to Rachel. A hesitation when it comes to Alan. When did *Love you* become a routine pretence with her husband, and not a real feeling? Maybe he feels the same way.

She slides back into the car. Slams the door harder than she needs to.

~

Beth sees the black pickup parked in front of the Morning Glory. She pulls in beside it, squeezes the steering wheel with both hands, hard, then releases it. Maybe she doesn't have to feel embarrassed around him. He never knew what she was thinking last night.

As soon as she steps through the door, Dan nods. She slides into the booth across from him.

"Special is cod." He looks at his half-empty plate. "Not

as good as my trout, but hey, what can you expect from amateurs?"

"Thanks for driving me home last night. Sorry it was such an ordeal."

"No worries."

The skinny waitress comes with the menu. "Special is pan-fried cod with boiled potatoes and coleslaw," she says. "Soup is turkey vegetable."

Beth doesn't even glance at the menu. "Just a bowl of the soup and a salad, please. Vinaigrette on the side. Thanks."

The waitress scribbles notes on her order pad and turns away.

"So you stopped by Mattie's this morning," Beth says.

"Nope." Dan looks up from his plate. "She tell you I did?"

"No, but when I went to see her, to apologize, she already knew I'd found the rosary."

He pushes at a boiled potato, then lays down his fork. "Like I told you, Mattie just knows things." He shrugs. "I've gotten so used to it, I hardly notice anymore when she answers my questions before I even ask."

"It's too strange."

"Not really. Might be simple ... the same way you know, and I know, the waitress will mess up something about your order."

"But that knowledge is based on experience. Mattie's is based on ... what?"

"She's had a whole lot more experience than the rest of us. And truth be told, it's not much of a mystery for her to figure out that you'd find that stupid rosary."

The waitress brings Beth's order: the iceberg lettuce is swimming in salad dressing. Dan looks at the salad, then lays a finger on the back of her hand. They both smile.

"Guess so," she says. Thinks, but doesn't say, But how did Mattie know that I'd lost it in the first place? She tastes the soup, adds salt and pepper. "She told me this morning that Muin has chosen me."

"For what?"

"Apparently she wants to go with me after Mattie dies."

He smirks. "Guess that lets me off the hook."

"Seriously, Dan. Is she dying?"

"Doubt it," he says. "Or not anytime soon. She's healthy as a horse." He leans back in the booth and takes a toothpick from his pocket. "So, push back any frontiers of science today?"

"Collected one fresh sample. I put it in your freezer with the others. Triple-bagged," she adds. "Hope that's okay."

"Anything to further the cause." His voice drops to a whisper. "Just don't talk about it too loudly."

Beth takes a spoonful of soup. It leaves a greasy film on her lips.

"By the way," he says, "there's a party tonight at the Bide-a-Wee. You should come and meet some of the local crowd … if you're interested."

"Thanks, but I should go out and do observations. I already skipped them yesterday morning and last night."

Dan taps the toothpick on the table. "Come afterwards then. Probably won't even start till after eight. There'll be music."

"I'll see how things go." Beth takes a bite of the salad, winces at the tartness of the vinegar. Chews and swallows. "Do you fish on any ponds besides Medicine Rock?" she asks.

"I fish anywhere there's fish."

She holds up another forkful of lettuce, lets some of the salad dressing drip off. "So you would know which ponds around here have otters?"

"Most of em do."

"It could save me a lot of time," she says carefully, "if someone could tell me where I might be able to gather samples from otters who aren't part of the group on Medicine Rock." She watches his face. His frown is deepening. "To confirm that there are enough otters in the area for a real study," she explains quickly.

"If you wanna know about otters, you should come to the party tonight. A couple of the guys do some trapping. They know all about the otters around here."

"I guess." But she doesn't want to talk to anyone about trapping. She knows most of the trappers are just trying to make a few extra bucks, but she doesn't even want to think about it.

"Or just ask Mattie," Dan continues.

"Sure," Beth says, "and she'll give me some sort of answer, but I won't know what she means."

"True enough." He laughs.

Emboldened by his laughter, she puts a hand to her mouth and clears her throat. "I've been wondering ..." Beth's words are slow and cautious. "You said that you'd take any excuse to get out on the water. Would you be willing to take me to a few other ponds?"

Dan sighs. "Why not? I'd love to have more shit in my freezer."

CHAPTER 17

Beth drives past the Bide-a-Wee. She just wants to see who's there and then she'll head back to the cabin to finish the notes she jotted after her observations. It's a mild summer evening; about thirty people are standing around or sitting on lawn chairs on the small patch of grass under the motel floodlights. She spots Dan. Playing a fiddle. She brakes, turns around in the library parking lot, and goes back to the Bide-a-Wee.

When she steps out of the car, Beth nods to the few people she recognizes: Clive, the postmistress with the severe black hair, the clerk from the liquor store, and the surly boy from the Irving station. She seeks out the empty canvas chair beside Clive.

"How's the work going?" he says slowly.

"All right," Beth says, glancing toward the musicians. "Didn't know Dan could play. And aren't those the girls from the Morning Glory and Price Chopper?"

"Yep. And the guy with the accordion is their dad, Fred. Owns the Bide-a-Wee. His wife's birthday is the reason for the party."

Beth slides back in the chair. So the two skinny girls with the bright red bangs really are sisters, talented ones at that. The waitress from the Morning Glory is singing to her own guitar accompaniment, her sister adding the harmony. Surly Irving boy edges closer to them, no longer surly.

At a break in the music, Dan goes to a cooler and pulls out two Black Horse. He walks over to Beth, opens a bottle, and hands it to her. "Glad to see you could make it."

"You never told me you could play the fiddle," she says.

"Wouldn't take it on the stage."

"Hey, who's this?" says the accordion player, now standing at Dan's side.

"My new boss," Dan says. "I'm helping out with her research."

Clive waves his good hand at Dan. "Go on, b'y. What kinda help could you be?"

"Hey, I'm right there on the cutting edge. Taking her out tomorrow to scout out otters on some of the ponds around here."

Beth can almost see the synapses connecting behind Fred's eyes. "So you must be that lady who's collecting otter shit," he says.

She smiles wanly and nods.

"That otter be interesting," Fred says. "Otterly fascinating," he continues, grinning at his own puns. "You otter be careful out there."

Dan catches Beth's eye and grimaces.

The sisters start playing again, and Dan and Fred go off to join them. Beth tries not to notice the attractive, dark-haired, forty-something who reaches out to touch Dan's arm when he passes. Whatever she says makes him laugh.

Beth also tries not to see how people are assessing her. The young woman sitting on the other side of Clive whispers into his ear. He holds up his good hand and talks behind it. It won't be long until everyone knows that Beth is "that lady who's here to collect otter shit."

An older couple approach Clive, and when he begins to introduce them, Beth stands. It seems impolite to talk up to them, but she forgets their names almost immediately, can recall only that the woman is the town librarian.

"So you're the one doing that research?" the woman says. Her husband has already turned back to the musicians. "From the university?" she continues.

Beth nods.

The woman's lips pucker like she's just bit into a lemon. "Our tax dollars at work." She offers a plastic smile. "Where you staying to?"

"Old Wells place."

"Out near Mattie MacKenzie? Met her yet?"

"Time or two."

"She comes into the library now and again," the woman says. "Never has much to say though."

The postmistress joins them. "Hi, Dorothy," she says, then turns to Beth. "How's the collecting going?"

"All right." Beth wonders whether she remembers the postcard or if Clive's information has already spread that quickly.

"Must be lovely to spend all that time outdoors, out on the water. Not being stuck inside all day."

"It is, actually," Beth says, "especially when I get a chance to watch them."

Dorothy's lips pucker again. "But what about having to pick up their … stuff? That can't be much fun. And what's the use of it all, really?"

The postmistress waves away the questions, and Beth likes her immediately.

"We see otters on our pond now and again," the postmistress says. "I think they're funny, but Harold, my husband, complains that they eat too many trout." She glances at Dorothy. "And leave their 'stuff' on the dock."

"Which pond?" Beth asks.

"Birchy. Just north of town a little ways."

"How many do you see?"

"Usually two or three. Sometimes as many as–"

"Beth's staying out to the old Wells place," Dorothy interjects. "Right there by Mattie's."

"That's good," the postmistress says. "If you need anything, Mattie'll help you out."

Dorothy frowns. "You think so, Agnes? She seems kinda crazy to me."

"What makes you say that?"

The librarian looks at Clive and then back to Agnes and Beth. "She always picks out the oddest books. Stuff no one else ever reads."

"And that makes her crazy?"

"Well, she keeps to herself out there in the woods. Hardly ever talks to anyone."

Agnes raises a painted black eyebrow. "Wish there was a few more folks kept their mouths shut till they had something to say." She turns back to Beth. "To answer your question," she says pointedly, "I sometimes see as many as six. But that's in the winter, when they're out on the ice."

Dorothy lays a hand on Agnes's arm. "What about her and Katherine?"

"What about them? Katherine was one of my favourite teachers. One of my son's too."

The librarian turns to Beth. "How's she seem to you?"

"Okay ... I guess."

"Sure, Mattie can be a little strange at times," Agnes says. "But then aren't we all?" She glances at Dorothy, then continues, "Long time ago, her brother drowned. She rescued his girlfriend, then took care of her for twenty years after. All alone out there in that cabin. That might make anyone a little cracked." She takes Beth's elbow and steers her away from the librarian. "Come on, let's get some of that birthday cake before it's all gone."

They step toward a table set near the motel's front entrance. In the middle, surrounded by other desserts, sits a huge chocolate cake covered with green candles and gaudy pink, blue, and yellow frosting. Beth opts for a small slice of cheesecake.

"Toppings are over there," Agnes says, pointing to a line of jars.

Beth spoons blueberry jam on the cheesecake and goes back to sit beside Clive. He studies her plate with his good eye. "Wouldn't eat that," he says. "That's Mattie's jam. Probably poison."

Beth's fork stops halfway between her plate and her mouth.

He slaps a thigh and guffaws. "Just tormenting you, girl. Go ahead. Enjoy."

Beth eats the cheesecake, wishing she had an espresso instead of a beer to wash it down. She watches the musicians play a set of jigs and reels. A few people are dancing. Beside her, a girl in a flouncy pink dress and sparkly pink sandals holds a plate with chocolate cake and ice cream; she leans back between her father's knees. Her small rosebud mouth, missing two front teeth, is ringed with chocolate. She bounces to the music, her gaze locked on the musicians. The plate begins to tip and, before Beth can say a word, the cake and ice cream slide down the front of the gauzy dress and the leg of Beth's khakis and plop onto the grass. The girl's lower lip trembles.

"No worries," Beth says, wiping at the dress and her own pants with a napkin. She twists around to smile an "okay" at the father and is startled by the severity of his scowl. He pushes the little girl away and steps to the table for more napkins. Fat tears roll down her cheeks.

"It's all right," Beth says. "We can clean this up and there's plenty of cake left. You can get more."

"No, she can't," her father growls, stooping to wipe at the mess on the pink dress.

Beth swallows. The harsh scowl, just like her own father's. A scowl, along with stony silence, covered all occasions, so that she could never be certain what she'd done wrong. Was it the muddy tracks on the kitchen floor, the glass of milk that slipped from her fingers, her running off to play with Jax when she'd been told to weed the peas? Was it because she was shy and scrawny, not chatty and pretty like her golden-haired cousin? Or was it because she wasn't a boy? The only thing Beth could be sure of was that she was a disappointment.

She goes to the dessert table, picks out a big piece of chocolate cake with thick multi-hued frosting. She brings it back to the girl. She wants to smash it into her father's pointy rodent face. Instead, she holds it out. "Here, sweetheart, there's plenty."

The little girl looks at her father uncertainly. His face still carries the same deep scowl, but he doesn't glance at his daughter, or at Beth. Beth sits down and rests a hand lightly on the girl's small shoulder. "It's okay," she says, "that stain'll wash out." The girl reaches timidly for the plate.

The girl's father doesn't say a word. Intimidation through silence. Beth knows all too well how that works.

While the little girl eats her cake, Beth smiles at her as often as she can catch her eye, then she helps herself to another beer and watches the musicians and dancers for another hour or so before she decides it's time to head back to the cabin. She can feel a headache starting, just above her left eye. She stands.

Dan raises a hand and shouts to her above the music. "Don't forget, boss. Seven tomorrow morning."

On the drive home Beth begins to see flashes of light at the periphery of her vision and knows that a migraine is coming on. Hopes she can make it back before it hits full force.

She's a little wobbly by the time she walks into the cabin. She rummages through her toiletry bag for ibuprofen, pops three with the water that's left in her bottle, then unwraps a Maxalt wafer from its foil pouch and places it on her tongue. Stumbles into bed and hopes the migraine will be gone by the time Dan comes to pick her up in the morning.

~

She startles awake, the sound of a gunshot ringing in her ears. She is curled into a tight ball and her cheeks are wet. Her head still throbs. In the dream she'd been wearing her favourite green overalls and standing in a field of newly mown hay, throwing a stick for Jax. He retrieved it again and again, dropping it at her feet. She threw it, hard, and he dashed off toward the setting sun, the light bright in her eyes. She called and called. Then the sharp crack of a rifle.

Beth straightens her legs and tries to relax. Begins to rock herself in the bed. It didn't happen that way. She hadn't been throwing sticks for Jax. Her dog got sick, eyes and nose running with slimy mucous like he had a bad cold. And then he just lay down and stopped wanting to go outside. She promised her dad she'd give him every dime of her babysitting money if he would just take Jax to the vet, but he wouldn't. The day he took his rifle down from the wall, she hugged Jax and wouldn't let go. Her father had to pry her arms away, and then he carried the dog outside. Ordered Beth not to follow. The sound of the gunshot split her heart wide open. A month later, when her mother offered to get her a new puppy, Beth refused. She hasn't owned a dog since she was twelve. Pirate is Alan's, not hers. She gropes her way into the kitchen for another Maxalt.

~

The night is black, a slender crescent of moon. She walks slowly, the scant light on the path like the beam of a small flashlight. The light veers off into the woods, and she follows, branches closing behind her. Thready clouds weave across the moon. Scarves of old man's beard draped on the spruce

147

sway back and forth, back and forth, grey moans riding the wind. Ahead, she sees a shadow moving through the trees. She follows. The shadow stops, lays a hand on Medicine Rock. A gleaming rosary dangles from the wrist. An otter stands upright beside the rock, which suddenly flares as if lit from within. Glimpse of a yellow dress. The shadow turns, blue eyes hollow, and Beth knows that if she looks long enough, deep enough, she will see a sadness beyond measure, another heart split wide open. And then the shadow is gone. The otter comes down on all fours and slips into the water. The black sky swallows the light.

Dan is sitting on the edge of her bed, mouth opening and closing, but his words are muffled. She tries to tell him about the shadow, the hollow blue eyes, but he leaves. And then Mattie is there, spooning something hot and bitter into Beth's mouth. It dribbles down her chin.

She sits at the table. Mattie stands at the sink, her hand wielding a knife that flashes in the sunlight. A brace of rabbits, one of them a cold, iridescent blue-grey, lie on a large cutting board. Mattie picks up the unskinned rabbit. The shiny black eyes are wide open. The head wobbles. She slices the skin around the neck, then makes a slit down the length of the belly. She cuts off the feet, bones crunching. Slides off the skin as if undressing a baby. She cups a foot in her palm, turns and tosses it toward Beth. *Good luck. You'll need it. You've started something you can't stop.*

Mattie sits down at the table with Beth. Alice joins them, her bald head wrapped in a yellow scarf. They sort through puzzle pieces. Mattie and Alice click them into place, one after the other. Beth's pieces are large, like those of a child's puzzle. She cannot make them fit. She turns to Alice, but Alice won't look away from the puzzle.

And then she is sitting on shore, the trees and water wreathed in fog, but she can see a full moon just above the horizon. The sun is rising behind her. A high-pitched chirp and then an answer. The otters climb out of the water and come closer, not warily, but as if she is one of them. Six of them, continuous *uhn-uhn-uhns*. She tilts her head, surprised that she can understand them: *We are here. We are all here. Now.* And then they are gone. Silver rings in dark water. She turns toward the rising sun and sees the backlit shadow of a woman. The light behind her makes a halo of her copper curls. She drops a brown and white feather, then turns and walks into the light.

~

Beth awakens to chocolate brown eyes staring into hers, a slobbery kiss. How the hell did Muin get into the cabin? Her head still aching but no longer throbbing, she nudges the dog off the sleeping bag and stands. Looks down. She's still dressed. She reaches for her glasses. And then she remembers. Damn! Dan is supposed to pick her up at seven. She rushes out of the bedroom, stops short, hand clutching the door frame.

Mattie looks up from the puzzle. "So you're finally awake."

"What are you doing here?"

"Dan came to get me. Said he couldn't wake you up this morning, that you were talking gibberish. You had him worried, girl."

Beth looks out the window. Already late afternoon. She's slept fifteen, sixteen hours?

Mattie snaps a puzzle piece into place. "Must've been some party."

"Wasn't the party. It was a migraine."

"Dan says he'll come by tomorrow morning. If you're feeling better."

"I'll be fine," Beth says. "There was no need to worry, but thanks."

Mattie snaps another piece into place. "Hope you don't mind me working at this. Been a long day." She glances at the folder of technical articles. "And your reading material isn't exactly gripping." She waves a hand over the table. "Frustrating though. Pieces don't always fit where you think they oughta." She stands and stretches her arms above her head. "If you're sure you're okay now, we'll be going."

Muin is sitting, staring up into a corner of the kitchen. Her tail sweeps the floor, back and forth. She stands and barks, tail still wagging.

"Looks like you have a guest," Mattie says.

"What?"

Mattie nods toward the corner. "Sure, it's not one of mine."

Beth looks up but can see nothing but cobwebs and water stains. She puts a hand to her aching forehead, then squeezes the bridge of her nose. No, she will not start believing everything Mattie says. She and Clive are two of a kind. *Just tormenting you, girl.*

Mattie opens the door and Muin bounds off toward the path.

Beth makes coffee then, every movement in slow motion. While she waits, she sits and rocks, fragments of remembered dreams floating through the chemical soup still bathing her brain: Jax and a gunshot; Dan; Mattie butchering rabbits; talking otters; Alice in the sunlight.

After two more ibuprofen, coffee, and an hour of sitting, she's not feeling so bad anymore. She doesn't want to waste the whole day, so she packs up her gear.

Walking slowly through the woods to the otter spot, Beth pauses at a patch of plump pink and green blueberries. She picks the lone ripe one and pops it into her mouth: an explosion of sweet blue sunshine. And then she sees it. An owl feather, brown and white, cradled within the blueberry bushes. Beth picks it up and smoothes it, the sound like a whisper.

~

The old female is alone; the others are far away, hunting for fish and crabs. Long before she sees the human, she scents her. Hears branches snap, leaves rustle. She watches from the tall grass near the lodge, then quietly slips into the pond and swims closer, barely rippling the water. She lifts her head and sniffs the air. No scent of metal, only human and plastic. And the heavy odour of grief.

CHAPTER 18

Dan picks her up at seven, the *Black Feather* on a trailer behind the truck.

"Morning," she says, sliding into the front seat. A thermos and a metal travel mug clank together. Dan's mug is already ensconced in the cup-holder.

He looks her over, his eyes narrowed. "How you feeling this morning?"

"Fine. Just a bad migraine after the party."

"You looked like shit yesterday morning."

"Thanks." She tries to smile. "I appreciate your going to get Mattie, but that wasn't necessary. I'm all right."

His frown is sceptical. "Okay then. As long as you're sure you're up to it, we're off to One Gunshot."

"I'm fine. Really."

They've lucked out on the weather: overcast but not raining, the cloud cover hinting, teasing, that it might clear away later in the day.

Beth pours herself coffee, sweet and thick with cream, and for the next thirty minutes, while they bounce over rutted dirt roads, they exchange barely ten words, which is fine with her. She can use the rest. She stayed too long at the otter spot last night, and while she waited for otters who never showed, she smoothed the feather and remembered Alice. They'd met when Beth was five months pregnant, Alice four, stretched out on yoga mats beside each other, learning how to breathe. It was Alice who laughed first. And then neither of them could stop, not even when Alice started braying and the instructor scowled at them. All that breathing practice turned out to be useless for

Beth. Rachel was delivered by caesarean, but by then, Beth had gained her first, and most enduring, friend in St. John's – a bond formed initially by laughter and "not being from here." Alice could always make Beth laugh. It was one of the things Beth loved most about her. Alice could make any problem seem less serious.

Back at the cabin, Beth put the feather on the chair beside the bed. Hoped she would dream of Alice again. And this time, Alice would stay. But Beth slept without dreams.

On One Gunshot Pond, Beth wades into the cold water in her sandals to help Dan unload the boat from the trailer. Her feet are almost numb, the skin bright red, by the time she climbs into the boat.

They circle the perimeter twice, slowly. There are no houses on the pond, but the shoreline and the forest behind it are nearly identical to Medicine Rock: jumbled grey rock backed by thick spruce and fir, a scattering of birch and alder. On the second trip around, Beth finally spots a few droppings on a large rock. They look dry and bleached out, at least a week old. She takes samples anyway, just to make things look good to Dan.

They load up the boat and move on to Crawling Stone Pond, the trailer bumping and rattling behind the truck. The fir and birch are so close to the road that branches scrape both sides of the pickup. Even before they unload the *Black Feather*, Beth finds scats. Three fresh samples. She pulls plastic bags from her backpack and marks them: *11 Aug 10: Crawling Stone, north shore boat landing.* Stoops down beside black droppings filled with fish bones and insect parts. Dan watches from a distance and smokes. No questions. No apparent interest in her work, but at least he's kept his teasing comments to a minimum. He's kept all his remarks to a minimum. Doesn't seem annoyed at having agreed to take her around to these other ponds, just quiet.

They put the Alumacraft in the water. It's easy to see how the pond got its name. A rock island sits in the middle. As small waves slap up against it, the island appears to crawl closer to shore.

After just twenty minutes of scanning the shoreline with her binoculars, Beth sees more droppings on top of an old beaver lodge. She points and Dan guides the boat closer, cuts the motor, and lifts the prop. They step out into the shallow water and pull the boat up onto the rocky shore. Beth collects two more samples and slips them into the cooler with the others. She finds a latrine about seven metres from the lodge, but all the droppings are old. She counts them and estimates a group of three or four. She examines the beaver lodge more closely. All the sticks, their ends bearing the tell-tale marks of large incisors, are sun-bleached, nothing fresh and new, and there's a hole in the side of the lodge that no beaver would ever allow to go unrepaired. An abandoned lodge, similar to the one on Medicine Rock, a perfect otter den.

Dan grinds out a cigarette on a rock, tucks the butt into his pocket. "Lunchtime yet?" he says, grabbing his own cooler, a small red one, from the boat. They sit down on the flat-topped boulders near the beaver lodge. It's nearly noon, and, as promised, the clouds are starting to break up. Patches of blue sky peek through.

Beth pulls bread, cheese, and a water bottle from her backpack.

Dan opens his cooler. "Here," he says, "brought enough for two." He hands her a sandwich – sliced turkey, provolone, tomato on fresh rye bread – and a chilled bottle of Black Horse.

"Thanks," she says, tucking her own skimpy rations away in her backpack.

"So how many more ponds you wanna go to?"

She tries to read his voice, and his face, for irritation or impatience. Hears, and sees, just a casual question. "Another two or three?" she says. And maybe a stop by the ocean, she adds to herself, wondering just how far she can push his generosity.

Dan takes a bite of the sandwich, chews, and follows it with a swallow of beer. Gazes out over the water, which, with the sunlight, has gradually changed from grey to dark blue. Just down shore, six black ducks bob, all in a line; three tails point skyward, come down, three others go up.

"What, exactly, are you trying to accomplish?" he says.

"Well ..." Beth lowers her sandwich. "There's not a lot known about otters in the wild. Not really. The basic social unit is probably the female and her pups, but their social organization also seems to be pretty variable, more variable than most other members of the weasel family. You know, weasels, mink, marten, wolverine–"

"I know what weasels are." His head is tilted to the side, brow furrowed, but he's smiling.

"If the DNA analyses work," Beth continues, "and if I can get funding to collect samples over a large enough area and throughout the year – maybe two years – I should be able to learn something about the composition of otter groups, how they change seasonally, how far members of the groups travel and if their ranges overlap."

"And that would matter because ...?"

"By finding out what areas they use most often, I can identify the landscape features and micro-habitats that are important to their survival. Knowing more about them helps us to protect them." A pat answer. She wants that to be true, but she knows it's not, not if there's no political will to save wilderness and wildlife. Beth takes a bite of her sandwich.

"But people around here aren't much interested in protecting them," Dan says. "They trap them."

Beth wipes her mouth with the back of her hand. "This type of research helps us to understand not just the otters here but also other species, like the otters in South America and Africa that are endangered. There are thirteen otter species in the world and all but five of them are endangered. We need to study species that are doing well to understand why others are in trouble."

Dan takes a swallow of beer. "I don't mind, you know, taking you around to other ponds. But do you really think that anything you do can make a difference?"

She stops mid-chew. Swallows. "You never know what's going to matter in the end." Almost chokes on Alan's words.

"Sometimes you do." He looks toward the black ducks. "Might as well spend every day of our lives fishing. While we still can."

"So you don't think anything's worth the effort?"

"Can't see that it'll do much good." He spreads his arms. "Unless you can figure out a way to make saving all this profitable." He smiles halfway, a curl of the lip, and raises the brown bottle in a toast. "And then you'll be famous. Probably win the Nobel, the Pulitzer … one a them big prizes."

~

It is early evening and the truck is approaching the "T" intersection at the bottom of Medicine Rock Pond. A left turn will take them to Beth's cabin, a right to Dan's house.

She's collected samples at five ponds. And finally screwed up the courage to ask Dan to take her out to the ocean. He agreed. Pretty readily, actually. But when the trips to the ponds took longer than they'd planned, they decided to leave the ocean sampling for another day. Beth is anxious to get the samples into Dan's freezer, but she hasn't decided yet whether or not she'll accept an invitation to his house. Will he even ask?

"Wanna see it?"

"What?" she says carefully.

"What's left of the big house Emma's family built. Not much there. Just the foundation and a stone fireplace, but a nice view of the pond."

She's tempted to tease him: *none a my business.* Instead, she says, "Okay."

He turns left at the "T" and after a few minutes, pulls to the side of the road and points. "That was the driveway."

They step down from the truck and pick their way along a narrow path through short, dense fir until they come to a wide opening with several enormous maples that must have been planted when the house was built. The light is golden, filtering softly through the trees. An old-fashioned rosebush covered with dark pink blooms stands by crumbling concrete steps. Beth touches the delicate petals, breathes in their spicy-sweet fragrance.

Dan stoops to clear away a patch of long grass. More crumbling concrete. He stands and sweeps his arm out and across. "Foundation was huge. Grandest house this pond has ever seen."

"Why'd they let it go to ruin?"

"After the accident, Emma's family never came out again. By the time they got around to putting it up for sale, the house was already rotting away." He pulls a cigarette from his shirt pocket. "Doesn't take long when nobody's keeping a place up." Flicks his lighter. "And people start scavenging."

She faces the pond; the remains of a stone fireplace and chimney stand to her right. She's probably looking through space that was once large glass windows onto an expansive view of the water. A clematis trails up the grey stone, the blooms a deep purple.

A loud *cronk-cronk-cronk* overhead, followed by a cacophony of caws. Beth looks up and sees a raven. Three crows – a murder – are harassing it. Dan is watching as well. When he walks down to the pond, she follows. There are a few old pilings in the water, all that's left of a pier.

Dan takes off his cap and wipes sweat from his forehead with the back of his hand. Puts the cap back on and chews his lower lip. Beth is sweating too, and the clear water looks inviting. She wishes she had the courage to suggest that they swim. Strip off their clothes and go into the cold water together. Naked. But she won't. A backbone of Jell-o. She wishes then that Dan would suggest it. If he would just ask, she would say yes.

"Look." He points with his cigarette. Out in the water, less than ten metres away, are three brown heads, three sets of small black eyes watching. Chirp. Chirp. Snort. And they are gone. Just gone.

"Well, there you go," Dan says, laughing. "Guess they're watching you as much as you're watching them."

The moment has passed. As they pick their way back to the truck, Dan tells her that he'll take her samples back to his freezer.

He drives to her cabin and drops her off. "See ya." And then he is gone. Just gone.

~

She huddles in a dark corner, peeking out from under a blanket. Watches as a slender young woman searches through the cabin. Her pale hair hangs loose, swings out when she turns. The rosary is woven around and through her fingers, dangling from her wrist. The green beads glow as if lit from within. She is wearing the yellow sundress with huge pink roses, and there is a dark purple bruise on her forehead.

With a wide sweep of her arm, the girl whisks carvings of ravens off the table. They clatter to the floor, then open their wings and fly to the window. Ebony feathers beat against glass: *thwump-thwump-thwump.*

The girl sees the puzzle. With thumb and middle finger, she flicks pieces off the table, slides an entire corner off the edge. She opens the journal then, grabs a pencil, and stabs the page. She throws the journal to the floor, opens a cupboard door, and there, in the dark, is the amber shine of animal eyes, low *uhn-uhn-uhns*, the smell of musk. She flings open another cupboard, pulls out pots and pans, tosses them. The crash and clank are deafening. In the quiet that follows, Beth hears beating wings and the distant strains of a flute. The girl stops and stands like a statue in a half-crouch, listening. She sees Beth then and bares her teeth in an ugly grimace, blue eyes filled with bright fury.

Beth cannot move, cannot scream.

She awakens in the dark, fading notes of a flute still in her ears. Beth lies still and waits for her heart to slow, its *thwump-thwump-thwump* like the ravens' wings against the glass. She sits up and reaches for her watch: 5:12. Light soon. Searches for the box of matches and lights the kerosene lamp. Carries it into the kitchen. The nightmare was so real she half expects to find everything in disarray, but all the cupboard doors are closed and the only bowls and pans on the floor are the ones she put there. The puzzle is spread out on the table, half finished, just the way she left it when she went to bed.

Beth builds a fire and prepares the coffee pot: a routine to calm her. But her hands are shaking. Coffee grounds scatter across the counter. She gathers them with a damp paper towel; a few catch under the counter's ridged metal border. She puts the percolator on the stove and sinks into the armchair. Her research journal is on the floor. Beth stares for a long minute, then finally reaches for it. Holds it in her lap and opens it slowly, but sees only her own handwriting. She rifles through the pages. Her own notes, all familiar, ending with last night: *11 Aug 10: clear and sunny, winds moderate, ~20°C, observed at A5, 19:42 – 21:50. None observed. No fresh scats on latrine.*

She lays the journal on the arm of the chair, idly flips open the back cover. Blinks hard when she sees scribbles on the back page: *Matthew d 1943 at 17, b 1926. Emma d 1963.* Scrawled across the bottom of the page are a few characters she cannot make out. She holds the page closer to the lamp: *1944,* or at least she thinks so. Preceding the numbers are what appear to be two letters, what look like a *b* or an *h* and an *a* or a *d*. The script is in her own hand, and messy, as if she'd been writing quickly.

Beth wraps her arms around herself, hugging her own chest. She doesn't recall making these notes, but she must have. Probably jotted them down shortly after talking with Clive, or after one of her visits with Mattie, when she was trying to make sense of her stories.

She stares at the rivulets of water running down the windowpane. Above the drumming of rain on the roof and the steady plink-plink-plink into bowls and pans, Beth hears the first slow blurps of perking coffee.

CHAPTER 19

When the weather clears, Beth spends a couple of hours surveying more kilometres of shoreline, still puzzling about the scribbled notes in her journal. Mid-morning, she finds herself paddling past Mattie's cabin. She beaches the kayak beside the aluminum canoe, drops her life-jacket into the cockpit, and climbs the path to the cabin, journal in hand. Maybe Mattie will know something about the odd notes.

She raps on the door, but hears nothing: no chair scraping, no barks, no paws clicking across a wood floor. She walks around to the garden. No Mattie or Muin there either. Everything is eerily quiet, just the chickadees in the birches, cheerfully singing out their own name.

She knocks again, then tries the door. It's unlocked. She should go in and make sure that Mattie is okay. She quietly steps inside. The kitchen is tidy, no dirty dishes, nothing left on the counter. She peeks into the bedroom, but Mattie's not there either. She goes back into the kitchen. Touches the kettle. Then the woodstove. Both are cool. Mattie and Muin have been gone a while.

When she looks up, she sees the other bedroom door, the one that's always closed. She should check in there too. Just in case. She lays the journal on the kitchen table and puts her hand to the doorknob, envisions cobwebs and animal skulls, jars of animal parts. Pulls her hand away, then shakes her head at her own foolishness.

The door opens onto an old-fashioned guestroom. White muslin curtains with wide ruffles have been drawn back from the window, and the sun is pouring in: dust motes float through the light. A white chenille bedspread covers a double bed that sits on a white metal frame. A hooked rug, in shades of rose and burgundy, lies in the centre of the wood floor, and against one wall is a tall wardrobe. An old vanity with an oval mirror and crocheted doilies sits beside it. A porcelain ewer and basin rest primly on one of the white doilies; on the other is a wooden comb and brush set. On the nightstand, also painted white, are a candle, a wooden flute, and a ribbon necklace with a small bone carving of an otter, similar to the one on the rosary.

Beth touches the otter, then holds the necklace up to her throat and turns toward the mirror, the surface yellowed and wavy with age. She sees, with dismay, just how worn and old she looks. She puts the necklace back on the nightstand and steps closer to the mirror, takes off her glasses and tries to smooth the web of wrinkles around her eyes and mouth. She slides her glasses back on and pushes at her short, grey-streaked hair. Greasy. No wonder Dan has shown no interest.

Her attention is arrested then by the small weaving hanging beside the vanity: a deep rose sky blending to purple then to indigo; a white crescent moon; Mattie's signature spider web in one corner; and an otter, in rich shades of brown, standing. There's a small white scar on its black nose. At its feet is a rust-coloured rock overlaid with fine grey threads, almost like another spider web. Beth leans in closer, finally discerns that the threads could spell out the word "hope." Maybe.

She steps to the wardrobe, hesitates, then opens one tall door, then the other. Clothes hang neatly from wooden hangers. On the left are pants and shirts, denim and flannel. Dresses, for someone small and slender, hang on the right. Beth flips through them, gasps: the yellow sundress – with huge pink roses.

She hears a scrabbling at the door, Muin's low woof. She closes the wardrobe and steps out of the room, but her hand is still on the doorknob when Mattie and Muin come into the cabin. Mattie is carrying a small metal bowl heaped with blueberries.

"Fancy meeting you here." Mattie's face is neutral, unreadable.

Muin noses at Beth's hands, and she wishes she'd brought a Milk-Bone. Anything to create a distraction from Mattie's close scrutiny.

Beth tries to smile. "Just stopped in to say hi." She shoves her hands deep into her pockets. "When you didn't answer the door, I thought I should check and make sure you were okay."

Mattie sets the bowl on the table and picks up the kettle. "How about a cup a tea then?"

"No," Beth says. "No thanks. I really should get back to work now."

"But you just got here … didn't you?" Mattie sits down at the table. At her right elbow is the yellow sugar bowl, the one with the pink cabbage roses. Beth stares. That's where the dream image came from. Has to be.

Muin settles at Mattie's feet. A large drop of clear drool hangs from the dog's mouth, momentarily suspended, then drops to the floor.

Mattie picks up Beth's journal. Holds it out. "Don't forget this then."

"Oh, yeah. Thanks." Beth reaches for the journal.

Mattie's grip is tight. "There's always a logical explanation," she says, letting the journal slide from her fingers. "Except when there isn't."

Beth hugs the journal to her chest. "For what?"

"Don't know. You tell me."

Beth steps toward the door, then spins back around. "I had a horrible dream last night." Her words come in a rush. "There was a young woman in my cabin, tearing everything apart."

Mattie's eyes widen, then she looks away from Beth, toward the window.

"She pulled everything out of the drawers and cupboards," Beth says. "When she saw me, she looked like she wanted to kill me."

Mattie watches two noisy blue jays come and then go. A nuthatch hangs upside down, poking at the feeder. She brings her fingers together, then moves them apart, as if playing the child's game of cat's cradle. "Strange dream," she says finally. "Guess you better get back to work now."

~

While the sun is still high and warm, Beth bathes in the pond, dips her head underwater to rinse the shampoo from her hair. She needs to get these distractions out of her head. She needs to focus on her research.

But what about that yellow dress? Or the bedroom set up for a couple long dead?

Stop. Focus. Otters.

Swimming out from shore, Beth breast-strokes slowly and keeps her eyes just above the water, trying to see the world from an otter's point of view. Just like her, they're a little near-sighted out of the water, so the view without her glasses might be fairly accurate, but they have small muscles in their eyes that reshape the lens for better vision underwater. That raw sensory input is manipulated by the brain into something the animal can understand.

So how might otter brains construct the world? At the most elementary level, they live in a world with no red. Blue, yellow, and green, but no red. So they don't even see the red of her kayak or the pink of the wild roses.

Pink roses. Jesus, don't go there again. Stop. Focus. Otters.

Certainly they would smell them though, far more strongly than people do. They can probably identify different bodies of water just by smell, and individual rocks and trees too, and whether a beaver lodge is occupied or not. She'd be willing to bet that an otter can tell from a single sniff of a scat just whose it is. And if it's a stranger's, the otter can probably know the stranger's age, sex, reproductive state, what it's eaten, its general health, and possibly a whole lot more.

She swims underwater and tries to spin as if she's an otter wrestling, but it makes her dizzy. She surfaces and rolls onto her back. She doesn't really have to stay here much longer. She's collected enough samples for an initial assessment of food habits. She just needs a few more fresh ones for the DNA tests, along with a trip to the ocean, to where the outlet of Medicine Rock Pond flows into the salt water. She'd also like to do a few more direct observations. They're not really part of this preliminary research, but watching them first-hand gives her a better understanding of them and their sensory world. Never mind what Mattie has to say about watching and not listening.

Beth swims back to shore. Thoroughly chilled now, she steps out of the water and wraps a towel around her. Uses a second one to dry her hair. She climbs the path to the cabin, damp feet picking up dirt and spruce needles along the way.

Muin is at the door, tail wagging as if welcoming her home.

"Go back to where you belong," Beth says in her teacher voice, mustering all the sternness she can. "I have work to do." She brushes off her feet, then opens the screen door and squeezes through. Muin settles on the step and watches her through the mesh.

Beth dries herself off and smoothes lotion everywhere she can reach. Smoothes an extra dollop onto her face and around her eyes. Slips on khakis and a denim shirt. She hasn't eaten since breakfast and she's famished. She opens a can of sardines, but before she can fork even one piece of fish onto a cracker, the whining and scratching begin, and then the low woofs.

What does it mean when a dog has chosen you? But isn't it Mattie who's chosen Beth? Does it matter?

She opens the door. "Okay," she sighs, "you win." Muin sashays into the cabin.

Beth finishes her meagre supper, clears away the remains, and stuffs the journal into her backpack. When Muin shows no inclination for going back to Mattie's, Beth lets her come along to the otter spot. Truth be told, she's glad for the company. She's still a little unnerved by her dream and that spare bedroom with the yellow dress.

She sits down to wait, and Muin settles beside her, as if she's glad for the company too. Beth drapes an arm around her. The temperature is still mild, but the sky has become a sullen grey, and the air is too still. Although Beth has covered every square inch of herself with thick fabric or insect repellent, the mosquitoes and black flies still manage to find unprotected skin. She swats and squirms, binoculars and voice recorder at her side.

Muin stands, ears forward. After another minute, Beth hears the excited chirps, and spots them not far down the shore. She puts a hand to the dog's collar to keep her from rushing forward, then clicks on the voice recorder: "19:46, A5, at least three or four in the water, coming from the beaver lodge, now about thirty metres away, swimming toward me. At least one pup." She searches anxiously for the second one. It's not the trapping season, but there are other hazards for the young and unwary. When she finally spots it, she relaxes. "A second pup is swimming beside an otter with a grey muzzle."

Beth hears chirps coming from the opposite direction. Her jaw drops. Another four or five are swimming from the northeast. The groups are approaching each other. If they stay on course they will meet almost directly in front of her.

"Chirping from both groups is almost continuous now. The two groups merge, and at least four or five touch muzzles. They begin wrestling in twos and threes. Continuous grunting now, with occasional chirps from the ones that are wrestling."

They are behaving like they all know each other: a friendly flotilla of otters. Where did they all come from? With all the activity, Beth cannot begin to tell one from another. She slowly releases Muin's collar. It's as if the dog understands that she needs to keep still and quiet. Beth lets the binoculars fall against her chest, slips her camera from her backpack and tries to take photos. Manages a few in the fading light, then takes up her binoculars and voice recorder again.

"They are all swimming past me now, toward the beaver lodge. No aggressive behaviour. An old one comes out of the water at the latrine; it is small and slender. It stamps its back feet, leaves a black scat, and urinates." Beth can see that the grey-muzzled otter is most likely a female: *the old grandmother.*

"She is standing upright and looking in my direction." Beth doesn't move. Just stares for what feels like a full minute. Is the otter looking at her? Or at Muin? When the dog starts to move forward, Beth grabs her collar.

"The old female snorts, drops to all fours, and goes back into the pond."

Peering through the binoculars, Beth is finally able to count nine. Counts them again: two pups, seven adults – or sub-adults. She can't be sure. A small otter could be an adult female or a sub-adult male.

"At 19:57 two come out of the water about six metres northeast of the beaver lodge. They rub on the grass and then begin to groom themselves and each other around the head and neck. Two other adults come out at the latrine, alternate their back feet in a little dance, and leave scats, one after the other. The first one, by its urination pattern, appears to be a male; the second is a female, maybe. They return to the water."

Within a few minutes they are gone. Simply gone. Water sprites.

Muin lets out a whine. "Yeah," Beth says. "I wish they'd stayed longer too."

She notes the time: 20:02. Takes out three plastic bags and marks them: *12 Aug 10: A5.* Also writes on each bag: *old female?, male?, female?* With droppings this fresh, she can also collect anal gland secretions – their musk – but the samples should be frozen quickly to be useful. She'll have to drive over to Dan's. Tonight.

~

The otters tumble and roll through the water, aroused by the rich banquet of smells and the energy of newness. A female touches her muzzle to a male's, and knows he has just eaten trout and a beetle. But she detects another scent as well: he's the one she mated with last spring, just after she gave birth to two pups. She paws his face, chirps. They turn and twist in the water, lunge and feint, grab and spin.

The old female is more wary. She'd scented the dog. The dog is familiar, and harmless, but she'd also scented the watcher, faint sweet odours of excitement and joy riding the wind, traces of sour fear and sadness woven within.

CHAPTER 20

Beth sees the pothole too late. Clenches her teeth in anticipation of the jolt when her left front tire hits it. Muin's forefeet slide off the passenger seat.

"Sorry, girl."

She's going only 40 kph, but eases her foot off the gas and flicks on the headlights. She's been debating it, but still can't decide if she hopes Dan is there – or hopes that he's not. Catching herself, she refocuses her thoughts on otters: the two groups coming together amicably, then wrestling and grooming; no squabbles. *A big ole family reunion*, Mattie would say. Although in Beth's experience of family reunions, there's always been a squabble or two. But if an otter harboured hidden resentments or grudges, how would anyone know – except another otter? They never appear to be annoyed or worried. They always look content to be doing exactly what they're doing: otters being otters. To the unscientific eye, Mattie's not wrong: *They're just happier than most folks.*

Of course otter happiness wouldn't be the same as human happiness, Beth reasons, but she has to confess that she's been willing to describe otters, at least to herself, as possessing *joie de vivre*. What is *joie de vivre* if not happiness? Her thoughts take a cynical turn: Maybe otters feel *joie de vivre* because they don't form long-term pair bonds. Males and females can simply enjoy the physical imperative of the moment – and then go their separate ways. No worries about whether or not they're *fine* with their partners. A simple life. But maybe not. They live in their own world, with their own way of making sense of that world – a mental life just as complex as her own perhaps, just different.

She glances at Muin. The dog is staring out the windshield as if helping Beth to watch for moose. What kinds of thoughts are going through her head? What kinds of feelings? There's a news story that has taken up permanent residence in Beth's heart. The article was brief, only a few details reported for their oddness: A young man went out into the desert with his dog – and hung himself from a cottonwood tree. Wasn't found for six weeks. In all that time, the dog maintained vigil, leaving the body only long enough to find water. Beth cannot get that image out of her head: the dog waiting by the body, guarding its companion and friend for six long weeks, day and night. Waiting for what? Hoping for what? How long would the dog have stayed had the body not been discovered? Beth can't think about the story without tearing up. She doesn't wonder what the dog was thinking: she wonders what it felt. Love and loyalty and grief aren't thoughts, they're feelings, unfathomable feelings that go to the very core of who we are. And if animals can feel love and loyalty and grief, what else do they feel? Almost impossible to know. But just because animal feelings are hard to study – and inconvenient to acknowledge when people want to use animals for food and furs and research – doesn't mean they don't exist.

Animals have the same basic wiring as people. Why wouldn't they have the same emotions?

It's dark by the time Beth arrives at Dan's house. The black pickup's not in the driveway. Relief? Or disappointment?

Muin stands. Her tail, going full force, sweeps Beth's face.

"No, girl," Beth says, winding down both front windows halfway. "You stay here. I'll just be a minute." She grabs the plastic bags from the cooler, retrieves the house key from under a paving stone, but then finds the door unlocked. She slips into the kitchen and turns on a light, puts the triple-bagged samples into the freezer with the others. Now to escape before Dan returns. She's already been caught snooping once today.

She turns from the refrigerator and sees the wall phone. She could take just a few minutes to call Rachel and Alan while she's here. She reaches into her back pocket. No, she can't. She left her wallet and calling card in the cabin, and she certainly doesn't want strange long-distance charges to appear on Dan's phone bill. She could check her email though. Just five minutes. Five minutes and then she'll be gone.

She creeps down the shadowed hallway to the study, cracks open the door. Screams and jumps backwards. Mattie's broken-toothed grin, lit by the glowing screen, looks like a jack-o-lantern's.

"Didn't think I was that scary."

"What," Beth gasps, "are you doing here?"

"I could ask you the same question."

"I ... I came over to put samples in Dan's freezer."

Mattie's brow furrows, then she laughs. "Otter poop in his freezer?"

"He knows all about it."

"I'm sure he does."

"So what *are* you doing here?" Beth says, still trying to catch her breath.

"He is my nephew, you know." Mattie turns back to the screen, closes a window with a click of the mouse, and the room becomes that much darker. She turns on the desk lamp. "I come here now and again to use the Internet. You can learn a lot from the Internet, you know."

She stretches her hands toward the ceiling, moves her head from side to side. "Long as you're here, you might as well stay for a beer. Dan's probably got some in the refrigerator. Or you could fix yourself a cup a tea. Plain black. On a real stove."

"No," Beth says, almost a whisper. "I should be going."

"But he'll be home soon."

Beth closes her eyes. "I really need to go."

"No time? Even for a beer or a cup a tea? You scientists sure work hard."

Beth hears barking. Mattie tilts her head.

"Muin came over to my cabin," Beth explains quickly. "And I didn't have time to bring her back before going out to do observations. I can leave her here, with you."

"Unless you need her."

"Why would I need her?"

Mattie pushes out her lower lip. "Just thought you could use some company. Guess Muin thought so too."

"I'm fine," Beth says, trying not to think about the dark cabin she'll be returning to.

"Okay then, leave her here." Mattie turns back to the computer. "Oh, and you might wanna use the bathroom before you go. I always do. Toilet flushes."

~

A slender crescent moon offers only scant light, and when she pulls up to the cabin, Beth grabs the flashlight from the glove compartment and points it at the door. Sees something white tucked in close to the latch. God, what now? She walks closer and grabs the piece of paper, unlocks the door and quickly locks it behind her. Lights the kerosene lamp and unfolds the note: WEATHER SHOULD BE GOOD TOMORROW. PICK YOU UP AT 7 TO GO TO THE OCEAN. Big block letters, almost a child's hand.

Note clutched in her fist, she looks all around the living room and kitchen, carries the lamp into both bedrooms. Nothing out of place, no drawers or cupboards ajar, but she wishes she'd kept Muin. She doesn't *need* her, it would just be nice to have company in the shadowy cabin.

Beth picks up the journal and settles into the armchair to transcribe her observations from earlier that evening. Pushes the switch on the recorder, rewinds, then plays the tape. She can hear the excitement in her voice when she describes the two groups coming together. Wrestling, chirping, almost continuous grunting: otter happiness.

By the time she checks and rechecks her notes, it's after midnight. She goes to the outhouse, then brushes her teeth over the sink. Strips down and crawls into her sleeping bag before blowing out the lamp. Every movement provokes a silky rustle from the sleeping bag and a groan from the sagging springs beneath the thin mattress. The floorboards creak, a curtain flaps softly at the window, paws skitter across the roof.

On the long drive back to the cabin, she'd come to terms with the idea of Mattie using a computer. Although it had surprised her at first, Beth can make sense of it. Mattie is certainly adventuresome enough to tackle a computer. What Beth had avoided thinking about, and what is now worming its way to the forefront, is her dream from last night and Mattie's spare bedroom. There is no making sense of that yellow dress. *There's always a logical explanation ... except when there isn't.*

Beth sits up, strikes a match, and re-lights the lamp, the oily odour of kerosene familiar now. She plumps the pillows behind her and reaches for the tattered copy of *Endless Night*. Reads. Until she comes to the part about the house being cursed. Where is Miss Marple? Beth wants Miss Marple right now, someone down to earth and entirely sensible. Someone who can always figure things out.

~

She wakes early, distressingly early. Longing in every inch of her body. She lies still and clamps her eyes shut,

desperate to re-enter the dream, to finish what she and
Dan had started. They'd been lying side-by-side, partly
naked under a soft sun. He was kissing and touching her,
fingers and mouth caressing her shoulders and breasts.
Her hands were on him. Her jeans slid down her thighs.
And then he was over her, his head haloed by the sun, and
they were just about to … and she awoke.

She wills herself back to sleep. No use. She props
herself on one elbow, gropes for the box of matches, and
lights the kerosene lamp. At least she'd dreamed of nothing terrifying.

She pulls on a pair of jeans and sneakers and runs
to the outhouse. When she returns, she builds a fire and
pumps water into the percolator. She'd enjoyed this routine at first, but now she's tired of it. And looking forward to getting back to electricity, indoor plumbing, hot
showers. But what about Alan? What about Dan? She feels
tight cords forming a knot just behind her breastbone.

She wraps herself in the sleeping bag and sits down to
wait for the coffee. Watches the dawning of what promises
to be a bright, clear day, the first rays of sun already warm
on her face. She feels lingering desire, a desire so strong
her body aches.

CHAPTER 21

Precisely at 6:59, Dan knocks on the door. When she opens it, Beth avoids looking into his face. He glances around at the pots and bowls scattered throughout the living room and kitchen. "Guess the place could use some work."

She pulls on a jacket. "Not sure if we'll try to fix it up. Or tear it down and build something new, like you did." She grabs her backpack. "Although Mattie said we shouldn't."

"Don't worry about that," Dan says, stepping out the door behind her. "She just doesn't like change."

Beth locks the door, then slides into the pickup, pushing aside a stack of napkins and old invoices, a thermos and two travel mugs. On the third grinding attempt, the engine finally turns over. Dan looks over his shoulder as he backs up. No boat this time. They'll walk to the outlet. She wants to check out the entire area close to where the river from Medicine Rock flows into the ocean.

"Mattie said you stopped by last night." He laughs. "I warned her not to tell anyone about the shit in my freezer."

"Sure didn't expect to find her there."

"She paddles over once a week or so to use the computer."

"Paddles?"

"Her canoe." Dan speaks matter-of-factly, as if there is nothing remarkable about a woman in her eighties paddling thirty minutes across the pond – and back – in the dark. "When the weather's bad, I drive her. Or pick her up on the snowmobile."

"Mattie at the computer," Beth says. "Not an image I ever expected to see."

He punches in the lighter and pulls a cigarette from the pack in his shirt pocket. "Sure, she even has her own email account. I check it for her and let her know when there's anything from the gallery."

While they drive the now-familiar route into town, they chat about the news, which turns out, not surprisingly, to be no news. Dan flicks on the radio. After days of virtual silence, Beth finds the loud ads jarring: needles to the brain. But the coffee is a comfort. Beth wraps her hands around the travel mug.

Just beyond the town, the road twists and turns, but heads generally north. The landscape is rolling and thickly wooded with spruce, fir, and white birch. Dense thickets of alder grow close to the road, perfect hideouts for moose. They pass innumerable bodies of water, ponds at first and then the deeply indented, slender fingers of ocean, the rocky shoreline marked by tide-lines.

By water, Medicine Rock Pond is only four or five kilometres from the ocean. By car, it's nearly fifty, and after driving for almost an hour, Dan pulls into a roadside park: a wide beach and a few decrepit picnic tables, a green barrel trash can. As soon as she opens the door, Beth can smell the salt water, the wet kelp. The surf is gentle, the rhythmic rattle and click of rocks as waves sweep in and then retreat, turquoise water near shore, dark blue beyond. Standing tall and severe in the distance are steep grey cliffs streaked with amber and topped by a narrow swath of spruce and fir. An eagle soars near the cliff's edge.

"Outlet's a click or two that way." Dan points to the east. "Tide's going out, so we have plenty of time."

Beth is wearing heavy-soled hiking boots, but walking over the fist-sized rocks is precarious, the rocks sometimes rolling out from under her feet, potentially ankle-turning.

It's a sparkling summer day though, and she tries not to spoil it by noticing the makeshift fire pits surrounded by broken beer bottles and crushed cans, or the plastic bleach containers and lengths of brightly coloured synthetic rope strewn on the beach. She looks instead at pieces of driftwood and toward the gulls flying overhead. They make shallow dives, then rise up to drop sea urchins onto the larger rocks. Fragments of green and purple shell lie scattered everywhere. Terns dart past, screeching, their calls incongruous for such graceful birds: beautiful harpies.

Binoculars in hand, she sometimes walks beside Dan, but more often behind, looking for signs of otters. They walk slowly, conversation minimal, words often lost to the wind.

About a hundred metres before they reach the outlet, she finds a few older scats on top of a flat rock. She bends over them and probes with a piece of driftwood – dried fragments of lobster and mussel shell, slender fish bones, scales, a couple of otoliths. She pulls out plastic bags. The samples will be useful for food analysis but not for the DNA tests.

The outlet itself is broad, at least twenty-five metres across. Beth walks the near side, searching for fresh scats and hoping to find tracks in the scattered patches of wet sand. While she follows the river about fifty paces back into the woods, Dan stays out by the ocean. She is looking for signs of otters as well as a place to cross. Finds neither. And the flies in the woods are fierce.

She hikes back to where Dan is standing. "Looks like I'll have to wade across," she says. "Doesn't look too deep."

"Probably deeper than it looks."

Beth takes off her jacket and boots first, rolls up her socks and pushes them into the boots. Unzips her jeans and slides them off. She's worn her swimsuit under her clothes for just this possibility. She doesn't look at Dan or try to assess whether he's watching. She pulls sport sandals from her backpack, straps them on, then unbuttons her shirt.

"Guess you came prepared." He peers into the water. "Careful of those rocks. They'll be slippery."

She holds her backpack over her head; she's already sealed her camera and voice recorder in plastic bags. She wades in. He's right: the rocks are slippery. She inhales sharply when the icy water reaches her thighs. She can feel the current pushing against her legs, but it's not strong. She takes a few more steps, wary of a deeper channel where the current might be stronger. The water is up to her waist now.

If she slipped and went under, would he come in after her? Rescue her and then, perhaps, kiss her? She considers slipping. On purpose.

Beth is now more than halfway across, and with every step the water becomes shallower. By the time she reaches the opposite shore she is shivering. She pulls a small towel from her backpack and drapes it across her shoulders.

It doesn't take long for her to find what she's looking for: fresh black scats, at least four, on top of a prominent rock. And near the rock is the perfect imprint of a small hind foot. The track shows all five toes and the webbing between them. She raises her arm in triumph.

Dan cups his hands around his mouth, shouts, "Long way to go just for otter shit."

Beth photographs the footprint and then bags the samples. She pulls her journal from its protective plastic bag and jots a few notes, walks about a hundred paces along the ocean and then back along the outlet until she comes to the trees – and the flies. Finds nothing more, but she's satisfied. She has what she came here for. The DNA analyses will confirm whether or not any of these scats are from the otters on Medicine Rock.

Steeling herself against the frigid water, she wades back across the outlet. When she reaches the other side, she dries herself off. This time, she knows Dan is watching, smoking and watching, a thumb hooked in his back pocket, cap tipped. "Get what you need?" he says.

"Think so. Can't be sure until I get the lab results back. And even if the DNA analyses work, the data won't be conclusive, only suggestive." She pulls her jeans over her damp swimsuit. It will be an uncomfortable ride back to the cabin. "Thanks for bringing me out here."

"Kind of interesting, being able to learn things from shit, I mean. And I don't know many women who'd hike for an hour, ford a river, and then let out a whoop when they found otter shit." He pushes his cap farther back on his head. "And I thought Mattie was strange."

Beth smiles and shrugs one shoulder. "It's just what I do." She sits down on a rock, brushes sand from her feet, and pulls on her socks and boots. "Found a nice track too. A small hind foot. Probably a pup." She stuffs the damp towel and sandals into the backpack.

They share a companionable silence on the hike back. Trailing behind him, Beth can feel sand inside her socks, rubbing under and around her toes. She walks slowly, still looking for signs of otters. And wonders why, even in his stained jeans, flannel shirts, and rubber boots, Dan looks better every time she sees him. She gazes toward the horizon, at the whitecaps in the distance. Knows that, with the help of her dream, she's well on her way to creating a schoolgirl crush on a man she hardly knows. She did that a lot in her teens and early twenties. Never mattered much that the boys, and then men, paid little attention to her. All she was after was the longing, the obsession. It was the intensity of the longing that made her feel alive.

She picks up a small, twisted piece of driftwood shaped vaguely like a bird's head. She knows next to nothing about the real Dan, the surly Dan of the curled upper lip, the *not-my-business* Dan. Maybe if she did, she wouldn't even like him. Maybe that's what she needs to do, find out more about him – before she makes a complete fool of herself and does something she can't undo. She tosses the driftwood into the water, sees a small white feather trapped between two rocks. She stoops to pick it up. Wishes she could talk to Alice. Alice would sort things out. She was a clinical psychologist, and whenever Beth asked for advice, Alice would pause, then say, *Do you want me to answer that as a therapist ... or a friend?* Alice wouldn't hesitate to point out just how stupid she's being. Beth holds up the feather, releases it to the wind.

When they get back to the pickup, Beth slips the samples into her cooler, then tucks her backpack down between her feet. "Thanks again. I really appreciate this."

"No problem."

CHAPTER 22

The drive back seems shorter, quieter. Dan leaves the radio off, but the silence is comfortable. Only vaguely aware of the passing landscape, Beth mulls a line of questioning that would be revealing but not intrusive. Before she can screw up the courage to ask him anything, however, they are approaching the "T" intersection at the bottom of Medicine Rock Pond. A right turn to Dan's, left turn to Beth's. She tugs at the damp swimsuit clinging to her midriff.

"I'm starving," he says. "How about some lunch? I'll drive you home after."

"Okay."

A right turn, then another fifteen minutes and they pull up to his house. Dan unlocks the door, then steps aside to let her go in first. She opens the freezer and slides in the samples, turns and says, apologetically, "Shouldn't be many more."

"Good. Don't wanna start confusing them with the sausage patties."

She grins. "You'd know that right away. They'd be crunchy." She turns toward the hall. "Mind if I use the bathroom?" She has dry underclothes in her backpack.

"Be my guest."

On her way back to the kitchen, they pass in the hallway. Dan touches her shoulder lightly, but keeps going.

Back in the kitchen, he opens the refrigerator and grabs the makings for sandwiches – sliced ham and turkey, bread, cheese, tomato, mayo – and the same cartons of coleslaw and potato salad from a few nights ago. Using his chin to hold the stack in place, he carries everything, along with two beers, to the kitchen table. Lifts an index finger to point at the cupboard. "Plates in there. Knives and forks in the drawer below." He sits down, opens a Black Horse, and gulps down half of it. He pulls out two slices of rye bread. As soon as Beth sets the plates and cutlery on the table, he grabs a knife and begins spreading mayonnaise.

"Starving," he repeats, grabbing slices of ham and slapping them onto the bread. "Looking for otter shit is tough work." He lays a slice of provolone over the ham.

Beth sits down across from him. He slides the packages of meat toward her. She reaches over them for a slice of cheese, lays it on the bread, adds tomato.

"Turkey? Ham?" he says.

"I generally try not to eat a lot of meat."

"You had a turkey sandwich just a couple days ago." A quarter of his is gone in one bite.

"I'm not a complete vegetarian," she says, levering the cap off the beer. "And I don't like being preachy about it."

"So you think people shouldn't eat animals?" He bites off another quarter of the sandwich.

"No, it's not that. Eating meat is part of who we are as predators." She takes a swallow of beer. "And I think hunting and old-fashioned farming can be all right. At least those animals get to have some kind of life. It's the factory farms that are awful."

"Okay, go ahead and be preachy, cause I'm not getting it." A third quarter of the sandwich disappears.

She places a slice of bread over the tomato and cheese, inhales slowly. "Animals on factory farms are treated like things that aren't even alive. Some of them live in tiny enclosures and never feel sunlight on their faces or grass under their feet. And ..." Beth looks up. He's not annoyed or scoffing, or even giving her a patronizing smirk. She continues: "And growing animals for meat takes a lot of grain and water. And energy. The single biggest way humans can reduce their carbon footprint is to cut back on the amount of meat they eat."

"No shit?" he says, then adds, "No pun intended." He finishes the last quarter of the sandwich and begins to construct another. "It'll take an awful lot of convincing to get people to eat less meat."

"The economy may do that all by itself. Meat will become too expensive. It'll be the food of the wealthy, a status symbol."

"Whoa! You're not too optimistic about the future, are you?"

She tilts her head to the side. "Who was it said that we might as well spend every day of our lives fishing?"

"Yeah, well. Fair enough."

Beth puts up a hand, palm out. "Okay, sermon over." Then opens the cartons of potato salad and coleslaw. "So now you know I'm an environmental pessimist, but that I'm also a woman who'll go to almost any length to collect otter scats." She chooses her words carefully. "But I know next to nothing about you."

"Not much to know. Born here, went away, came back. And you already know I like to fish. And can play the fiddle. Sort of."

Beth picks up serving spoons and puts them into the salads. "There's got to be more than that."

"Not really."

"Everyone's life is more complicated than that." She takes a bite of her sandwich.

"Not mine."

She wipes the corners of her mouth with a thumb and middle finger. "I don't believe that."

"I don't like complicated. I like simple." Dan slices a tomato.

"But what about all those years in the army?"

"Trust me. Nothing interesting there." He adds the tomato to his sandwich, slaps a piece of bread on top. He takes a long swallow of beer, finishing off the bottle, then goes to the refrigerator and pulls out another one. Holds it up. "Nothing environmentally destructive about drinking beer is there?"

Beth raises an eyebrow, then spoons potato salad onto her plate. "You were in the army for more than thirty years. Something interesting must have happened."

"Seriously, just routine work. Nothing remarkable."

"Nothing? In thirty years?"

He bites into the sandwich, chews, swallows. Beth folds her hands and lays them on the table.

"You're just gonna keep asking, aren't you?"

She nods.

"Okay," he sighs. "Once upon a time there was a wife. She didn't like the military life, all that moving around. Only lasted three years. And that's all there is to it." He finishes the sandwich and pulls the red and white pack of Macdonalds from his shirt pocket. "Mind?"

Beth does, but shakes her head no. Nibbles on a slice of cheese. "Children?" she asks quietly.

He lights a cigarette, sits back in the chair, and swings an ankle over one knee. He'd look relaxed if his foot weren't jiggling up and down. "Not from the marriage."

Beth looks at him sidelong.

Dan picks up the beer and rubs a thumb over the heavy-haunched workhorse on the label. "Wouldn't even know him if I passed him on the street." Picks at a corner of the label. "Look, I'm not big on talking about myself."

Beth takes a bite of potato salad and watches him while she chews.

"Kid must be at least … what? Almost forty by now. He was nineteen before I even knew he existed." He takes a long draw on the cigarette, exhales to the side. "If he hadn't run off, I wouldn't even know about him at all. All water over the dam now."

"What's his name?"

He squints at Beth. "You really wanna hear this?"

"Yeah, I do."

His foot jiggles up and down, up and down. "So Sharon, my girlfriend when I was eighteen …" He laughs, but without humour. "Not even my girlfriend, really. More like a one-night stand. One last fling before I went into the army."

The ash is building up on the cigarette. Beth pushes an ashtray toward him.

"So Sharon tracked me down somehow, and some guy woke me in the middle of the night to tell me I had a call from Toronto. When I got to the phone, it took me a few minutes to even remember who she was." He takes a swallow of beer. "Anyway, she tells me I have a son who's now nineteen, and he's run off."

"And that's the first you knew of him?"

"Yep. And Sharon tells me she thinks he's run off to find me, his long-lost daddy." He shakes his head. "I was just thirty-seven or thirty-eight then, stationed in Cyprus. Don't know how she even tracked me down."

"So what happened?"

Dan uncrosses his legs, brings the jiggling foot to the floor. "He never contacted me. And Sharon never called again. End of story."

"You weren't curious?"

"Look, I never knew the boy, never even knew he existed." He scrapes a fleck of tobacco from his lower lip. "If he'd been younger, I'd've offered Sharon some money or something. Maybe even tried to meet him. But the kid was already nineteen. Didn't need a dad by then."

"But you might have grandchildren somewhere."

"So you think I should care about a son I never even knew I had? Never even wanted?"

"Well … yes."

He puts his hands on his knees, leans forward. A thin contrail of smoke curls upward. "Not my business. None of them are my business." He stubs out the cigarette. "Now that you've got all your samples, I spose you'll be heading back to St. John's."

"I'm staying on for another couple of days. I'd like to get a few more observations."

"Planning to see Mattie again? She's gonna miss your visits."

CHAPTER 23

Awkward silences, punctuated by equally awkward conversation, on the drive to her cabin. But their combined efforts at chit-chat lead Beth to suspect that both of them are trying to apologize without having to say the words. When she slides out of the pickup, he leaves with a wave and a "See ya," but also a half-smile.

It's late afternoon. She should drive into town and call Alan, let him know she's planning to come home in a few days. Eventually, she'll also have to tell him that they might be inheriting a dog, a big dog. But no need to worry about that now.

She grabs her keys and locks the door. Slides into the Toyota. Stares out the windshield at the faded red clapboard, the crumbling window frames. Maybe what they have together is as good as it gets when you're fifty-three and married for twenty-five years. At least they don't hate each other and they don't have children somewhere they don't care about.

By the time she gets to the Irving, Beth has decided to call Rachel before she calls Alan. Her daughter picks up on the first ring. "Hi, Mom."

"Hi, sweetheart." Relief sweeps from Beth's forehead to her toes. "How are you?"

"Good. I'm standing in the checkout at Safeway right now. Sorry I couldn't answer when you called before. I was in the middle of experiments. And I couldn't call you back. What's with the no-reception thingy anyway?"

The chatter Beth loves. She smiles into the phone. Instant forgiveness.

"Oh, and thanks for the postcard," Rachel adds. "Cute. How's your stuff going?"

"Pretty well," Beth says. She can hear chaotic noise in the background, clanking carts, announcements of specials. "I think I've got enough to put together a decent research proposal."

"That's great, Mom."

"A lot depends on whether the samples are good enough for DNA analyses. Those can be tricky."

"How's the cabin?"

"Roof leaks and there's no electricity, but it's private and has a great view."

"Is there a beach? Can you swim?"

"It's rocky, but good for swimming. The water's clear."

"Cool. Maybe I'll have to come home next summer. Take some friends out there for a weekend."

Rachel, home for the summer. Beth closes her eyes and luxuriates in the thought for just a moment, then says, "How are things going with that new guy?" Her eyes snap open. What would she say if Rachel were to ask *her* that question?

"Over and out," Rachel says. "But that's okay. He wasn't all that great and I'm getting kind of tired of Vancouver anyway. Everything's so expensive. I might apply to graduate schools closer to home."

"That would be wonderful."

"Yeah, it'd be nice to be closer to you and Dad. Oh, I'm up to the checkout now. Gotta go. Love you."

"Love you too, sweetheart. Love you too."

Beth stands a while, cradling the phone. Then she squares her shoulders and calls Alan. As she waits through five long rings she makes patterns in the dirt at her feet. A Friday evening, he should be home. The answering machine comes on and she listens impatiently through her own message, then says, "Hi, Alan. Just me. Everything's fine."

She pauses, expecting him to pick up. When he doesn't, she continues: "Almost done here. Just want to get a few more observations. I'll probably head home Monday or Tuesday, but I'll call first, so you'll know when to expect me. Just talked to Rachel. She's thinking about graduate schools closer to home. Isn't that great? See you soon."

Just before the receiver hits the cradle, her hand stops short. She lifts the receiver back to her mouth. "Love you," she says quickly. "Bye."

~

13 Aug 10: A5, clear and sunny, winds moderate, ~18°C, 19:08 – 20:25. None observed. She flips the journal closed and stands. Rubs her aching hip and shakes out the tightness in her knees. She hadn't really expected to see them, not after seeing nine the evening before. They could be almost anywhere now. Might even be out at the coast, dining on flounder and crab, leaving more footprints in the sand.

No observations meant plenty of time to think. Too much time. And now, she wants to get back to the cabin before dark. If she didn't feel so silly – and if it weren't dangerous – she'd leave the lamp or a candle burning all night.

To distract herself while she was waiting, she'd begun to plan the house she and Alan could build to replace the cabin. Nothing fancy. Maybe something like Dan's, small but well-appointed: floor to ceiling windows onto the pond, a fireplace, a stove and refrigerator, an indoor bathroom. They could even ask Dan for advice. If she could just introduce him to Alan, that would put a quick end to her schoolgirl fantasies. Learning about his former wife, and the son he doesn't care about, the child of a girlfriend he can hardly remember, should have done it. But it hasn't. And she *will* ask the power company to bring in electricity. Then she can store her own samples in her own damn freezer. She won't need Dan at all.

~

The dog follows a faint but familiar scent, tracks it through dark trees skirting the pond. When she gets to the outlet, she smells the strong musk of otters – and forgets the other scent that brought her here, to the river. But the old female does not forget. The scent of the young woman is one she recognizes, a presence that has lingered here forever, searching, a presence who knows the otters, and the dog, intends harm to neither.

The dog bows down, resting her head on her large front paws. An otter pup approaches her, touches his muzzle to hers, then they leap up to chase each other, into the water and out, splashing, chirping, barking.

Later, worn out with chasing and wrestling, the dog sleeps among them, cradled by tree roots and warm wet fur. Sometime in the night, when it begins to rain, the dog wakes and remembers why she came here.

~

Beth is on her second cup of coffee when she hears tapping on the door. Opens it to find Mattie, rain streaming off her green slicker. She is holding her hands in front of her, rubbing them together. "Have you seen Muin?" she asks. Beth shakes her head.

"She's been gone all night," Mattie says. "I was hoping she was here, with you."

"Come in," Beth says, opening the door wider. "You're getting soaked."

Mattie steps inside. Her wet sneakers squish. Rain drips off the slicker and forms a puddle around her feet.

"Is there somewhere else she might wander off to?"

"No." Mattie's hands are still for a moment. "Well, yes. But this just feels different."

Just feels different. Beth's not sure how to weigh this, but Mattie seems genuinely worried.

"I better get back," Mattie says. "I left the flag up for Dan. As soon as the rain lets up, he'll go out fishing. I want him to go out in the truck and search. Or ..." She looks out the window at the Toyota. "If you would go out in your car then he can go out in the boat and search. If Muin's anywhere near shore, she'll come out when she hears the motor."

"But–"

"But what?"

"Never mind."

~

Bumping along the narrow dirt road, Beth tries to steer clear of the deepest ruts. Even so, the bottom of the car scrapes rock now and again. She's been driving slowly for hours, the radio off so she can listen for barking, although the wipers' smack-smack-smack drowns out all but the loudest sounds. Every few minutes, she stops the car, gets out, and calls. Waits hopefully for an answering bark. Sometimes, she can hear the distant whine of a motorboat and knows it's Dan. Who else would be out in this weather?

He'd answered her knock on the door in nothing but blue jeans. "More shit already this morning? Freezer's getting pretty full."

"Muin is gone. Has been all night. Mattie wants you to go out in the boat while I search by car." Beth could hear, and smell, coffee brewing.

He ran his hand through sleep-tousled hair. "But Muin's always gone."

"Mattie says this *feels different*."

"What's that supposed to mean?"

"I don't know, but she seemed really agitated."

"Not a moment's peace," he sighed. "Not even on a Saturday morning."

Beth avoided looking at his bare chest. Even more spare than she'd imagined.

193

She glances at the gas gauge: half a tank. She can drive for hours yet. And she will. She'll stay out after dark if she has to. It surprises her just how much she cares about that goofy dog. Sure, Muin can be a nuisance, but she's also affectionate and lovable. And she's chosen Beth – whatever that means. But Muin's also a gorgeous purebred who's friendly with strangers. Someone might have decided to take her in. And keep her. Beth envisions her in a stranger's car, confused and already missing Mattie, wanting to come home. Sees, in her mind, Muin hurt, in pain and shivering, lying in a ditch somewhere with no protection from the rain. Beth begins to tear up. She can't even think about sitting at Mattie's table and not having Muin underfoot, of not smelling her distinctive doggy odour. She can't imagine how lonely Mattie would be without her. Just thinking about it makes her heart ache, which surprises her too – how much she's come to care about Mattie. She might be strange – and sometimes a little spooky – but she's never boring. What did Matthew mean? *You're here to help her.* Mattie seems pretty self-sufficient, so Beth can't see how she could help, except, perhaps, with her loneliness. Wait. Did she really just think that? Mattie as *he*? Beth hears a loud scrape. Cringes. And hopes she hasn't put a hole in the muffler or tailpipe.

She brakes. The road ahead is too deeply rutted for the low-slung Toyota. She studies the map on the seat beside her, a topographical map showing the old logging roads. If she's kept track of the twists and turns correctly, and the distance, she should be near the north shore of Medicine Rock Pond, just a little ways north and east of it. The trees are thick here, but the sky overhead has lightened and the rain has slowed to a drizzle. She'll get out and walk. She has to do something.

Beth pulls on her raingear, grabs a flashlight from the glove compartment, and slips it into the backpack along with the map. She slings the backpack over one shoulder and begins walking, but all she can hear is the swish-swish-swish of the raingear, so every minute or two, she stands still and calls: "Mu-u-e-e-n. Here, girl." Her breath makes white puffs in the air. It can't be more than ten or twelve degrees. "Here, Muin. Here, girl. Mu-u-e-e-n." She waits for an answering bark. Her hair is getting soaked, but she can't put her hood up. With the hood up, she won't be able to hear anything at all.

She comes across a pile of debris dumped at the side of the road: a threadbare, gold velour sofa; an ancient cabinet TV; an old grey computer monitor; a stained mattress; torn black garbage bags spilling out old issues of *Sports Illustrated,* phone books, and Sears catalogues. Who throws their trash out in the wilderness? She answers her own question: The same kind of person who'd steal a dog.

She continues walking for nearly an hour. Damp since early that morning, her clothes are sticking to her skin. The search is beginning to feel like looking for the proverbial needle in the haystack – despite Muin's size. Beth doesn't want to give up, but she's not sure this is the best way to find the dog – or even if she's still lost. Muin could be waiting at Beth's cabin right now. No, Mattie would be going back and forth between the cabins, if only to keep herself busy, and surely she and Dan have worked out what colour flag she'll put up if Muin returns. As long as Beth can hear the drone of the motorboat, she knows Dan's still out searching. So she'll keep searching too.

A quiet rustle, the snap of a twig. She stands still, heart and throat clenched tight. Hears it again, leaves and branches moving. She calls out, "Muin?" Then sees, up ahead, a furry black rump waddling off into the brush. Beth almost weeps. Any other time, she'd be thrilled to get a glimpse of a black bear, but not today.

She walks for another hour, keeping to the meandering road. No point in going off into the woods. It would just be harder to walk, and for all she knows, Muin is miles away. Or even in St. John's if someone has picked her up. Or dead. Beth balls her hands into fists to keep herself from crying. Her heart hiccups. Jax. She'd taken a hammer and nails and made a cross, painted it with the dates: '63 – '69. Put the cross and a handful of wild daisies on the grave. Beth swipes at tears.

She looks up and there she is, standing stock-still in the middle of the road – as if the massive dog had simply materialized out of wind and earth and rain. Beth drops to her knees and Muin bounds forward. Beth buries her face in the smelly wet fur. She puts her hands on either side of the broad head. "Muin," she says sternly, but can't continue the scolding. The dog licks the tears from her cheeks.

She pulls out the Milk-Bones she'd stuffed in her backpack, and while Muin chomps one down, Beth considers her next move. She should try to signal Dan, otherwise he'll be out searching the whole time she and Muin are walking back to the car and driving to Mattie's – more than two hours. But to signal him she needs to get out on shore.

She pulls out her map and compass. If they head south-southwest, they should come out on shore somewhere near Medicine Rock. Can't be much more than half a kilometre through the woods. She checks her watch: 15:32. Plenty of time to go to the pond, signal Dan, and get back to the car before dark. She folds up the map and steps into the woods. Muin happily follows, especially when Beth pulls out another Milk-Bone.

She holds the compass before her, on a south-southwest bearing. Within fifteen minutes they are standing on the north shore of the pond, just east of the outlet and

Medicine Rock, which, in the grey light and drizzle, looks almost black. She scans the pond. Dan's boat is nowhere in sight. She decides they'll wait there for an hour. If Dan hasn't shown up by then, they'll head back to the car. She pulls up her hood and sits down on a rock, calls Muin to her side, but the dog backs up and barks.

"What's wrong, girl?"

Muin runs toward the outlet, barks, and then comes halfway back. Beth pulls another treat from her backpack. Waves it. Muin won't come, even for the Milk-Bone.

Beth groans. Not another Lassie moment.

Okay, she could follow Muin for a short way. They'll be just as visible walking along the shore as they are sitting, maybe more so. She stands and walks toward Muin, who now trots along silently, leaping across the rocks, which, sharp-edged and slippery, are far more difficult for Beth to navigate. It takes her nearly ten minutes to cover the short distance to the outlet. Once there, Muin bolts straight back into the woods.

"Damn it, Muin. Come here." Beth can hear the dog crashing through the undergrowth. She stamps her foot. "Come here, Muin." Her love for the dog, and her relief at having found her, are quickly morphing into anger. She doesn't want to follow Muin and miss Dan, but she doesn't want to lose the dog either.

She lifts the binoculars and scans the pond. Still no Dan. She decides to go into the woods a short way, but not far, even if it means losing Muin. She'll stay near shore and signal Dan, and then both of them can search on foot together. At least they'll know the dog is somewhere nearby.

She calls for Muin again, then follows the answering bark into the dripping trees, gloomy with old man's beard. She spots her standing beside a small pile of rocks, near to where she found the rosary. Beth approaches slowly, calling to Muin. The dog stays put, looking alternately at

Beth and the cairn. That's how Beth sees it now, a cairn: grey and ochre rocks, all about the size of a grapefruit, piled knee-high.

"Good dog, good Muin," Beth croons until she is standing by the dog's side and has grabbed her collar. She turns toward the cairn. On the top stone, an ochre one, someone has painted a spider web. The paint has worn away and some of the lines are barely visible, but Beth can make out the word "hope" within the web.

Muin lifts her ears. A few moments later, Beth hears it too: the motorboat. They run toward shore. As soon as they emerge from the trees, Beth waves her arms wildly. She pulls the flashlight from her backpack, flicks it on, and waves that too, but Dan is turned away. Muin barks, but the outboard drowns out the sound. Beth adds jumping to arm waving.

Dan turns the boat in a wide arc. Finally spots them and steers the Alumacraft toward shore, cuts the motor and drifts in. Muin swims out to greet him.

"Where the hell have you been?" he says. The words are harsh, but Beth can hear his relief. Dan steps out of the boat and pulls it partway up on shore. Muin emerges from the water and shakes, and even in their raingear, Dan and Beth take a step back.

"This where you found her?" he says.

Beth points back across the woods. "Not far from here, but back on the old logging road."

"Doing what?"

"Nothing ... that I could see."

Dan tugs on the bill of his cap. "Well, at least you found her."

Muin has both front paws on the gunnel, ready to jump aboard.

"Okay, girl. Hang on a minute." He turns to Beth. "If you're okay to get back to your car on your own, I'll take Muin back to Mattie. I've never seen her like this."

Beth tucks damp hair behind one ear. "Got out here by myself. Guess I can find my own way back."

"Why don't you stop by Mattie's later? I'm sure she'll wanna thank you."

"Maybe. If it's not too late."

Muin jumps into the boat. Dan pushes it into the water and climbs in. "Thanks, Beth. Mattie's gonna miss you when you go."

And what about you, Dan? What about you?

CHAPTER 24

Now that she's no longer consumed with worry about Muin, the walk back to the car seems endless. She should have gone back in the boat and then asked Dan to drive her to the car. Still would have taken more than two hours, but at least she'd have company and a ride. But she has to consider: Dan never offered.

Beth trudges on, each step accompanied by the annoying swish of raingear. When she finally reaches the Toyota, she has to drive for nearly an hour, on bad roads skirting the pond, to get back to the cabin. It's nearly seven by the time she unlocks the door.

She changes into dry clothes. Looks with longing at the bed and thinks about just falling into it, but twenty minutes later, flashlight in hand, she is standing on Mattie's doorstep. She hears Muin's low woof, and when Mattie opens the door, Beth can see a pot of something bubbling on the cookstove. There are three places set at the small table: Dan and Mattie have waited supper for her. Muin nuzzles her hand and Beth feels tears welling. Hides her face by reaching for Muin's shaggy head. "What a bad dog you are."

"Come on now, sit down," Mattie says. "You must be gut-founded."

"I know I sure am," Dan says, rubbing his flat belly. "Mattie wouldn't even let me have a taste. Moose stew," he adds.

Beth breathes in the rich aroma and suddenly realizes that she is famished, emptied out by the whole ordeal. Mattie dishes up three large bowls, then sits down. Beth takes the seat across from Dan, while Muin settles in her customary place under the table. All of them move their feet aside, simultaneously, as if their steps were choreographed. Dan picks up a fork and digs into the stew.

"Dan says you found her not far from the outlet?" Mattie says.

"I was just walking and calling, and then there she was." Beth blows on a forkful of hot stew, takes a small bite – moose, carrot, potato, turnip, onion, and some subtle flavours she can't identify. She glances at the dried plants hanging from the ceiling, hesitates, then takes another bite. She is too damn hungry not to eat.

Dan sets down his fork and arranges, then rearranges, his knife and spoon. "Mattie," he says slowly, "it's time you started tying her up."

"No."

"Look, I can fix up a sturdy line between two trees. One that'll let her walk on a chain up and down the line."

Mattie shakes her head. "No. She's never run off before. Not like this. Must've had her reasons."

He picks up his fork and points it at Mattie. "That's exactly why she needs to be tied."

"She won't do that again."

"And how do you know that?" He looks as if he wants to poke her.

"Just know. That's all."

Dan lets out a beleaguered sigh. "Muin needs to be tied. I can't be chasing all around after that dog. And Beth won't be here to find her for you."

Mattie turns to Beth. "Where you going?"

"Don't change the subject." Glaring at Mattie, Dan shoves a huge bite of stew into his mouth.

"Where you going?" Mattie repeats.

"I've finished my research," Beth says. "At least for now. I'll be heading back to St. John's in a couple of days."

"You're not done here."

"Classes start soon. I need to get ready."

"But you're not done here," Mattie insists.

Dan shovels stew into his mouth, bites off thick chunks of buttered bread, keeps his eyes down.

"I've taken as many samples as I need to write a proposal," Beth says.

"That's not what I'm talking about." Mattie taps the back of Beth's hand with two fingers. "It's your other work."

"What other work?"

"You know."

"No, I don't," Beth says.

"You can be thick at times."

"Look who's calling who 'thick,'" Dan mumbles, around a mouth full of bread.

"You said that you came here to learn about otters." Mattie taps Beth's hand again. "Know anything more now than when you first came?"

Beth pulls her hand away. "Mattie?"

"Well, do you?"

Dan stands and tosses his napkin on the table. "Thanks for supper, but I need to get going." Points a finger at Muin. "*You* stay home." Muin scrambles out from under the table and follows him to the door. Dan lets the screen door slam behind him.

"I do have a job and a husband to get back to," Beth says.

"But you want to stay."

Muin turns her head toward Beth and whines. Mattie takes a bite of stew, chews slowly, swallows. "Nothing to feel guilty about. Everybody has those kinda thoughts one time or another. And he is a good-looking boy."

"Don't be ridiculous!" Heat rises up Beth's neck and into her cheeks. "He's just been helping with my research."

"That's good. Because whatever it is you're supposed to be doing here, it's not about Dan."

Beth stares at the bowl in front of her, takes a small bite of carrot but can hardly chew. When she finally allows herself to look up, the first thing she sees is Muin. She makes an effort to swallow and then clears her throat. "When I found Muin," she says, "and we walked out to the pond, she went straight to Medicine Rock. And then headed back into the woods. To the place where I found the rosary."

Mattie toys with a piece of turnip.

"She stopped beside a pile of rocks," Beth continues. "A cairn or a shrine of some kind. On one rock, someone had painted a spider web incorporating the word 'hope.' Looked a lot like your work."

"Did it now?" Mattie lays down her fork.

"Is it?"

Mattie pushes the bowl aside. Exhales through narrowed lips. "Was a time in my life, girl, when I needed to be reminded of hope, when every day was an act of faith." She taps her fingers on the table as if counting. "Must be what? More than sixty-five years now."

"When Matthew drowned?"

"Thereabouts."

"Why would Muin go there?"

At the sound of her name, the dog comes and lays her head in Beth's lap.

"She sees him. Follows him sometimes." Mattie looks toward the blue baseball cap hanging by the door, then back to Beth. "Muin and me ... we live with ghosts."

"Memories," Beth says gently. "You mean that you live with memories."

"I mean what I say."

"But ghosts are just products of our imaginations," Beth says, "our fears." She thinks of Alice. "Or our deepest desires."

"You sure of that?" Mattie puts an elbow on the table and rests her chin in her palm.

"Reasonably so."

Mattie picks up the box of matches. Slides it open and takes out one match. "Would you agree that scientists discover new stuff almost every day?"

"Sure."

"Stuff that sometimes changes the way we think about everything else?" Holding the match like a cigarette, Mattie points at the bookshelf.

"Yes," Beth says, a little more tentative now.

"For thousands and thousands of years, everybody knew about ghosts." Mattie strikes the match and lights the kerosene lamp. "Then, in the past two hundred years or so – yesterday, if you're Medicine Rock – a few scientists come along and say: Ghosts? What foolishness!"

She adjusts the height of the wick. "How long till some scientist discovers a ghost?" Pale light shadows the corners of her upturned lips. "Then we'll all be able to see em again."

~

Beth picks her way along the path. Every time she hears a rustle of leaves, she can't stop herself from shining the flashlight toward it. The minute she steps into the cabin, she lights the kerosene lamp and every candle she has – until the living room and bedroom are glowing with soft yellow light. An open bottle of pinot noir stands on the counter. She pours a glass, then checks to be sure the door and all the windows are locked. Checks again. Sits down in the rocking chair – Katherine's chair – and sees her own pale reflection staring back at her from the black window. Like someone outside looking in. Or a ghost. She turns the chair away from the window. Her toe beats a steady tattoo on the wood floor.

How long till some scientist discovers a ghost? She sips the wine. There's not one shred of scientific evidence, and it's likely there never will be, but she can't completely discount the possibility either. Lots of perfectly sane people harbour a vague belief in the possibility of ghosts, or in something loosely resembling the notion. Nothing scary about it. Not really.

Okay. So what about animals then? Considering the issue scientifically, if there are human ghosts, there's no biological reason why there wouldn't be animal ghosts. And that raises the question of souls. If we grant them to humans, there's no reason not to grant them to animals too. And what would that mean for how we think about, and treat, animals?

Mentally, she throws up her hands. Maybe otters do have souls. Maybe they've created some sort of otter god they worship. Maybe there are born-again pups. She should be laughing, but alone in the cabin, with shadowy light creeping up the walls, she's not amused by the thought of animal souls or animal ghosts. Or any other kind of ghost, for that matter.

Beth goes to the bedroom and grabs her novel. Sits down again in the rocking chair and reads a few pages – but can remember nothing. She lays the book aside. She doesn't need any more mystery anyway, certainly not a novel titled *Endless Night*. She moves the lamp to the table and sits down at the puzzle, one thousand pieces, still only half-finished. She picks up a blue piece that's mottled with white, tries at least six different ways to fit it into a snow-capped mountain. Sets it aside and picks up another piece, one that looks like it should be part of a spruce, but she can't make that one fit either.

Mattie's words niggle: *Know anything more now than when you first came here?*

How had she ever imagined that coming here and spending a few weeks studying otters would change anything? Seems naïve now, presumptuous and benighted. Especially in light of what she's managed to accomplish so far: to collect samples of otter shit no one but she really cares about; to become thoroughly spooked by a lonely old woman's ghosts and a yellow dress; and to invent a romantic fantasy to replace her tired old marriage. She cringes. Damn. She thought she'd been hiding her feelings, when all along she's been telegraphing everything like a moonstruck schoolgirl. She's let herself become a pitiful cliché.

The rain starts, pinging against the windows like a spray of BBs.

CHAPTER 25

She gets up, makes a fire, and prepares the percolator. Wraps herself in her sleeping bag and waits, watching the sun rise on a morning that is warm and clear, as if the rain the night before had washed the air.

A restless night, but no dreams. And sometime during all that tossing and turning, she decided that she has everything she needs to write a proposal. This morning, she'll check the otter spot one last time, then stop in to say goodbye to Mattie. She'll retrieve the frozen samples from Dan's and call Alan from the Irving. She can be in St. John's before dark.

~

Beth sees Mattie in the clearing, kneeling beside Muin, who is nose to nose with a small otter. Beth lifts the paddle and lets the kayak drift. Muin bends into a play bow: head down, hind-end up, front legs straight out. But the otter has seen Beth. It snorts, then galumphs down to the pond, thick tail bobbling, and enters the water with hardly a ripple. Muin follows at a gallop and plunges in. Chirping, the otter circles the dog, touches its muzzle to hers as if to start a game of wrestling, but then dives. Muin watches, ears forward, but when the otter fails to reappear, she swims out to Beth, who paddles to shore and beaches the kayak beside Mattie's canoe. Muin comes out of the pond and shakes, showering water in a wide arc: rainbow flashes in the morning sun.

Mattie straightens slowly, unfolding herself as she works out the kinks from hips and knees. She cups the dog's chin. "Guess the old grandmother's not in the mood for play this morning."

If Beth didn't know better, she'd think Muin looks disappointed. Maybe she is.

"Do they come here often?" Beth says.

"Often enough. That was the old grandmother. When I told her you were leaving, she said you can't. You have too much to learn yet."

"Indeed." Beth crosses her arms. "She have anything to say about what, exactly, I need to learn?"

Mattie chuckles. "Just playing with you, girl." She nods toward the cabin. "Time for a cup a tea?" She holds up a hand. "Or water? I got lotsa water."

Beth follows Mattie and Muin up the trail and into the cabin. There is a new weaving in the loom: loden, cobalt, mahogany, and ivory. It is less than a quarter finished, but Beth can see the stylized spider web in one corner. Just off centre, what looks like an otter's webbed foot is taking shape.

Mattie points her chin at the loom. "That's for you."

"Me?"

"For finding Muin."

"That's not worth a weaving."

"Is to me." Mattie pumps cold water into a jar. "But it won't be done for at least another week, so I guess you'll just have to stick around."

"I have to go back, Mattie. Classes start soon. But I'll be out this fall for a few weekends."

"I'm gonna miss our little chats." Mattie brings her mug and Beth's water to the table. "Talking with you is a lot like talking with Katherine."

Beth sits down across from Mattie and picks up the jar of water. Stares at the yellow sugar bowl, the pink roses, the brown crack trailing between them.

Mattie adds a spoonful of sugar to her mug. "I miss her, you know. The way you miss your friend."

Beth has never mentioned Alice, has she? She stands up. "Can we go outside?"

"Sure. It's a grand morning." Mattie grabs a dish towel. Outside, she wipes the rain off both Muskoka chairs, then settles into one, mug of hot tea resting on the arm. The fragrant steam smells of raspberries. Muin noses around in the grass where the otter was, then plops down near Beth's feet.

Mattie sips the tea, pursing her lips at the heat, then sets down the mug. "The old grandmother and I were having a chat before you got here. She says you're worrying about the wrong things."

"Hmmm. She happen to say what I should be worrying about?"

Mattie lifts her hands, palms up. "I'm just the messenger, love." She lays an arm on the chair and drums her fingers. "She could mean that you should stop worrying about whether or not what you do matters. And just do. You can't know what matters."

Beth rotates the jar, moving it out of the puddle of condensation. Alan's words. If only it were that simple.

"The earth is so much more than any of us can know," Mattie continues. "Everything is. Including otters. Which means you're wrong."

"About what?"

Mattie shrugs. "I'm wrong too. All of us are wrong. And most of the time we don't even know what we're wrong about." She puts a hand to her forehead to shade her eyes and watches a pair of loons and their chick swimming in the middle of the pond. "Could be that people trying to understand the world – I mean really understand it – is like Muin trying to understand long division. Might be something we just can't do."

The dog stands and puts her head in Beth's lap. Beth scratches her behind her ears. One of the adult loons releases an echoing yodel.

Mattie smiles. "But there's hope in that."

"Hope in ignorance?"

"No, not in ignorance. But in maybes. Possibilities."

Fingers buried in Muin's fur, Beth closes her eyes. Alice was full of maybes: *I'm not sure, but I wonder if ...* In the end, in those last horrible days, Alice had needed to believe in possibilities. Beth tried, but she could believe in nothing but her anger and her grief.

Mattie turns to Beth. "To lose hope is a failure of imagination."

"It might help our imaginations," Beth says bitterly, "if hope paid off now and again, if we got one shred of evidence that it matters."

"Maybe we do, but we just don't see it." Mattie takes a swallow of the cooled tea and watches the loons for a long moment.

Muin lifts her head. A few seconds later, Beth hears the crunch of gravel and then the creak of a truck door opening. The dog trots toward the pickup.

"Oh, hey," Dan says to Beth while he fends off Muin. "Didn't expect to find you here. Thought you'd be out collecting more *samples* for my freezer."

"Just stopped in to say goodbye."

"Don't forget your samples then. I don't wanna be left with a freezer full of otter shit." He turns to Mattie. "Anything you need in town?"

"Just the dog food and the bird seed."

"Okay then, see ya." He turns toward the truck, then spins back around. "Long as you're still here," he says to Beth, "wanna go fishing again?"

"I'd planned to pack up and leave today."

"Your loss." Dan looks up at the sky. "Great day. I'm gonna go out after supper and try for a salmon. Might even see otters. You never know."

Beth is listening hard, but can hear no innuendo. Doesn't see a smirk or even a knowing glance at Mattie.

"Okay," she says slowly. "I suppose I could stay on for one more day."

"I'll bring the boat around at seven."

She allows herself to look at Mattie only after Dan has left.

Mattie clicks a thumbnail against her broken tooth. "Long as you're staying, wanna help me pick some crackerberries?"

"I thought they made you sick."

"Guess you were wrong about that too."

CHAPTER 26

Beth tosses the line out over the water. Doesn't really care that she's not casting right. She only pretended to listen to Dan's careful instructions earlier. She wants to talk, but Dan is far more interested in fishing. Fishing in silence, apparently.

Beth is bone-weary of being alone with her own thoughts. She'd made a trip into town that afternoon and stopped at the Irving to call Alan. He didn't pick up. On a Sunday afternoon? She tried his cellphone. He didn't answer that either. But she didn't have the energy to worry about what that might mean.

She went to the liquor store and picked up another bottle of wine, as well as a six-pack of Black Horse, and some ice for the cooler, just in case. In case of what? She chose not to worry about that either.

Back at the cabin, Beth put the beer on ice, then went into the pond and bathed. Tried to wash the black soot from under her fingernails. She searched among her clothes for something reasonably clean and flattering. She doesn't own anything remotely sexy. Why would she want sexy? One more thing she chose not to worry about.

True to his word, Dan came by precisely at seven, and they've been fishing near the outlet for nearly an hour. So far, there hasn't been a single rise, salmon or trout. Beth pulls in her line, then holds the fly rod idly in one hand. "So what do you know about the cairn?" she says.

"What cairn?" Dan casts, then flicks the line.

"I found it yesterday, a pile of rocks about fifty paces back from Medicine Rock. Near where I found the rosary."

"Was hoping I'd heard the last of that damn rosary. Hasn't been stolen again, has it?" He says the words like it's a little joke between them. He pulls in the line in measured increments.

"I took it back to where I found it." She brushes a mosquito off her cheek. "But what about the cairn?" she says.

He examines the red and silver fly at the end of his line. "Never seen it. Never heard of it."

Not my business.

He reaches for his tackle box. "How do you know it's not just a pile of rocks? Not like there's a big shortage around here."

"No," Beth says. "They were piled there deliberately. All of them are the same size and the top one's been painted. The paint has worn away, but you can still make out the word 'hope.' Sort of."

Dan removes the fly from his line and clips on a small blue one with a bit of yellow feather.

He casts the new fly over the water.

"It's Mattie's work," she continues. "She said so last night, after you left. She told me she made it a long time ago, just after Matthew drowned. A memorial of sorts, I guess."

"There you go. No more to it than that." Dan's line goes taut. He pulls it firmly but gently. The fly releases, a long blade of grass snagged in the hook. His shoulders sag.

"Yesterday," Beth says, "when I found Muin, she was hell-bent on going there."

"No big mystery to that." Dan removes the grass from the hook and lets it drop into the water. "Mattie usually brings Muin along when she comes out to Medicine Rock."

"She comes out here?"

"Sometimes she canoes." He examines the blue and yellow fly. "Other times, I bring her out in the boat or on the skidoo. I go off and fish while she does whatever she does."

"Why didn't she say that last night, when I told her where I found Muin?"

"Cause Mattie is Mattie. She never keeps anything simple if she can make it complicated." He turns to the other side of the boat and casts again.

"But when she told me about Medicine Rock, she made it sound like it was just some old place people from long ago used to visit."

"Mostly is," he says. "I doubt that anyone but Mattie comes out to the rock anymore. But she always comes out here at least once around mid-August."

Beth tips her head, puzzled.

"Anniversary of Matthew's drowning."

"Oh." She wraps both hands around the fly rod. Fumbles a cast. She pulls the line taut, but knows by the feel of it that she hasn't caught a fish. The fly has hooked into weeds or a submerged log. Dan reaches for the line and tugs gently to work the fly loose.

Beth pulls in the line. "Mattie told me that Muin might have been following Matthew's ghost when she ran off."

"And you believed that?"

"Course not. I just find it all strange. And, to be honest, a little creepy."

"Strange. But not creepy. That's just Mattie."

"What about the spare bedroom then?" she says. "You can't tell me that's not creepy."

"What's creepy about the spare bedroom?"

"The wooden flute and the bone necklace on the nightstand? The clothes in the closet?"

"That's just Mattie's stuff." Dan looks at her sideways. "Why the hell were you in there anyway?"

She turns away. Fumbles another cast. The fly plops into the water less than two metres from the boat. "When I stopped by a couple days ago, I couldn't find Mattie. I was looking around to make sure she was okay."

"In the spare bedroom?"

Beth keeps her gaze on Medicine Rock. In the softening light and lengthening shadows, the face she'd imagined before, the old man's profile, has morphed into an old woman's. "Let's go ashore," she says. "I'll show you the cairn."

"Why?" He pulls a cigarette from the pack in his shirt pocket.

"You're not even curious?"

"Not really." But he slides the cigarette back into his pocket and stows their fly rods, tips up the prop and rows the short distance to shore. Beth helps him pull the boat partway out of the water. He reaches for a flashlight and waves it toward the woods. "Lead on, Macduff." Smirks. "I think there might've been a ghost there too."

"Very funny." She lays a hand on Medicine Rock and points. "About fifty paces straight back from Medicine Rock."

"That's not Medicine Rock."

"It's not?"

"It's that one over there." He points to a flat grey rock sitting squarely in the middle of the outlet. It has a few green and rust striations, but it looks like all the others, only larger.

"But there's nothing special about that rock," she says.

"Hey, I didn't name it."

Beth is disappointed, but she's not sure why. "Okay then," she says, "the cairn is about fifty paces back from this rock."

In just a few minutes they are standing beside the pile of rocks. Dan flicks on the flashlight and points at the painted rock on top. "It's Mattie's work, sure. But you already knew that."

Beth leans in closer. Tucked between the painted rock and the pale one beside it is a brown and white feather like the one on her nightstand. She reaches out to touch it, her chest squeezing her lungs so tight she can hardly breathe. Alice?

"All right, I've seen it," Dan says. "Can we go now?"

Hoo-hoo-hoooo, hoo-hoo. They both look up. A great horned owl is sitting in a spruce just a few metres away. The bird swivels its head and looks down on them with round yellow eyes that seem to have gathered within them every photon of available light. They shine brighter than the flashlight, which Dan has pointed at the ground. The bird ruffles mottled feathers and clacks its bill – a warning – then spreads wings that are nearly as broad as Beth is tall and glides silently into the dark.

"Well, there's your ghost," Dan says. He sets off toward shore.

Beth hesitates, debating whether or not to take the feather. Decides to leave it where it is. She's already taken enough from this place. She follows the bouncing light beam over the mounds of sphagnum and through the ferns and underbrush.

A high-pitched chirp.

"Stop," she calls out in a whisper, but Dan is already standing still. He turns off the flashlight. Beth can hear the steady *uhn-uhn-uhns*, but it takes a full minute for her eyes to adjust to the dark. She finally spots a small otter standing upright on the real Medicine Rock, muzzle silvery grey in the faint light.

"The old grandmother," she says softly.

The otter chirps again then drops down and slides into the pond. Disappears in a ring of dark ripples.

"Why here? Why now?" Beth says. "And standing on Medicine Rock of all places."

"It's just an otter, Beth. And it's here. Just like we are."

"But it's the same one that was at Mattie's this morning. It's like a sign ... or something."

"A sign?" He laughs. "Now you're sounding like Mattie. Making something that's simple into some big complicated mystery." He takes a step toward her. He's standing so close she can smell his shirt: wool, dry leaves, wood smoke. "Look," he says more gently, "you've been spending way too much time with her."

Dan reaches out and gives her arm a squeeze. "Come on, let's go."

She feels the presence of his hand, then the absence.

He flicks on the flashlight, points it toward her. "Jesus, Beth, you look like you really have seen a ghost." He reaches out and squeezes her arm again. "Why don't you come back to the house for a while? Have a drink and calm down. I'll drive you home."

~

The old female swims to join the others. When they see the light beam, even the pups grow still. They sniff the air − strong scent of humans and fear. They hear voices above the sounds of the water churning around the rocks in the river. They touch each other's muzzles. *Uhn-uhn-uhn, uhn-uhn-uhn.* Growls of a motor, then a stink so strong they can taste the bitterness. The otters come out of the water and hide among the grasses and dark shadows. They begin to groom themselves and each other, comfort in the touch-touch-touching.

CHAPTER 27

Within twenty minutes, Dan is tying the *Black Feather* to the pier. He turns off the small light on the bow, and they climb out of the boat and walk around to the back of the dark house. He unlocks the kitchen door and flicks a switch. Beth blinks. The bright fluorescent light banishes any lingering sense of ghosts in a way that a kerosene lamp and candles can't.

He grabs a Black Horse and a bottle of white wine from the refrigerator. "You look like you could use this. Or maybe something stronger?"

She runs a hand through her hair. "No, wine is good."

He uncorks the bottle and pours, hands her the glass, then points his beer toward the living room. Beth sinks into the armchair. She sets the chilled glass on the end table, turns up the collar of her jacket, and wraps her arms around herself. Dan steps to the fireplace and opens the flue.

"Please don't bother," she says. "I'll be fine."

"No trouble. I'll just build a small one to take off the chill." He smiles. "And to scare off any ghosts."

"I feel pretty silly now."

"No worries. Mattie can have that effect on people." He adds kindling to the slender splits already in the fireplace. Flicks his lighter. The kindling smoulders, then flares. He feeds pieces of birch bark to the small flames. "Been a long time since she's had someone actually pay attention to what she says."

Beth watches the fire grow. Her shoulders begin to unhunch. "What's troubling," she says, "is that sometimes

221

– even though I can't follow her logic – I find myself agreeing with her. Maybe I'm getting to be as nutty as she is."

"Could be." He grins. "You do spend your days collecting otter shit."

Beth laughs. "And you let me store it in your freezer. So what's that say about you?"

He takes a swallow of beer. "Seriously, Beth, don't worry about trying to find logic in what she says. There is no logic. It's just senility talking."

"You don't really believe that."

"No, but she is a little unhinged." He adds a few more splits to the fire. "She likes to keep everybody off balance. I learned a long time ago not to listen to her." He pokes at the fire with a piece of wood. "Even Katherine ignored half of what she said. But she did have a way of keeping Mattie more ... reasonable."

He steps out into the kitchen and turns off the fluorescent light, comes back to the fire and adjusts the small logs with the poker, adds a larger birch junk.

Beth takes a sip of wine and stares into the flames. She does feel silly now. She's allowed herself to get caught up in Mattie's strange web of beliefs about ghosts and animals who bring messages, to the point where she's beginning to see odd coincidences – the appearance of otters, owls, and brown and white feathers – the same way Mattie would. Dan's explanations are perfectly reasonable: As a teenager Mattie was derailed by her twin's drowning, and over the decades, she's become eccentric, fabricating the illusions she needs to survive.

"She'd love this," Dan says, poking at the fire. "Us talking about her."

"Hard not to."

"But you came back here so you could stop thinking about her and her creepy ideas." He points at her glass. "More wine?"

"Thanks."

While Dan fetches the wine, Beth goes to the bathroom. Finger-combs her hair and studies her face in the mirror. The light is harsh, highlighting wrinkles she doesn't want to see. Smile lines, Alan calls them, kindly. No, she will not think about him right now.

She returns to the living room and finds that Dan has placed her glass on the end table beside the sofa. Everything is perfect: wine, a crackling fire, soft light surrounded by a darkness that is warm and comforting rather than scary, Dan sitting on the sofa. Everything she would have imagined ... if she had allowed herself to imagine it.

She unzips her jacket. "Lovely fire."

"Yep." His ankle rests on one knee, foot jiggling.

She takes off the jacket and lays it aside. He looks up at her from the sofa. She picks up the wineglass and sits down beside him.

"So you're heading back tomorrow?" he says.

"That's the plan."

He picks at the label on the Black Horse. "Not much point in hanging around any longer, I spose."

"Well, I can always use more observations." She runs her fingers up and down the stem of the glass. "And I might try to get out here a few weekends this fall. I'll probably need more samples."

"Guess there's always a need for more shit." Dan speaks the words gently, another joke between them. He finishes the beer and uncrosses his legs to set the bottle on the floor. "Beautiful time of year just to hang around and fish."

"Well ... maybe I *could* stay on another day or two." She turns to face him. He leans closer, puts a hand to her chin and tips it up. She closes her eyes, then feels his hand drop. Her eyes spring open.

He scrubs his face with the hand that had cradled her chin. "Damn," he says softly. Sitting back, he swings his ankle back onto his knee, takes her hand in his, and looks down at their interlaced fingers. "I like you, Beth." His foot is going like a sewing machine. "But we're after different things."

She hugs the wineglass to a stomach that is doing somersaults. "I'm not after anything," she says quickly, stupidly.

Dan releases her hand, stands, and walks to the kitchen. "I like simple," he continues, "and you would make it" – he opens the refrigerator, a rectangle of light in the dark – "complicated." He grabs another beer. The refrigerator comes on, the hum loud in the silence. "I hate talking about this stuff," he says into the dark.

He levers the cap off, a soft pf-f-ft. Takes a long swallow, Adam's apple bobbing. He uses the back of his hand to wipe his mouth. "My idea of a great arrangement would be for you to come out here now and again. I could help out with your research, and we could have … fun. No strings. But you'd want the strings. And that gets tangly."

He sits down beside her, a little farther away this time, and stares at the fire. "I don't wanna be a jerk, Beth." His face contorts in what could be an effort to smile. "Been there, done that. And there's probably a few women who would be glad to give me the T-shirt."

Beth looks up from her wineglass, sees Mattie's weaving above the mantle, the black outline of the raven just visible. "So … basically, you want to live your life without complications."

"Easier that way. I've done complicated."

His eyes are narrowed, and she wonders who he's remembering: the girlfriend, the former wife, or someone else? She feels an odd alliance with these troublesome women.

"Might be easier," she says, "but kind of empty too."

"Beth, I'm not the one who's unhappy."

The fire has burned down to embers. Ugly goose-bumps are popping up on her forearms. She reaches for her jacket. "Maybe I should go now."

~

Wisps of fog drift past. They travel in silence through a dark tunnel of trees, two completely separate entities now, two different conversations in their heads. Beth stares into the black night. She's replayed what Dan said, several times, and has come to the odd conclusion that he's like an otter: wants to enjoy the physical imperative of the moment with no worries about what comes after. The comparison would make her laugh if she didn't feel like such a fool.

After a ride that seems to go on forever, they finally reach the cabin. Beth opens the door of the pickup. Dan reaches out to touch her arm. "I can still help out with your research, you know."

She looks away. The adult equivalent of *We can still be friends:* the mortification of a teenager. She slides out. "Thanks." But she's not feeling grateful for anything.

He keeps the headlights pointed toward the cabin until she unlocks the door. "See ya," he calls from the open window. "Have a safe trip back to St. John's." And then he is gone.

Beth turns the knob, too numb to be scared, but then she lights the lamp and holds it up like a torch. She carries the lamp into the bedroom. Sees the brown and white feather lying beside her paperback. Alice. Alice would have told her she was being an idiot. Alice would have saved her from humiliation.

CHAPTER 28

She is paddling through murky water as viscous as molasses, every stroke an effort. The blue cap shades her face from the bright sun overhead, but in front of her, grey fog swirls around a girl standing on a pier, a girl wearing the yellow dress. Another person, hair short and dark, and wearing a red plaid shirt, steps out of the fog, eyes and mouth tight with anger. Pushes the girl's shoulder. She cartwheels into the pond.

The dreamer tosses the paddle aside, stands, and jumps, tumbling through the thick fog. As soon as she hits the surface, the molasses water swallows her. She can no longer see the canoe. Or the girl in the yellow dress.

Her lungs are bursting. She has to breathe. She has to. She opens her mouth. Sweet, brown water pours in. Weightless, she floats, and watches the blue baseball cap drift from side to side, like a feather in a gentle breeze.

Beth awakens and tastes the sourness of last night's wine on her tongue, but something else too, something sweet. That goddamn yellow dress. That blue cap.

She lies still and listens to the rain drumming on the roof and the plaintive plink of water dripping into pans and bowls. Who will empty them when she goes back to St. John's? Because she's leaving today. For sure.

She gropes for the flashlight. Looks at her watch: 5:16. Slides on her glasses and lights the lamp. Sits on the edge of the bed and studies the clothes piled on the floor, finally pulls out a sweatshirt and jeans, then adds a rain jacket and sneakers before she runs to the outhouse. It's raining hard: big fat drops coming at a forty-five degree angle.

When she returns to the cabin, she builds a fire and prepares the coffee pot, then packs up the few boxes and cans left in the cupboards. She sits down in the rocking chair, listens to the perking coffee, and tries to forget the dream. She watches grey light seep into the cabin. Begins to realize there's a gaping hole in her chest, like a cartoon cannonball has been shot right through. She misses Alan. Why isn't he answering his phones?

A light tapping on the door. She jumps up. Has Dan come back to dump the frozen shit in her lap? She approaches the door cautiously. Cracks it open. It's Mattie, in a wide-brimmed rain hat, and Muin.

"Glad I caught you before you left." Mattie steps into the cabin and digs deep into the pocket of her slicker. "Thought you'd want this."

Wary, Beth takes a step back.

Mattie opens her hand to reveal a carving, just eight inches long, including the thick tapering tail. "Rowan," she says, holding out the otter on the flat of her hand, "wood of good fortune. Most folks call it dogberry."

Beth's touch is tentative, as if the wood might burn her. The otter is stylized, yet carefully detailed, down to a small scar on the tip of the nose. "It's ... it's beautiful."

Mattie lifts her hand higher. "Here, take her now."

Beth turns over the carving, sees the signature. *Matthew MacKenzie.*

"He made it for you." Mattie takes off her hat and hangs it by the door. Muin shakes, drops sizzling when they hit the stove.

Beth points to the percolator.

"No thanks. Never touch the stuff." Mattie winks. "Poison, you know."

"Water then?"

"No thanks." Mattie hangs her slicker beside the hat, then slips off her boots. Muin sniffs at the packed box on the counter, at what's left of the carton of Milk-Bones Beth intended to take home to Pirate. Beth reaches into the box and offers one to Muin, who carries it over to the stove. The odour of wet dog replaces the aroma of coffee.

Mattie studies the puzzle still laid out on the table. "Not making much progress, are you?" She sits down in the rocker and folds her hands in her lap. "So ... catch anything last night?"

Beth pours coffee into a mug and sinks into the armchair. She places the otter on the arm of the chair. "Not a thing," she says carefully.

"So things didn't go so good then."

"Not really."

"And otherwise?"

"Otherwise?"

"Just wondering." Rocking steadily, Mattie glances around the room. Muin's crunching is audible in the silence.

"What?" Beth blurts. "You put a love spell on me. Or a curse or something?"

Mattie chuckles. "That's a good one."

The idea is so ludicrous Beth can't stop herself from laughing with her, even though she half believes Mattie would try it. She almost wishes she had. Then none of it would be her fault. She wouldn't have to feel so stupid for indulging a teenage crush.

Muin rises from beside the stove and goes to Beth, turns and offers her hips for scratching. Beth buries her fingers in the dog's fur. The shaggy tail thumps against her legs.

"Sure," Mattie says, "you and him got things to work out, but I'm thinking you'll be okay. A lot of things aren't what they seem."

Beth knows, somehow, that Mattie is talking about Alan, not Dan. She studies the contents of her mug as if there might be leaves there she could read, but there is only opaque brownness. She can't predict the future. And neither can Mattie.

Mattie picks up *Endless Night*, fans the pages one way, then the other. "Good story."

"Haven't had time to finish it yet."

"Don't wanna spoil it for you, but when you're about halfway through, you think you've got it all figured out." Mattie lays down the book. "Then, at the end, you find out that nothing – not one thing – was what it seemed to be."

Beth looks over the rim of her mug. "At least Agatha Christie's always logical."

Mattie snorts. "You sound like Katherine." She studies the weaving. "All that logical stuff you and Katherine and Agatha like so much is just one part: the warp. The weft is the mystery. Leave out either one and the whole story unravels."

Beth rubs a thumb along the arched back of the carving. "I dreamed last night that I drowned."

"Spose you came close. Not a good idea, going out with him again."

"I jumped into the water to save a girl in a yellow dress," Beth says carefully. "Someone had pushed her off a pier."

Mattie stops mid-rock. "Come on, Muin. Time to go." She stands and pulls on her slicker and hat, ties the straps under her chin. "Guess you'll be heading back to St. John's as soon as this rain lets up."

Beth reaches awkwardly to hug her, then holds up the otter. "Thanks."

"I'm just the messenger, love."

After she closes the door behind Mattie and Muin, Beth places the carving on the table and goes to the bedroom to finish packing. Closes her eyes when she sees the feather on the chair. The owl had clacked its bill at her last night, warned her. She just didn't heed the warning.

She shakes out the sleeping bag and stuffs it into the sleeve, punching it harder than she needs to. When she pulls the drawstring tight, a familiar discontent takes hold: nothing between her and Alan has changed just because Dan rejected her.

The sleeping bag slips from her hands. The gaping hole in her chest is not from missing Alan, or from Dan's humiliating rejection, but from a different kind of absence.

CHAPTER 29

The heavy rain let up hours ago, but Beth has waited until mid-afternoon to drive into town. Because she doesn't know yet what to say to Alan, how to explain to him why she has to stay. She doesn't understand it herself.

Monday afternoon. She considers calling the home phone instead of the clinic or his cell, then she could just leave a message. She wouldn't have to answer his questions.

The light mist is just heavy enough that she has to keep the wipers on. When she gets to the Irving, she sees a small sign taped to the phone cubicle. She has to get out of the car to read it: *Out of Order.* A message from the universe. Her whole life is out of order.

She knows there's a pay phone outside the Morning Glory but worries that Dan might be there.

She cruises slowly past the library, the Bide-a-Wee, the churches, the liquor store, and Price Chopper. Doesn't see a phone cubicle anywhere. Turns around and goes back to the Bide-a-Wee. Every motel has a pay phone, doesn't it? Circling the parking lot, she almost wishes she'd see the black pickup parked behind the motel, in the middle of the day, out of sight. Then she'd have an easy story to tell herself about what kind of man Dan is. She could focus all the scattered energy of humiliation into outrage and disgust, could be grateful she'd dodged a tawdry affair. But she doesn't see the pickup. Or a phone.

Left with no other choice, she drives to the café. Slides out of the car and stands by the silver metal box. Mist dots her glasses. There is a small spider web in the bottom corner of the cubicle, the silk strands perfectly outlined with tiny drops of water. A struggling daddy-long-legs is enmeshed in the centre. Beth wants to pluck it from the web, to effect a rescue. She pulls at one long leg; it comes off in her fingers.

She leans her forehead against the phone, listens to the dial tone. Finally punches in the numbers of her calling card and the home phone.

Don't pick up, Alan. I don't know what to say.

Please pick up. Please. I need you now.

The answering machine comes on. Tears well, but she's not sure if they're from relief or loneliness. "Hi, Alan. Things are–"

"Hi. Hope you're calling to tell me you're on your way home."

"Well ..." Beth almost sobs. "The research is going okay, but–"

"What's wrong?"

"Nothing," she says quickly. "There's just a lot to tell you." But how will she ever begin? More important, how will she end? "But everything can wait until I get home. I just wanted to let you know that I have to stay just a little longer. More research."

"More research? I thought you said you had enough to write your proposal."

"I still need just a few more samples. From out by the ocean," she adds. "Should be just a few more days."

"You sure there's nothing wrong?"

Beth can't discern whether it's suspicion or worry she hears in his voice. Maybe it's her own guilt whispering.

"You still there?"

"Yes." She watches the spider creep toward the daddy-long-legs still struggling to pull itself free. "What are you doing home on a Monday afternoon?"

"Knocked off work a little early."

"You feeling okay?"

"Just needed some time."

Time for what? "Alan ..."

"I miss you," he says.

She can hear the deep truth of it in his voice.

A long sigh. "But you need to do what you need to do," he says. "Stay as long as you need to. But no longer. Call me before you leave. And be careful on the drive home. And watch for moose."

She runs her fingertips along the ribbed metal cord tethering her to the phone. Comfort in the rituals, in the unneeded admonitions to be careful. But a genuine caring too.

"Promise me you'll be careful, Beth."

"I promise."

"Because I love you."

"I love you too." For the first time in a long time she feels like that could be true. She hangs up the receiver. A soft click in the cradle.

~

Beth picks up the carved otter and strokes the tapered tail. Thinks about walking to the otter spot just to get out of the cabin for a while. She's done enough thinking about Alan. She felt some clarity when she hung up the phone, but she still doesn't know how to explain to him the emptiness she feels. She can't explain it to herself.

The heavy overcast makes it seem later than it is. Only 16:05. Early for otters to be out and about, but she could go out in the kayak and look for signs, anything she might have missed in all her previous searches. She has to do something. She fills her water bottle at the pump and packs her backpack.

Paddling south from the cabin, she slows when she gets to the otter spot. Scans the shoreline: no fresh scats to indicate they've been here in the last day or two. She continues south around the small bay then heads out into the middle of the pond and circumnavigates two small islands. Finds nothing but the ever-present bare rock and scrubby spruce, sandpipers probing the shallows. When she crosses to the west shore, she spots some fresh scats and a small rubbing site about fifty metres north of Mattie's cabin. She lands the kayak and makes notes in her journal, but resists the temptation to take any samples. The last thing she wants is to have to go back to Dan's again.

Beth slides back into the kayak. Another hour of slow paddling and she is at Medicine Rock. The water in the outlet is high from all the rain, noisy as it pushes against and around the rocks. She lays the paddle across the bow and closes her eyes. Christ, was it just last night that she was here with Dan? It feels like a lifetime ago. She wishes it were a lifetime ago.

She lands the kayak near the tall maroon boulder she mistook for Medicine Rock. The overcast has descended as light fog. She can see only one clear boundary: a jade ribbon of spruce and fir separates grey sky from grey rock and grey water. Beth wipes her glasses on a corner of her shirt, slides them back on. The view doesn't change.

She walks back into the tangle of spruce and fir and, within a few minutes, finds herself standing before the cairn, staring at the ochre rock on top and the word "hope." Beth cannot reconcile the Mattie she knows now with the hopeless young woman, girl really, who built this cairn for her brother, and then sacrificed her entire youth to care for his damaged girlfriend. Mattie should be a tragic figure, but she's not, even after nearly seven decades of grieving. How could building a cairn and painting a rock have helped her?

Beth picks up the brown and white feather, smoothes it with a soft f-f-fth. She went to Alice's memorial service, even took charge of planning it, but none of that helped. All she could feel then – all she can feel now – are anger and loss. For Alice's suffering and for all the years stolen from their friendship.

When Beth finally looks up, she is surrounded by dense fog. She carefully places the feather between the two rocks, then turns and starts off toward Medicine Rock, listening hard for the sound of rushing water. Can't hear any, and the undergrowth and mounds of moss look unfamiliar. She turns and retraces her steps back to the cairn. Looks again at the ochre rock, the fragmented word, and the brown and white feather. She hears a chirp, an answer, and then a snort. She turns toward the sounds and begins walking. Everything looks just the same, the undergrowth, the mounds of moss, all unfamiliar, but before she's gone twenty paces she hears the river, and in another minute she is standing beside the kayak. She looks around, hoping to spot the otters, but she cannot see beyond a few metres, can hear nothing but churning water.

She rummages in the backpack for a flashlight, flicks it on, and secures it under the elastic cords on the bow to make the kayak more visible to anyone else caught out in the fog. If she hugs the shoreline, it will lead her right back to her cabin. Shoving off, she takes one last look at the real Medicine Rock. In the fog and twilight, it looks completely ordinary. Nothing special about it at all.

She paddles slowly through an eerie silence. The shorebirds have stopped piping. No chickadees, nuthatches, or juncos call out, no raucous jays or crows. No chattering red squirrels. No hum of a motor. Not even wind rustling birch leaves. Only the soft gurgle of water as it parts for the kayak and the paddle. She hugs the shore so closely the hull grazes barely submerged rocks. The loud scraping is unnerving. She feels alone, like the last living being on earth.

She hears it then: the faint sounds of a flute, a series of trills and twitters, repeated again and again. The high-pitched notes are coming from in front of her. Abruptly, the music stops. Beth peers into the fog and can see a dim glow up ahead – like another kayak or canoe with a flashlight attached. She paddles cautiously toward the light. The soft glow becomes larger, then as suddenly as the music stopped, the light goes out. Beth stops paddling, drifts. Nothing now but dense fog. And dark silence.

The bow of the kayak bumps against the metal pole of a pier. Beth sees the stern of an aluminum canoe and looks up to the right. The soft glow is moving up toward what must be Mattie's cabin, and then it goes out again. Beth beaches the kayak beside the canoe and flicks off the flashlight, climbs the path. She hears Muin run to the door and bark, and when Mattie opens it, she is wearing the blue baseball cap.

Mattie takes a step back and opens the door wider. "You're shivering, love. Come in now and have a cup a tea. Kettle's already boilt."

"Thanks for the light," Beth says.

"Seen the kayak crossing the pond earlier. Thought you might need it."

"You weren't, by any chance, playing a flute?" The question, spoken aloud, sounds absurd.

Mattie laughs. "No, love."

"Matilda then?"

"She don't know how to play." Mattie sets a steaming mug on the table. "Come on now. Sit down. You looks half froze." She picks up a block of wood and sits down in the rocker. The floor around her is littered with curled shavings.

Still wearing her life-jacket, Beth sits down at the table. Muin settles beside her, the weight of her head on Beth's feet. Beth wraps her chilled hands around the mug. "I could have sworn I heard a flute."

Mattie flicks a shaving to the floor. "Probably did."

"No, must've been a bird, its song distorted by the fog. Could've been a winter wren, I suppose. Kind of sounded like one."

"You keeps getting in your own way." Mattie lays the wood and the knife in her lap and holds up a thumb and a forefinger, measuring off half an inch. "You needs that little bit a proof. When really, girl, it's all around us."

"Proof of what?"

"Mystery. Sure, for all your science, you wants to believe in mystery too."

Beth unzips the life-jacket and slides it off. "Dan says just the opposite. Tells me I'm creating a big mystery out of things that have a simple explanation."

Mattie snorts. "What's he know?" She interlaces her fingers, moves them apart. "Think about it. How many assumptions do you have to make for his version of things to work out?"

The kerosene lamp flares. The shadows on the wall lengthen.

"Not one of them assumptions can be proved," she continues. "But that don't bother you. Cause they're all *logical*. But making the single assumption that there's mystery in the world? *That* bothers you." She picks up the knife and the wood again. The blade glints in the lamplight.

"But once you open that door, you can believe in anything."

"Yep. Can't always know what's possible. Or impossible." Mattie waves the knife at Beth. "To make it easier, maybe you can just think of mystery as the stuff we don't know yet ... and maybe can't know."

Beth lifts the heavy mug. Sips the red tea. It tastes like rosehips. She watches the steam curl upward. "Dan showed me the real Medicine Rock last night," she says. "I didn't expect it to be so ... ordinary."

Mattie drops another shaving to the floor. "I don't really know why, but I'm guessing that's cause people long ago knew that mystery lives side by side with the ordinary." She shrugs. "Or maybe it's just cause they knew that every rock can be a Medicine Rock."

Muin stretches in her sleep, lets out a series of small woofs. She flicks her front paws as if she is dreaming of paddling through water.

"You like the carving?" Mattie says.

"I can't really see what you're working on."

"Not this one. The one Matilda brought over."

Beth runs a finger around the rim of the mug. Clears her throat. "It's beautiful," she says softly.

"She told me about your dream." Mattie angles the knife to make a deep gouge, the tip of her tongue showing at the corner of her mouth. "The one where I drownded."

Beth shifts in the chair. Pulls her life-jacket back on.

"She can't forgive herself for that." She looks up at Beth, eyes shadowed by the bill of the cap. "Maybe you can help her."

"Help her?"

Mattie lays the wood and the knife aside. "Matilda never meant no harm. Not really. I forgave her a long time ago, but Emma ...? She's another story."

"But I thought you saved Emma."

"Matilda did. Sort of. But only her and me, and Emma, knows the whole of it. And Emma can't forgive her."

"For what? I thought you took care of her for twenty years."

Mattie picks up the pipe and the pouch of tobacco. "It's a long story, love, so if you gots to rush off to collect more shit or something, now's not a good time."

"No, no, it's okay." Beth's words are tentative.

Mattie reaches into the pouch, takes out a big pinch of tobacco, and packs it into the bowl. "Emma's father thought I were plenty good enough to swing a hammer, plant a rosebush, or mow his grass … but not near good enough for his daughter." She slides a match from the box. "Don't know how he found out about us, but when he did, he forbid her to have anything to do with me."

She strikes the match and holds it to the pipe, inhales a few shallow draws. The tobacco glows red. "So we was planning to run off." She shakes her head, slowly. "And damned if Matilda didn't want to come with us. Thought she couldn't live without me." Mattie pushes the cap to the back of her head. "And who knows? Maybe she were a little bit in love with Emma herself."

Beth pulls the life-jacket closer, zips it against the chill.

"We're two halves of a whole, see, so I knew exactly what she'd do." Her words are a cloud of grey smoke. "If we didn't agree to take her with us, she'd go to Emma and threaten to tell her father about us running off."

Beth takes a mouthful of tea, sweet and bitter.

"So when I seen she was gone," Mattie continues, "I went after her in the canoe. Seen them on the pier, arguing. And I guess you knows the rest."

Beth mis-swallows and nearly chokes.

"I jumped in after Emma. But I can't swim, see." Mattie's thin smile is wistful. "And Matilda wasted too much time trying to find me when she should've been looking for Emma. She didn't know Emma'd hit her head on the pier."

CHAPTER 30

Beth sits in the rocking chair and watches the sky, the clouds above the rising sun glowing pink and tangerine. A restless night, but at least there'd been no dreams of yellow dresses or blue caps. She spent hours, though, turning from one side to the other, punching the pillow, kicking off the sleeping bag then pulling it back on, all the while trying to puzzle out why Mattie told her about her role in the drowning. Sixty-five years of guilt? But Clive and Dan both claimed that Mattie rescued Emma, not pushed her.

Beth rubs her temples. Feels a headache coming on. So why did she dream it that way? And what in the world is she supposed to do to help?

~

She spends the morning in the kayak poking around the pond, trying to convince herself that she's doing something useful, that she has a reason to be here. By mid-afternoon she's famished. She paddles back to the cabin and checks the box of food she packed the day before: half a bar of dark chocolate, Skippy, a few saltines, a tin of sardines, rolled oats, and the box of Milk-Bones, nearly empty now. Cheese and bread in the cooler. Every bit of it unappetizing. She decides to drive into town.

On her way out of the cabin, Beth picks up the carving. She places the otter on the front seat of the Toyota and touches it now and again as she drives. She stops at the Irving to fill up the car and sees that the *Out of Order* sign is gone from the pay phone, but there's no one she wants to call. Not yet anyway.

Just as she's pulling out, Beth sees the black pickup approaching. Her stomach lurches. The truck comes closer. Dan nods. Beth lifts one finger from the steering wheel to acknowledge his nod. The truck passes, heading out of town.

So this is what her grand passion comes to? The lift of a finger, a nod. She almost laughs at herself. Almost.

She parks at the Morning Glory, and before she gets out of the car, she runs her fingertips over the carving, as if for good luck. Or a thank you. At least now she doesn't have to worry about running into Dan here.

She is just sliding out of the car when she hears the crunch of gravel behind her. The door of the black pickup creaks open. Dan leans out, holding the door between them like a shield. "Knew by all that shit still in my freezer that you hadn't left yet." He has one foot out of the truck, the other still in, as if he needs to be ready to pull his foot back in and slam the door, quickly.

"S-sorry," Beth says. "Just another day or two."

"No worries. Just teasing." He opens the hand gripping the steering wheel and then closes it again. Looks at his knuckles and opens the door a little wider. "Just wanted you to know that I meant what I said about helping with your research. That's the most interesting thing I've done since I came back here."

"Thanks," Beth says. "I guess."

"Almost makes me feel like I might be doing something useful." He looks away and adjusts his cap, as if embarrassed by his admission. "Even if I'm not, at least it's fun. And that counts for something."

"I guess."

"So you'll let me know when you come back this fall?"

"Sure."

"And if you get that grant, you'll be needing an assistant. Lots of ponds around here with otters. Good fishing too. I'd like to help keep it that way." He pulls his foot in and closes the door. Starts backing out, then rolls down the window. "See ya," he calls out.

Beth stands for a long minute and stares at the receding tailgate, trying to take in what just happened. So it comes to more than just the lift of a finger and a nod: it comes to one more person who gives a damn. Maybe that's not so bad.

She is smiling when she opens the screen door. Clive gives her a lopsided grin and a nod. Sliding into the booth, she glances at the congealed gravy on his plate. "That the special today?"

The left side of his mouth turns down. "Roast pork and mashed potatoes," he says slowly. "Wouldn't recommend it."

The skinny waitress brings a glass of water and a menu. "I'll just have the soup and a salad please," Beth says. "Vinaigrette on the side."

"How's things with the otters?" Clive articulates each word carefully.

"Good," she says. "I think I have what I need for now. Enough to write a proposal anyway."

"Proposal?"

"I'm hoping to get funding to do more research here."

"So you're planning to come back?" he says.

"Hope so," Beth says. "And even if I don't get funding, we'll still come out to the cabin now and again."

"How're you finding that old place?" He picks up his cup, hand shaking.

"Cabin needs repairs, but it's a beautiful spot."

"It is that." Clive lifts the cup to his lips. When he sets it down, tea slops onto the saucer.

"Guess we'll have to decide whether to fix it up," Beth says, "or tear it down and build something new."

"Hate to see that old place go."

"That's what Mattie said."

"Lotsa memories for her there."

"More than forty years of friendship," she says. "I guess it would be hard to see that go." She picks up the glass of water.

Clive fixes his one good eye on her. "Not just memories of Katherine," he says. "That's where Emma lived after. Where Mattie took care of her."

Beth almost drops the glass. Cannot stop the cascade of dream images: an angry young woman in a yellow dress searching the cabin, throwing pots and pans, stabbing her journal. A girl in a yellow dress tumbling from the pier.

"Too many memories maybe," he says. "Not long after Emma died, Mattie sold that cabin to Katherine. Moved into the one she's in now."

The waitress brings the order and sets down the bowls and cutlery. Beth stares at the bits of celery and onion floating amidst rice and small squares of chicken. "Did Katherine ever mention anything about ghosts in the cabin?" she asks quietly.

"Ghosts?" Clive frowns. "Katherine was a history teacher. She didn't go in for that kinda thing."

Beth picks up a fork and pokes at lettuce swimming in oily vinaigrette. "Did you actually see the accident? When Matthew drowned?"

Clive shakes his head. "Only ones actually seen it was Mattie and Emma's little sister, Lily. She come running outta the house when she heard the screams."

"How did it happen anyway?"

"Way I heard it, Matthew and Emma was out fishing. Or maybe they was just sneaking off for a little time together." Clive tries to wink his left eye. It closes only halfway.

"Both of them?"

"That's the way I heard it. Canoe overturned somehow

and Matthew drownded. Couldn't swim, see."

"Nothing else?"

His good eye stares off to the side. "Only that Mattie managed to save Emma. Now she could swim, but she'd hit her head somehow when the canoe overturned. That's what Lily saw. Mattie holding Emma in her arms."

"Why was Mattie even there?"

"Jealous, see. Probably spying on em."

Beth folds the corner of a napkin. "Do you remember anything about there being an argument between Mattie and Emma?"

"Never heard nothing about that," he says, "but Mattie being Mattie, she probably did fight with Emma." He pushes his heavy glasses up on the bridge of his nose. "I were just a youngster at the time, about the same age as Lily. Big news for a while, but then talk died down. As it always does."

He lifts the cup to his mouth. A brown drop falls from the cup to the table. He sets down the cup with a loud clink. "I do remember that only a handful of folks went to Emma's wake. Guess everybody felt like she'd already been dead for twenty years."

Beth stares at the drop of tea on the Formica tabletop. "Where was she waked?"

"In your cabin."

Clive reaches for his cane and pushes himself to his feet. "Well now, you have a safe trip back to the big city." He lifts a finger. "And watch for moose."

CHAPTER 31

Beth unlocks the cabin door, slowly, and wonders where, exactly, Emma was waked. Probably in the middle of the living room. Maybe under the weaving. She's always assumed Mattie made it for Katherine. Maybe she made it for Emma. A peace offering.

She turns away from the door, reminding herself, once again – just like she did a hundred times on the long drive from town – that it doesn't matter that Emma died in the cabin and was waked in the living room.

She looks at her watch: 18:42. Two hours until dark. She could leave for St. John's right now. She closes her eyes. No, she cannot let things she doesn't believe in send her scuttling back to the city. She'll sit outside and watch the sunset, then go to bed early. Pack up and leave first thing in the morning.

Beth goes inside and grabs a jacket and binoculars. Walks down to the water. The slanting light coming from behind her gilds the spruce and fir across the pond. To the north, loons call, probably the mated pair with their youngster. The yodels echo across the quiet water. She breathes deeply, pulling in the scent of fresh water and balsam.

Two ravens fly overhead, almost wingtip to wingtip. One veers away from the other and turns in a spiral. The other dips a wing, then it too spirals. It looks as if they are playing, delighting in the warmth and golden light of a summer's evening.

It looks as if. Always *as if.* Beth wishes she could know.

She hears a chirp, then another. Raises her binoculars and spots them about thirty metres away. Brown heads all in a line. With their tails arched and just breaking the water, they look like a multi-humped sea monster. They swim closer. Beth can hear their steady *uhn-uhn-uhns*. She scans the group for the two pups and the old scar-nosed female. One. Two. Three. All there, along with three others. They seem like old friends now, and Beth imagines that they've come to watch her. Maybe the otters have a whole catalogue of observations and they sit around debating why humans do what they do. *Uhn-uhn-uhn, uhn-uhn-uhn.* Good luck with that.

They approach to within a few metres. Beth knows they see her, undoubtedly smell her too, but they don't seem alarmed.

Uhn-uhn-uhn, uhn-uhn-uhn. Relaxed conversation. What *are* they saying?

Two otters, small but larger than the pups, come out of the water and stamp their back feet. Each leaves a black scat: gifts. More samples to collect if she wants them. She's so close she can smell the musk, and can tell by the way they urinate that both are probably females. Maybe Mattie is right: they're sisters, both daughters of the old grandmother. They slip back into the water and a pup and the old female come out. They begin to groom, themselves and then each other. The others dive and catch fish, eat them in the water, bones crunching. Two begin to wrestle, rolling and tumbling, splashing and chirping. A third joins in. Beth grins.

They do nothing out of the ordinary. No words come into Beth's head, and there are no strange behaviours or vocalizations: just otters being otters. No worries about their partners being fine or about accomplishing anything worthwhile in their lives. No worries about the fate of the earth. Who wouldn't feel *joie de vivre* when you're content just to be?

Beth lowers the binoculars. But she can't really know what they're thinking, whether they're worried or not. We're all trapped in our own heads. Can't even know each other's minds – Alan's, Dan's, Mattie's – let alone those of another species. Maybe otters do worry about the fate of the earth. Maybe animals know things we don't, things we cannot know and can never know.

The pup leaves the old grandmother, enters the water, and joins the wrestling. The old female turns toward Beth, stares at her for a full minute, then slowly approaches, moving her head up and down, sniffing the air. Beth can see her nostrils move. The otter puts her black nose to Beth's shoe, backs up and snorts, then leans forward and pokes the shoe with her muzzle. *Uhn-uhn-uhn, uhn-uhn-uhn.* Beth doesn't move, doesn't make a sound, but her heart is galloping. The otter takes a few steps forward and sniffs the back of Beth's hand. The long whiskers tickle. *Uhn-uhn-uhn, uhn-uhn-uhn.* Standing upright, she lays one webbed paw on Beth's shoulder and gently pokes her cheek with her silvery muzzle, the whiskers brushing Beth's face like a spider web. She sniffs at Beth's eye, her eyebrow, and then at her ear. *Uhn-uhn-uhn, uhn-uhn-uhn.*

For just a moment, Beth can see herself through the otter's eyes. Not her greying hair or her sunburnt nose, but the profound sadness and worry written in the lines around her mouth and eyes. Beth can smell it too, an acrid pungency like mildew. She wrinkles her nose against it, but then feels comfort in the paw on her shoulder, in the nuzzles to her ear. The taut cords behind her breastbone uncoil, and she feels light, as if she could float on the breeze like a feather. The pungent odour dissipates, replaced by the cinnamon sweetness of wild roses.

The old grandmother drops down and galumphs back to the water. And Beth is back in herself. Can smell only the otters' musk and the evergreen fragrance from the carpet of needles beneath her.

A minute later they all swim off in their sea-monster formation, disappearing into the dusk. Beth sits and watches until the last of the golden light has faded. She cannot take in what has just happened. It feels significant, full of meaning. But what meaning? She hears Mattie's voice whispering, but isn't sure if it's in her own head or in the wind or in the small wavelets caressing the shore: *A whole new way of being alive to this world.*

The sky darkens to indigo and a chill creeps into her joints and back. Beth rises awkwardly on legs gone numb and climbs the path to the cabin. When she reaches the door, she spins around and goes to the Toyota. Grabs the carving from the front seat.

Inside, she lights the lamp and places the carving on the table. She digs her journal out of her backpack. Picks up a pencil: *17 Aug 10: ~18°C, clear, winds light, observed from shore in front of cabin, A1, 18:46 to 20:50, 6 otters approached from south at 19:08.* She writes quickly, trying to capture every detail: *The old female touched my shoulder with a front paw and then sniffed my face and my ear, grunting the whole time.*

Beth taps the pencil on the page, chews the eraser, then writes: *Their visit felt like a blessing.* She draws a line through *felt*, replaces it with *feels*. Then crosses out the entire sentence. Writes: *THEIR VISIT IS A BLESSING.* She stares into the lamplight. Mattie's right: the otters are more than she can ever know, more than anyone can ever know.

She flicks through the journal, turning pages marred by dirty smudges and crinkled by drying raindrops. With a renewed sense of purpose, she begins to outline a research proposal. She wants nothing more right now than to be able to spend days and days just watching them, trying to learn some of what they know about being alive.

Beth works for more than an hour, until she comes to the bottom of the last blank page. She closes the journal, lays it on the table, and then checks to make sure the door is locked. She picks up the carved otter and places it on the chair beside the bed. Feels oddly comforted by the thought that the old grandmother is watching over her.

~

When she came close to the watcher, the old female could detect no scent of harm, only femaleness and sadness. The otters went away then, to fish and to play, but on their way back to the lodge, the old one returned to this place. She can still smell the strong scent of human, but also something high and sweet in the nose, the scent of now, the fragrance of joy.

The otters swim toward the lodge. The old female chirps. Her grey muzzle nudges a pup's belly, pokes his cheek. Paws reach to grab. The female pup joins them. They twist and turn in the water, rolling in somersaults. Then come onshore and chase each other over rocks. Over and around. And then back into the water.

The moon is high above. The old female rises up through ebony water, breaks through the surface of one world and into another. Silver drops fall from her whiskers. She's surrounded by shimmering ripples as five other heads surface. Amber eyeshine all around. They come out onto the grass and rub bellies and chins. Turn on their backs and rub themselves dry in this world of earth and rock and grass. They enter the lodge one by one, touch each other's muzzles. Scent of daughters, mothers, sisters, brother. Scent of one pup, two. *Uhn-uhn-uhn, uhn-uhn-uhn.*

CHAPTER 32

Beth awakens to the sounds of strong winds whipping through the birches. Woven within the wind, a sweet voice is singing a lullaby, the strains so faint she could not make out the words if the song were not so familiar: *Too-ra-loo-ra-loo-ral, Too-ra-loo-ra-li, Too-ra-loo-ra-loo-ral, Hush, now don't you cry*. The song she crooned to Rachel in the middle of sleepless nights.

Alert now, she lies perfectly still. Can hear only the wind and the creak of the rocking chair, back and forth, back and forth. She stands, heart thudding, and tiptoes to the doorway. The rocking chair is empty. But still rocking. The living room window is open and the wind is blowing against the back of the chair.

Beth breathes out and steps to the window. The chill wind makes her shiver. She lowers the sash. Lays a hand on the back of the chair, then sees the journal lying on top of the half-finished puzzle. The wind has flipped open the back cover. Beth reaches to close it, but sees the scrawls: *Matthew d 1943 at 17; b 1926. Emma d about 1962 or 63*. She still hasn't figured out when she wrote that. She holds the page closer to the window, turns it left and then right, upside down, and then finally, right side up again, until she's pretty sure the last few scribbles are *b* and *d, 1944*.

She looks out the window again and sees two women walking away. The wind is blowing one woman's long pale hair sideways. Her arms are wrapped around a bundle and she shakes her head to clear the hair away from her face; she is wearing the yellow dress with the huge pink roses. A tall woman with copper curls has an arm draped around the other's slender shoulders. She throws back her head and laughs, then turns and looks back over her shoulder.

Beth runs to the door and fumbles to unlock it. She throws it open, but they are gone. Simply gone. In bare feet and T-shirt, she runs toward the place where they disappeared, but it's Muin who emerges from the trees. She barks at Beth. Backs up and barks again.

"Is something wrong?"

Muin whines and then barks.

"Something with Mattie?"

Beth runs inside and pulls on clothes and shoes, then bolts out the door. Halfway to Mattie's, she stumbles on a root, falls, and scrapes her knee through her jeans. Muin comes back and pulls at her jacket. Beth is gasping by the time she reaches the cabin. She leaps up the steps and flings open the door. Mattie is slumped at the table, arms folded beneath her head.

Muin nudges Mattie's elbow. She slowly straightens.

"Oh my god," Beth wheezes, "are you okay?" Her heart is pumping so hard her chest hurts. Her side aches. "Is something wrong?"

"No, love, something is right."

Beth leans against the chair, still trying to catch her breath. She sinks down onto it.

Mattie turns and raises a finger. "I know."

"What?" Beth says cautiously.

Mattie rolls her shoulders and stretches as if just waking up. "Looks like you could use some tea," she says. She points her chin toward the counter. "And I've got some raisin squares going stale. Think you could choke one down?" She stands and shuffles to the counter. Muin follows. Mattie pulls a teabag from the Red Rose box, puts it into a mug, and pours in steaming water. She scoops a raisin square onto a plate, considers, then adds a second one before setting the plate and the mug on the table. Following the raisin squares, Muin sits attentively at Beth's knees.

Beth stares at the plate. Hears the wind testing the clapboard.

"What?" Mattie says. "You think there's poison in them too?"

"It's not that."

"What then?"

Beth rubs her scraped knee. "You said you know. What do you know?"

"What you learned from the otters last night."

"But how could you?"

"Just do." Mattie looks out the window, then back at Beth. "Your dreams don't belong just to you."

"I wasn't dreaming."

Mattie shrugs. "Asleep. Awake. It's all the same." She brings a mug to the table and sits down across from Beth.

Beth stares into the steaming tea. Wonders if she is in a dream. Maybe everything that happened last night, everything that's happening this morning is all a dream. She rubs her scraped knee again. It hurts. She lifts the mug. The hot tea scalds her lips. No, she is not in a dream. She wraps her hands around the mug, needs something solid to hold onto. She takes a small bite of the square and chews slowly. Muin whimpers, her gaze going back and forth between Beth's face and her plate.

Beth swallows. "The other night," she says, "why did you tell me what you did about the drowning?"

Mattie watches her over the rim of her mug. "I didn't tell you anything," she says quietly.

Beth runs her tongue over her teeth. "Mattie?"

Mattie sets the mug on the table and turns toward the birdfeeders just outside the window. "You'll have to ask Matthew."

"He said that I should help you. How?"

Muin goes to Mattie and licks her hands. Mattie stares at the birdfeeders, now occupied by two juncos, buffeted by the wind but clinging tight. Absently, her fingers work through the fur around the dog's ears. Three chickadees and a purple finch come and go. Muin looks at Beth, then back to Mattie. She circles and settles on the floor.

"I know what you've seen in your dreams." Mattie leans forward in the chair and puts her elbows on her knees. "That I'm no hero, that it's my fault they all died."

"All?" Beth takes a small bite of the raisin square.

Mattie closes her eyes, hands clasped so tightly her fingertips are red against her white knuckles. "One day – late winter it was – Emma just lay on her side all day, curled up and moaning." She opens her eyes and stares down at her hands. "I thought it was stomach cramps. So I made her some teas and bundled her up to take to the outhouse. That's when I saw she was all bloody down there. When I went to change the sheets, there she was." She rubs her hands together, pulls them apart. "I thought she was stillborn, but then she curled a tiny finger."

The square is a sweet gooey paste in Beth's mouth.

"Had to be a seven-month child at least, but no bigger than a newborn pup." Mattie leans her forehead into her clasped hands as if she is praying. "I washed her and bundled her. Even tried to squeeze milk from Emma's breasts and give it to her in an eyedropper, but she never took more than a few drops. I made weak teas of anything I could think of that might strengthen her." She holds out her arms like a cradle. "And I never stopped holding her."

Beth cannot move, even to take a swallow of tea to wash the paste from her mouth. The strange notes in her journal: *b* and *d, 1944.*

"She opened her eyes just once. Stared at me for the longest time, as if she knew everything: why she had no mama, no papa, why she was dying." Mattie shakes her head. "Only lived for three days."

"And you named her Hope," Beth says woodenly. "And she's buried under the cairn near Medicine Rock."

Mattie balls a fist, knocks it against the table. "If only I'd known earlier and been prepared, I might've been able to save her."

"She was too little, Mattie. You couldn't have saved her."

"Emma's belly was hardly swelled. She didn't even seem to know. When she was alive." Mattie smoothes the skin on her cheeks with both hands. "But after Emma died, she started visiting, angry I'd let her baby die."

She turns to Beth, and for the first time Beth sees fear and anguish in Mattie's eyes. "Or maybe she was just angry that I didn't let her and the baby drown with Matthew." Mattie looks away. "Or that I'd ever pushed her at all."

"And it was in Katherine's cabin that Emma came to you?" The question hangs in the air, a tangled thread. Beth watches Mattie, doesn't want to see the nod.

"Katherine never saw her." Mattie smiles ruefully. "She couldn't see ghosts."

"I think I heard her this morning," Beth says softly. She hears her own words as if they belong to someone else. "Rocking, and singing to the baby."

Mattie closes her eyes. "Maybe that poor girl is finally at peace."

"Was probably just the wind," Beth says in a rush.

"No, love. Wasn't the wind."

"I'm not sure."

"Yes, you are."

"But ..." But what? She heard that lullaby. She heard Alice's braying laugh. She saw them.

"Don't be getting in your own way."

Mattie stands and Muin stands with her. She lifts the blue baseball cap from the hook beside the door. Settles the cap on her head, then sits down again. "You're not done yet, you know." It's as if she has gone out the door and Matthew has taken her place at the table. "You have more work to do."

"But what about Hope?" Beth says. "We were talking about Emma and Hope."

As if his hands were made of lead, Matthew lifts them and lays the weight of them on the table. "Matilda worked and worked to save my baby girl. Even when she knew she couldn't, she kept on trying."

"Why name her Hope then?"

"Matilda chose that name ... she had to."

"But she died."

He looks at Beth, his eyes a deep, unfathomable green. "So did Alice." He pushes the pouch of tobacco toward Beth. "You needs to take some of this to where it belongs." Taps a finger on the pouch. "And a bit of prayer wouldn't go astray."

"Prayer?"

"It's not what you think," Matthew says. "It's not about talking, it's about listening." He grasps Beth's forearm. "It's just like the otters, girl. You finally listened to em. Now listen to everything else you love."

He releases her arm and waves his hand in a wide arc. "To the water, to the sky, to the earth. To Rachel and Alan ... and Alice." He winks. "Muin too." He reaches down to cup the dog's chin. "You got things to say, dontcha, girl." Her tail wags.

"It's all one weaving, one story." He sits back in the chair and tugs at the bill of the cap. "Don't need to say one word. Just listen. And then put your hand to the weaving, girl. Every little thread matters."

~

Beth stands beside Medicine Rock, her own Medicine Rock. In the noonday light it's the old man's profile she sees. Clutched in her hand are the three tobacco ties Matthew made for her. Each tie contains a pinch of tobacco wrapped in yellow calico, bound with a length of pink yarn.

Tmawei, he called it. And *nechwa*. Didn't explain.

Just put it down by the rock, he said. And listen. Tis a prayer all by itself.

Beth closes her eyes and breathes in the sweet scent of wild roses. Water is grumbling and complaining as it churns around rocks in its rush to the sea. The rocks hold fast. When she opens her eyes, she sees the juvenile eagle watching her from a tall spruce. Beth has interrupted its pursuit of lunch yet again. But maybe not. Maybe the young eagle is here for the same reason she is. And doesn't understand it any better than she does.

She lays one tobacco tie at the base of the rock. For her love of the earth and all wild things.

She turns and walks toward the cairn. That's where she'll put down the second tobacco tie, beside Alice's feather. For Hope and for hope. For all that we do not know and for the hope that lies in the heart of that unknowing.

The third one she will keep. A prayer all by itself. A reminder that Alice is still with her. And that she is laughing.

When she returns to this place, she'll have the right words. Or maybe she'll just listen. Maybe it's enough just to be. Here. Now.

Uhn-uhn-uhn, uhn-uhn-uhn: We are here, we are all here. We are.

Acknowledgments

Thanks:

to the Newfoundland & Labrador Arts Council and to the City of St. John's for supporting this novel;

to Marnie Parsons for her careful and insightful editing;

to all the good folks at Killick Press. They've been a pleasure to work with;

to the host of people who read and commented upon seriously flawed early drafts: Katie and Ken Pittman, Amy and Megan Kratz, Debra Durchslag, Denise Wildcat, Anna Kate Newman, Mark Callanan, Pat Byrne, and the Wisconsin Train Wreckers Writing Group – Michele Bergstrom, Tom Joseph, David Brainard, Joey Wojtusik, Mark Gaedtke, and Tara Nolan;

to Sharon Bala, who deserves a special thank you for offering not one, but two thorough readings, perceptive commentaries, and a number of long, inspirational conversations while hiking and snowshoeing in Bowring Park and on the East Coast Trails.

Newfoundland and Labrador
Arts Council   ST. JOHN'S